THE UNADJUSTEDS

MARISA NOELLE

Library of Congress Number: 2019902211

ISBN: 978-1-948115-03-2

For Riley, Lucas & Quinn:
may you always reach for the stars.

For Neil: you inspire me every day.

CHAPTER ONE

"Get it down! Get it down!"

The crowd shrieks around me, jostling each other to reach the front.

A girl with swan wings tunnels past me, her feathers brushing my cheek as she takes off toward the school. A boy with scales stumbles and falls on me. I regain my balance and continue fighting my way to the front of the growing crowd.

"Get it down! Get it down!" The chant grows louder.

A fairy type with wings from a morpho butterfly flutters above the crowd, smiling and clapping in rhythm with the chant. I spot a few unadjusteds among the gathering who hang back at the edges, their fearful expressions far different from the glee of the adjusteds, or as I like to call them, the *altereds*. They think they're a class above, some perfect version of a human being. But really, they're just a bunch of mutated DNA.

I push against the stab of sharp wingtips and pointed

elbows, trying to find a gap, trying to catch a breath. Anxiety trembles through my limbs and I hesitate, the crowd pinging me in all directions. An agonized wail from the thickest part of the melee gives me the spur I need. With my head down, I barrel my way to the small clearing. I brace myself, already knowing what I'll find.

"He's foaming!" someone yells.

The fairy's hands fly to her mouth and she screams. She kicks at the air, her ponytail bobbing about her shoulders. Two towering bulks in football jerseys laugh at her and slap each other's backs.

More screams ripple through the gathering. Finally, I break free from the crushing crowd.

My heart drops.

A boy falls to his knees as thick, white foam pours from his mouth. His eyes bulge and his face turns beet-red. His hands clutch at his neck as though he can wrestle away the pill's effects. *Just like Diana.*

"Someone call an ambulance!" I bark at the immobile group. "Now!" I toss my cell phone to a girl with pixie ears then kneel so my eyes are level with the boy's. Gripping his shoulders, I force him to look at me.

"You're not alone," I say, placing my hands either side of his face. "Please fight. Try. Hold on. The ambulance is coming." *Don't be another Diana.*

I shudder against the memories. The foam and the bulging veins.

2

It's happening all over again.

Blood trickles from the boy's nose, dripping onto his fresh, white T-shirt. He drops sideways, falling from my grip. His head smacks against the cement.

The pixie girl shouts into my cell phone about the blood and the foam and the gurgling and the choking. Just like I did for Diana over two years ago. But I already know it's too late.

"What did he take?" I ask the kids now silent at the front of the group. "Which nanite pill did he take?"

"Bulk," the fairy says quietly. She folds her wings into her back as her feet touch the ground, one foot tucked neatly behind the other.

I look toward the dying boy as his body convulses. He took the bulk nanite pill. He wanted to be a football player, big and strong and immortal with rock-hard skin. It's a level ten nanite. The paperwork involved takes months, not to mention the expense. All for nothing. His body rejected the change. It happens sometimes.

He reaches a hand toward me, and I hold it as he chokes out one final syllable, but I can't tell what it is through the gurgling blood.

His hand falls limp. His bloody eyes see nothing; not the lone black bird flapping in the bright blue sky nor the crowd of worried students slowly shuffling backwards toward the school.

He's dead.

Quiet conversations wind through the group, spreading the news, their voices rising with the drama of it all. The school will be wild with the gossip by lunch. *Gossip*.

I sit back on my heels as numbness sets in. That's better than the anxiety. Images of Diana's face as she collapsed on the floor right outside our lockers worm their way into my mind. The disbelief in her pupils, quickly followed by the fear.

It's the fear I remember most. Not how she choked on her own vomit or popped an artery and bled from her nose, eyes and ears. The fear. The last thing she said was "I don't want to die." But she did. And there was nothing I could do about it.

I force the thoughts away before the tears come.

Something digs between my shoulder blades. I turn to find the guard who escorts me to school every day. He grunts something indecipherable and gestures toward the school doors. When I don't move, he nudges my back harder with the rifle.

I glare at the guard. The nanite prerequisite for joining President Bear's security force has turned his skin partially green and changed the bone structure of his face until he resembles more troll than human. They're known for their obedience and aggression.

The guard points toward the school doors again, two massive arches of twisted glass and chrome that allow bulks and winged altereds to enter easily. A few yards

4

above the school's roof are the lowest of the competition hoops. Every year, contests between the winged altereds take place there. They compare how fast they can go around the aerial track or how small they can make their wings, and the rest of us watch from the bleachers atop the building.

The crowd disperses. Anxiety scratches inside my chest. I measure my breaths to a slow count, easing my growing fear. As kids file in through the archways, the morning sun glints off the glass and an American flag flutters in the breeze. Good old US of A. Good old American Dream. Reach for the stars and all that. Well, they've been reached for, lassoed, and wrestled back to earth, where they've become the opposite of twinkling, optimistic dreams.

In the distance, sirens pierce the air and draw near. The ambulance arrives, more of a truck than a van to fit the larger altereds. Two paramedics scamper to the boy's side within seconds of parking their vehicle. One of them grimaces as they go about the business of picking up the dead boy and putting him on a gurney. The other shakes his head and makes the sign of the cross. But there is no God here.

The guard points again. This time I follow him as the paramedics cart the dead boy away.

The guard halts at the entrance, and we part ways as I push through the front doors, jostling amongst the wings and tails and the snapping teeth of my altered classmates. We file into a more orderly line to let the scanners hanging from the ceiling read our retinas. The alarm on the metal detector blares, as it does every morning when I walk through it. Even though I'm prepared for the noise, the alarm drills into my head, making my heart skip a beat. A few kids look around, muttering about fire alarms. Then they see me and look away again.

Everyone knows I wear an ankle cuff. Mrs. Montoya, my unassuming Social Studies teacher, nods at me to go through. She pats my hand as I pass and glares at an altered dashing by whose wings dig into my cheek.

I pass the line of lockers favored by the bulks, each one big enough for me to fit inside without touching the walls. Above them is a smaller row, which the fairies tend to use. I stick to the bottom row, where I can stay out of their way. I open my locker and rest my head against the cool metal of the door. My skin is hot and flushed. A sign the anxiety is still hovering. A medley of opposing emotions circles inside my brain and I can't seem to settle on one. It would be so much easier to just not care. Take a pill. Be like everyone else. But I can't do that. I promised Diana.

I grab my gym bag from my locker and throw a sweatshirt over my shoulders to ward off the chill of the air conditioning.

The flap of several pairs of wings sounds above my head. I look up. Annabelle and her crew hover in the air, their gazes locked on me. I know one of them is going to drop a book or something.

I open my mouth to hurl an insult, but Annabelle's bulk boyfriend storms down the hall and glowers at me. I snap my lips shut and dash down the hall in the other direction. I don't usually run, but I don't have the energy to deal with them this morning.

When I push open the door to the practice gym, the smell of sweat and chalk rushes at me, calming my angry heart. Sensei Claus stands in the middle of the room, barefoot, dressed in his black karate uniform, his short hair trimmed into a crewcut. A few pairs of kids around him engage in one-on-one combat. Thuds and grunts reverberate around the high-windowed room, though no winged altereds are here. They aren't built for karate; all those delicate wing bones break too easily.

On the far side of the room, a gymnast springs onto a trampette, flips in the air, sails over a vault, and slams down on a crash mat. Chalk dust gusts into a small cloud around her head. Another boy swings around the highest of the uneven bars, around and around, his body a blur. A sixty-inch TV monitor raised halfway up the wall to record our training is on standby mode.

Claus nods at me as I slip into the locker room and change into my gym shorts and T-shirt—always cumbersome with the ankle cuff. I can never follow the latest fashions, all those skinny jeans and leggings. They don't fit over the cuff, small as it is. I wish I could cover it up. It blinks at me constantly, a permanent reminder that President Bear has my family by the balls.

I find the black karate belt nestled in the bottom of the locker, but I don't need it today for training. I slam my locker closed and march back into the gym, throwing my sweatshirt to a bench.

"You must clear your mind before you spar with me," Claus says, stroking his thin mustache. It mirrors the seriousness in his searching eyes. I always have the impression he's thinking about something else, something deep and important, like the answer to the universe. Until he'll say something insightful and I'll realize he's been watching my every move.

I push my shoulders down, pleading with myself to let go of the anger. Of the vision of blood and death I walked away from. Because of *them*.

"There was a nanite death," I say, trying to keep my voice steady. "Just now, outside school."

Claus' lips thin and disappear inside his mustache. "How many does that make?"

I wipe my slick palms on my shorts. "Second one this month."

Claus lowers his voice, his German accent softening.

"I hope you're not planning on… I know your sixteenth birthday is coming up."

"Today, actually." I lift a shoulder and sink a toe into the crashmat.

Claus puts a hand on my raised shoulder, gently pushing it back down. "Happy birthday."

"Thanks. And no, I won't be taking a nanite." I lower my voice so it's covered by the thuds and slaps of my sparring classmates. "I won't *ever* be taking a nanite." I keep the last part under my breath, thinking of Diana.

"Good. Because you're almost as good as me." His smile is warm under all that mustache hair, but a frown travels the length of his forehead. "Not sure I could keep up if you took a speed nanite or something."

A challenging grin creeps over my lips as I tie my hair up into a ponytail. "Oh, I'm better than you already, old man."

His mustache twitches. "Even with that cuff on your ankle? Doesn't it weigh you down?"

"Like an extension of my leg." I balance on one foot, pushing onto my toes, swinging my cuffed leg around like a ballerina, though I'll never be as graceful as my best friend's younger sister, Lyla.

While I admire the muscle definition on my supporting leg, Claus takes me by surprise and sweeps my legs out from under me.

"Never lose your focus."

9

It's the only mistake I make that session. I push the death out of my head. Not just the one outside, but all the ones that came before. The ones close to me.

I force my best friend Matt out of my mind too, knowing I'll see him later in class. He always pops up when I can't afford to think about him. It takes a concentrated effort to rid my mind of his startling blue eyes.

After twenty minutes of feet kicking shins and arms spinning faster than any Karate Kid movie, Claus shows me a new routine: a complicated series of blocks and sweeps with a few snap punches and a roundhouse. He indicates I should copy it.

"*Mouichido*," Claus says. *One more time.* Having spent time in Japan, the Japanese is as familiar to him as his German mother tongue.

I perform the routine once more, then Claus moves in to block my front thrust kick and shields my high knee rise. And on it goes, him mirroring my actions in perfect synchronization. But I know he's going easy on me. He's a 5th Dan. A master.

At the end, Claus dips his head. "*Rei.*" *Bow.*

I lower my head in return, resisting the urge to wipe the sweat from the nape of my neck. Then I make my way to help with the more junior kids, like I do in every session, because they need to be as prepared as I am. One day, President Bear won't always be in charge, and

He calls to the rest of the kids in the gym, and we all walk to the far end toward the wall-mounted monitor. Picking up the remote, Claus thumbs the power button. The whispered conversations fall quiet. Students gather around us. Kyle's breath puffs against my neck.

The screen comes to life, and the presidential seal fills every inch of it. My stomach clenches and ice slithers down my throat. A panic attack hovers, thick and immediate, like it does every time I see that damn symbol.

"Terror attack?" Kyle whispers in my ear.

I shrug. I know it will be far more personal than that. The last time President Bear gave an unannounced public message, my mother was thrown in prison. My mind races in time with my accelerated heartbeat. I picture my dad working in his underground lab. Is he watching the same message?

"Da-da-da-dum…." one of the bulks calls, laughing.

"Shhh." Claus glares at those making noise.

I look at my toes, bracing myself, knowing deep in my gut something bad is going to happen. Seconds tick by. "What's going on?" Kyle whispers.

"I've no idea," I say, watching as the presidential seal is replaced by a room in the White House. The camera pans to a horde of journalists in temporary seating, their faces tense, jotting notes on smart phones. The bell rings, signaling we should be in homeroom. Claus crosses his arms, one elbow resting in the crook of the other, his forefinger tapping his cheek.

"This is bad, isn't it?" Kyle asks.

With the knife still in my hand, I turn my head toward him. "Always."

On the screen, the president's arrogant face looms from behind his desk in the Oval Office, the Stars and Stripes hanging to his left to remind us of his stance: patriotism and loyalty above all else. The scar under his eye is bleached a pale color but no less ugly than a raw wound. He's never taken a nanite to heal it.

The ice in my throat hardens. I squeeze my eyes closed.

Then he speaks, his patronizing voice familiar. It's a voice that fills my dreams. No, not my dreams—my nightmares. It's a deep, barking voice, well-placed to scare a bunch of fresh army cadets into dropping out. The voice that condemned my mother.

"This is a national announcement. All unadjusteds age twelve and over will now be required to take a nanite pill to enhance their abilities. With threats and competition from overseas, we must do more to further the strength of our country." The president's red eyes stare into mine, as if the message is just for me.

A dizzy spell washes over me, and I reach out a hand to Claus, who holds my arm. "Breathe, Silver."

On screen, the president continues. "The nanite

16

representative agency is on its way to every school right now. They will assign each eligible unadjusted a ticket number. You are not permitted to leave before you have your ticket. This ticket will tell you which day within the next two weeks you will be assessed for an appropriate nanite level. You'll notice some of those assessments start today. Nanite reps and soldiers are on their way to each school in every city to aid the process…"

Kyle inhales sharply. I hold my breath, afraid I'll collapse if I let it out.

"Once this assessment is complete, we will proceed to residences to evaluate the unadjusted adults. I expect each unadjusted individual to join the strength of the adjusted superbeings. Failure to comply will result in unfortunate circumstances."

A muscle in Claus' jaw pulses. He's an unadjusted too. And Matt…

President Bear's red, inhuman eyes stay fixed on mine. Even his pupils are red, and they seem to whirl with fire. Today is my sixteenth birthday. It's almost as if he planned it this way, to make as much impact on my life as possible.

"Our country is the most powerful in the world. Your loyalty and patriotism is expected. But in case you need a reminder of what happens to traitors…"

An image of my mother's face fills the screen. An old image. From two years ago, when she was arrested for treason because she refused to produce more nanite pills. I haven't seen her since. They won't let me near her.

I'm not even sure if she's still alive.

CHAPTER TWO

We stand in the gym, my friends muttering, me staring into President Bear's menacing face. The image of my mother is reduced to the top right corner. I want to go up and put my finger to the screen, just to touch her.

"They can't do this," I whisper, gripping the knife even tighter.

A few eyes turn to me.

Claus shuts off the monitor. A tense silence holds the group breathless for a few moments.

"Can he really do that?" Kyle asks. Although tall and already a brown belt, his skinny frame quivers with uncertainty. What does he have to worry about? He's already taken a speed nanite.

"It's not our place to question the will of the president," Claus says, his voice low. His eyes scan the altereds' faces.

"Dude, didn't you just set a record?" someone at the

back of the group asks Kyle. "The mile, wasn't it?" Karate isn't Kyle's only strength.

"I…" Kyle's mouth gapes open. "I chose the speed nanite. But it shouldn't be forced on someone if they don't want it."

I've always planned to escape. Maybe it's going to happen sooner rather than later. The cuff around my ankle weighs heavy and my calf twitches with the need to run.

"No, it shouldn't be forced on anyone." The hilt of the knife digs painfully into my palm, but I don't release my grip. "So much for living in a democracy."

Kyle turns to face me. "What are you going to do? You're unadjusted."

I manage a shrug before my shoulders collapse. I bite down hard to prevent a tear escaping. Sliding the knife up my sleeve, I survey the group. Speed, strength, resilience, armored skin, to name a few of the abilities in the room. Besides Claus and a small freshman girl and me, there isn't a single other unadjusted.

"I don't want to take a pill," the freshman says. She'd be perfect for a pair of fairy wings. "I lost both my brothers to nanite pills. They're not safe!" She sobs, then runs from the room.

"What's the alternative?" Kyles says quietly.

"You get arrested," Claus says. "Or detained. You heard the president. He speaks in euphemisms.

'Unfortunate circumstances?' You'd be lucky. Just look at Silver's mother."

Everyone's eyes find me. Why does he have to bring that up? The picture of her from two years ago is bad enough. On trial. Refusing to make the pills that are improving our country. Which is fine if you're talking about organ regeneration or the eradication of cancer. But no body odor? Running faster than a speeding bullet? Skin more impenetrable than a tank? The ability to fly to the clouds? It's all greed. My mother drew a line.

"Whatcha gonna choose, Silver?" A bulk crosses his arms and sneers at me. "You've always been on the feisty side. Maybe the light of a firefly?"

Foolish. Everyone I know who's taken the firefly nanite never gets a wink of sleep.

"I can't even believe there are any unadjusteds left," the bulk drones on, his biceps crossed over his ten-pack. He may tower over me by about two feet, but I'm not intimidated.

"Twenty percent," I snap. "Which is four more than the percentage of blondes in the world."

"Won't take long to improve you all, then." The bulk cracks his knuckles. "And we might as well cull the blondes while we're at it. All that bimbo airhead thinking." He grins.

I want to punch him, but instead I grit my teeth and fist my hand around the secret knife.

"Silver…" Claus reaches for me.

I sidestep around him. My stomach churning, I back toward the doors just as they burst open. Matt stands in the frame, his floppy hair falling past his eyebrows, his blue eyes finding mine. He nods. A brief nod that tells me he's thinking the same thing I am.

"Let's go," Matt says, waving me over.

Only Kyle tries to follow me. "Silver, you don't have to leave. Just wait. They can't do this. You'll see." Sweet Kyle. He places a hand on my bare arm.

Suddenly, agony ripples through my calves, doubling me over, making my breath catch in my throat. The world spins. Dark splotches overtake my vision. Nausea sloshes in my stomach.

Kyle removes his hand. "Silver?"

I snatch a breath. Then another. Energy seems to light my muscles on fire. Panic attack?

Kyle frowns, hands raised, eyebrows shooting up. "Dude, what happened? Are you OK?"

I force a smile onto my lips, massaging the cramp out of my calves. "It wasn't you. Just a panic attack. I get them sometimes." Then I turn and flee.

Matt grabs my hand as we dash into the hallway.

"Where are we going?" I hold tight to his hand and let him pull me along. He will have an answer. Matt will know what to do. He always does.

"Away from here," he says over his shoulder.

Doors fly open all along the hallway. Students spill out of the classrooms, whooping and hollering. We weave through a group of bulks high-fiving over our heads, under a group of fairies with butterfly wings skimming the ceiling, and straight into a student running on the same course.

"Watch it!" the student growls.

I yank on Matt's hand. "Wait! My cuff. I'm never going to make it through the doors without setting off the alarms."

Matt elbows my side. "Don't worry about that."

The unadjusted kid who growled a warning at us makes a run for the front doors, but a security guard tasers him.

A few seconds later, as we push past a group of band kids with more fingers than necessary, the fire alarms wail and sprinklers rain down on us.

"Did you do that?" I ask, a thrill running through me.

Matt grins at me. "Come on!" He pulls me toward the fire exit.

Together, Matt and I sprint out the emergency doors.

Outside, we run around the school building. Avoiding the main entrance, we make a beeline for the chain-link fence at the end of the football field. A swirl of summer rain clouds scud across the sky. Army drones buzz all over the city's roofs. Shaped like mosquitos, their elongated noses carry a revolving camera. Thankfully, they're not pointed in our direction—for now.

"Silver, wait up! You're running really fast!"

"Isn't that the point?" I pump my legs harder until I reach the fence.

"I can't keep up with you."

I wait at the top of the fence. We clamber over it and drop down to the dirt path below.

"You OK?" Matt tilts his head toward me and nudges my foot with his. "When did you start running so fast?"

I shrug. "Must be those protein drinks. And I've been training in the gym with Claus."

We take off down the street. Around the corner, heading toward the city, all hell breaks loose.

Altereds run down the streets, shouting and whistling at each other. Bulks and ogres in National Guard uniform carry machine guns and march down the busier streets, yelling at anyone in their way. A tank rolls by, its caterpillar wheels crushing trash left in the gutters. A girl with swan wings flies by just over our heads in the no-fly zone. The area is supposed to be for deliveries to the local shops.

Matt jostles from foot to foot. "Shit, Silver. Where do we go?"

I glance at my flashing ankle cuff. I'll never get more than a mile without the tracking mechanism activating.

President Bear and his army of guards will be on me. How the hell did I think I could get away?

A shop window shatters to my right, glass fragments cascading to the floor. One of the marching guards lets off a pop shot. A scream echoes down the street. A whiff of gunpowder snakes toward me. Another bulk soldier pushes an unadjusted to their knees and slams his rifle into the unadjusted's head. I feel for the wall at my back. Solid and rough, offering no hidden alcoves.

"You go," I say to Matt. "The guards will be after me."

He turns his blue eyes on me. The eyes I've always been jealous of because they're the beautiful blue of Caribbean seas, not the silvery grey of a January ocean I was born with. "I'm not leaving you."

He pushes me around the corner of a street and into an alley. A couple of dumpsters spill their contents into oily puddles. A stray dog limps by on three legs. It also has three eyes.

Matt kneels at my feet and places a hand on my flashing cuff. He fiddles with the buttons, releasing a high-pitched, electronic whine. He scowls. "If only I had something sharp."

I pull the knife from my sleeve and remove the sheath. "You mean like this?"

Matt whistles. "Exactly. Where did you get a thing like that?"

"Claus."

Matt tuts approvingly and grabs the knife from my hand, setting to work on my cuff.

A bulk jeep careens by the mouth of the alley, spilling soldiers like lava. My chest tightens and my heart thunders. My feet won't keep still.

I need to run.

"Hold still, Silver." Matt pats the back of my twitching leg.

"I'm trying. Can you get it off?"

An announcement blares over a loudspeaker. "All people are to remain inside. Your nanite representative will be with you in due course."

Soldiers march by, pointing their weapons at fearful faces. "Stay inside! Do not make me use this on you!"

Matt glances up at me, a grimace on his face. "This is going to hurt a bit."

I swallow. "Hurt? Why does it need to hurt? Haven't you been working on this stuff in that weapons and robotics class?"

Matt's lips twitch. "It has an anti-tamper shock dispenser."

"Anti-tamper…" An electric current zaps my ankle, shooting all the way up to the back of my knee.

"Ouch." Matt shakes out his hand, then sticks his thumb and forefinger in his mouth. He hands back the knife.

The ankle cuff clatters to the tarmac, its red light

flashing manically. Matt stomps on it until the light dims and dies.

"Cell phone?"

I shake my head. "Left it at school."

He removes his own from his back pocket, chucks it on the ground, and stomps on that too.

I grab Matt's hand and scan the mouth of the alley. "Let's put a little distance between us and that cuff."

We take off again at a fast walk to avoid raising suspicion, keeping to what little shadows the mid-morning sun offers. We stick to the back alleys, climbing over dumpsters and slipping down high walls. Matt's panting breaths follow me toward the park, which stands between us and my home.

When we skirt into the street, a bulk points at us. He shouts, but a commotion in a shop at his rear draws his attention away. The adrenaline pulsing through me feels exactly the same as a panic attack.

A few minutes later, we reach the park, but soldiers march through the grassy lawns here too. Matt pulls me under the cascading fronds of a weeping willow.

"We need a plan," I say. "I can't run all the way to my cousin's like this."

Matt dips his head and stares at me through his hair. "Your cousin's?"

I look at my best friend. All the secrets I've kept from him tumble through my mind. "I was going to escape.

My second cousin has a hunting lodge upstate. Thought I'd just get there and think about how to get my mom out." I smooth loose strands of hair away from my face and set my jaw. "But I need to go back for my dad first."

Matt shakes his head, smiling.

"There *is* a plan," he says, tapping the trunk of the willow. "But it doesn't involve your cousin."

I look left and right, then step close to him. "A plan for what?"

"For the unadjusteds to escape the classist rule of the alts."

I suck in a startled breath. "How?"

"People have been talking about leaving the city for a while now, in case something like this happened." His eyes dim as he surveys the park through the weeping branches. "We found a cave system where we can hide until we figure out what to do. But with this announcement coming sooner than we thought, everything's gone to hell. It's a mess. Megan's just turned twelve. She can't be forced to take a nanite."

I think of Matt's sister, who's had a wheelchair since she was three. She was offered a regeneration nanite after the accident, but they're risky for kids. And now, she wouldn't swap her chair for anything. "Where is this cave?"

"Through the forest."

I blow my cheeks out. "Our forest?"

He nods.

"Matt, there are wolves in that forest now. Altered wolves." My fingers fly to the zipper of my sweatshirt and fiddle with the clasp.

"I know. But we don't have a choice now." Matt's eyes narrow. "You heard what President Bear says. Failure to comply will result in *unfortunate circumstances*."

"My mother," I whisper, the words thick in my throat.

Matt clenches a fist. "Or worse."

I peer through the branches of the willow. Everything remains quiet. "How do we get there?"

"Enter at the north end. It's a three-day hike to the ruined village, then another three days directly southeast. You remember how to use a compass?"

"Yes, of course." It wasn't that long ago, before the altered wolves turned aggressive, that Matt and I spent a week camping under the stars. Orienteering. Then I realize I'm not the only one who's been keeping secrets. I poke his chest, then flick his forehead. "Why didn't you tell me about this?"

Matt grabs my fingers, then picks a leaf off my sweatshirt. "I didn't want to put you in danger with your mother in prison."

The spindly willow branches move in a gentle breeze, bringing the scent of the fragrant leaves, but also another hint of gunpowder.

Questions spin in my mind, and I cross my arms over my chest. "Were you going to leave without me?"

"Never. But I can't go with you now." Matt uncrosses my arms and pins my wrists. "I need to go back for my family."

"So I'll meet you there?" I shrug out of Matt's grip and rake my fingers through my hair, trying to imagine a few days without Matt. Longer if one of us doesn't make it. The thought of the separation sends a flare of pain to my chest.

He lifts my chin. "Yes."

We huddle closer to the trunk of the tree, hoping the branches conceal us as a group of bulks charge by. I press him closer into the shadows.

"Before you go, I have something for you." He digs his fingers into the pocket of his jeans and removes a small wrapped box, the paper pink with flying fairies. He points to the fairies, a lopsided smile lifting one side of his mouth. It's my favorite of his smiles, the one I once spent hours looking up silly knock-knock jokes for when he was sick one winter, just so I could see it again. "I thought you'd enjoy the irony."

"I don't think there's a cheerleading team in the country that doesn't have fairy wings now."

Matt chuckles. "Overgrown, dress-up butterfly wings."

I finger the small package, wanting to savor the moment but knowing we can't delay much longer.

"Open it," Matt whispers.

I tear open the paper, ripping right across one fairy's face. Inside is a black jewelry box. I lift the lid and my breath catches in my throat. I reach out to touch the delicate silver chain. The pendant is a single musical note, an eighth note.

"On account of your last name, Melody," Matt says. "And your love of guitar."

"It's beautiful, Matt. Thank you." My hand floats forward and rests on his chest. I feel his heart beating under my hand, slow and steady. "This is the nicest present anyone's ever given me."

"You're very welcome." Matt kisses me lightly on the top of my head in a rare gesture that fills me with warmth.

He plucks the necklace from its box and stands behind me. I lift my hair out of his way. Matt fumbles with the clasp but connects it on the second try. The pendant hangs three inches below my collarbone. It feels like it's always been there.

"And now we need to go." Matt grabs my hands. "I'll see you at the cave, right?"

"Yes."

He presses his thumbs into my palms. "With your dad?"

"I promise." I wrap my hands around his thumbs and squeeze.

Matt tilts his head, gives me his lopsided smile again.

But this time it's lined with tension. He takes a step backward, still hanging onto my hand. "I'll see you in a few days. A week, max."

I nod, then he dashes out from the cover of the tree.

"Bye, Matt," I whisper.

Gathering the courage to move, I lift the pendant to my lips and kiss it once before I start toward my apartment. Barking commands of distant soldiers and gunshots return to my consciousness. But for now, the park is empty. I'm going to have to run for it.

CHAPTER THREE

Weaving through the bushes and trees, I end up on the quieter streets. I stick to the shadows as my apartment building comes into view.

Here, at the edge of suburbia, the streets hum with silence. A curtain flaps in an empty window and a fly follows me, circling my head until I swat it away. A kid's bike with four pedals lies abandoned on a front lawn. A face appears in a window, and I scuttle down the deserted street. The army must still be battling their way through the streets to detain unwilling unadjusteds and aid the Nanite Enforcement Agency.

When a shout from a neighboring street makes me jump, I move toward the front doors of my building. But I don't call the elevator to go up to our penthouse apartment. Instead, I dash down the stairs to the basement lab where my father works.

Ignoring the lick of anxiety curling around my heart, I nod at the two armed guards flanking the heavy steel door. They grunt at me as I key in the ten-digit code to gain access to the lab. The doors whoosh closed behind me.

"We need to—" I call as I burst into the room, then clamp down on my jaw.

Instead of my father sitting at the workstation, it's Earl, one of my dad's remaining colleagues. His dark hair is slicked back and his broad face pores over papers on his desk. Computers whir around the room. Fridges and centrifuges line the back worktop while the low hum of the chairs provides an undercurrent as they heat or cool the fabric of the seats.

Earl swivels toward me in his chair. His eyes are greyer and colder than tombstones. "Silver! Back so soon? I know President Bear will be generous if you want a high-level nanite. He said as much."

"Like he was generous with my mother?" I snap.

There's a flicker in his cold eyes. A hint of emotion. "We all miss your mother." Standing still, I scan the room for my father. I glimpse a figure in the distant glass office. He's on a hologram call, and the 3-D image of the vice-president is hard to mistake. And not just because of his whip-like tail.

Ignoring the remark about my mother, I focus on the problem at hand. "So, you've been involved from the start?"

Earl smiles his bland serial-killer smile. "Of course. I've been the liaison between President Bear and the nanite reps. It's such a great thing for our country. Personally, I don't understand all the fuss. So many unadjusteds running around the streets. Honestly. How do they think they're going to escape an army of bulks?"

Bulks. Up to nine feet tall. Forearms bigger than my thighs. Heat resistant, fire retardant. Impervious to broken bones. A level ten nanite.

Unadjusteds certainly couldn't escape an army of bulk soldiers.

"I assume you've already taken something?" I ask. Earl's eyes skirt the length of me. I cross one leg behind the other to conceal the missing cuff. Earl doesn't have one. He never stood up to President Bear. "But I always thought you were against self-experimentation."

"Maybe in my youthful, naïve days." Something flickers in his pupils. My ankle itches and I long to reach down and scratch it. "But I've done my fair share now."

"I'm sure you'd be granted a level ten." The abilities at the highest level run through my head. Invisibility. Telekinesis. Teleportation. They're all formidable.

"As would you." He stares at me. I want to lower my gaze, but I'm afraid he'll see all my lies. I keep my chin high and my lips tightly closed.

With my mother in prison, I'd be lucky to be assigned a level one, despite what Earl says. I know Bear; he'll never allow it. It'll be horns or long fingernails tapered to points. Something useless.

The predatory smile slips back onto his face. "What are you going to take?"

"If I get a choice… intelligence," I lie.

Earl claps his hands. "Just like your dad."

I shift my foot, my bare leg aching with the weight of my treason. "I prefer the more human enhancements."

A phone chirps on the work top. President Bear's face fills the screen. I try not to flinch.

"Gotta go!" Earl says. "The president needs me." He swaggers past me toward the door.

He taps a photo on the wall as he walks by. The digitally enhanced photo widens the grins on all their faces. It shows my parents and the rest of their team back in the glory days. I recognize the one who was executed, the original pioneer of genetic modification. It was my parents who invented the nanite delivery method. Two of the other scientists were arrested with my mother. The four who remain also live under armed guard, escorted to their front doors like my dad and me. Apart from Earl. He's willing to do anything the president asks.

Dad comes out of the office. "Thank God you're here." He rushes over to me, grabbing my shoulders. His watery blue eyes are shiny. "You didn't have to take one yet, right?"

"Nope. Assessment first." I shake my head. "But I ran before they could give me a ticket and put me in the system. Not that that means anything. I'm sure President Bear will make a personal call for me."

"You might be right." Dad sighs. "It's chaos out there. Unadjusteds being gunned down in the street. I didn't realize so many would run." He squeezes me tighter. "You're OK now." Being held in my father's arms, I can almost believe everything *is* OK. Down in the basement lab, away from the chaos of the streets, the world appears normal. But it isn't.

I step out of Dad's arms. "Did you know about this enforced nanite business?"

"Of course not," he replies, one hand massaging the back of his neck.

I jab a finger at the worktop. "We have to go. Now."

"Go where?" Dad spreads his hands. "Did you not just hear about the unadjusteds being gunned down? Rounded up and taken to processing facilities?"

"We go away. I'm not taking a nanite. Matt says there are people meeting at a cave system beyond the Great Woods. We go there."

Dad frowns and sinks his lanky frame onto a stool. "We can't leave your mother. If we escape, they'll kill her."

"We don't even know if she's still alive," I whisper, picking up a glass paperweight on Dad's desk. I turn it over in my hands. Inside is an etched figure of a spider mashed into a centipede. "They haven't given us proof of life for over a year."

"But if she is…" His hand flies to his chest. "President Bear promised if I…"

I narrow my eyes. "President Bear makes lots of promises. None of which he keeps."

"But it's your mother." Dad rests a fisted hand on the desk. "I have to hold hope that one day she'll come back to us."

"But she's been gone two years already, and we haven't been allowed to visit her once!"

"If I keep making the pills, keep doing what I'm told, maybe that will change," Dad says.

"Maybe?" I want to punch something. "Maybe? You're willing to bet it all on a 'maybe?'"

"It's all I've got." Dad dips his head. "President Bear promised—"

I scowl. "How can you believe anything that vile man says to you?"

Dad slams his fist down twice. "Dammit, Silver. It's not always about you."

I take a step back. My mouth drops open. I can't remember the last time Dad raised his voice. "I know that," I hiss through my teeth. "I know that very well. It's about *all* the unadjusteds. We all need to make a stand. Not just Mom on her own. Maybe then something will change."

"I wish it was that simple." Dad lowers his head. "If I fight, then they'll take me too. I can't leave you here alone."

"I already am. You're here eighteen hours a day," I say. "I hardly see you."

"Because I'm trying to make up for what your mother—"

"Mom did the right thing!" I slam the paperweight on the desk, where it breaks in half. Dad glances at the soundproof doors. "Nanites are the devil's work. She was right to refuse making them."

Dad picks up the two halves of the paperweight and absently fits them back together. "I need more time…"

"Dad!" I stick out my leg. It takes him a moment to see what's missing. "I *have* to run. Even if you don't come with me."

His hand darts to his mouth. "Oh, Silver. What did you do?"

"I'm not taking a nanite! Besides the fact I could foam out, just like Diana. And another kid at school this morning. I won't let something like that define who I am. I am enough, just how I am." I struggle to keep my voice even. The anxiety hovers, so I press my hands hard against the worktop, seeking reassurance from its solidity.

Dad stands and stares at my bare ankle. "What are we going to do?"

I take his hand. "We have to run. Together. *Please*."

I watch the deliberation play out on Dad's face. He stares into my eyes. First his cheeks sag, then he runs his hand through his hair. Finally, a spark ignites in his pupils.

Dad nods and lets out a shuddery breath. "I didn't think it was ever going to get this bad. Not really."

"With President Bear in power, it was always going to get this bad." I kneel at his feet and start fiddling with his cuff. "Right, let's get this thing off you."

Dad shakes his head. "There's no way, it's set with anti-tampering shocks…" I stick the tip of the knife where Matt showed me. "Where did you get that knife?"

"Claus." I grit my teeth and apply pressure. "Wait for it."

"Ouch!" Dad says as the cuff drops to the floor. I copy Matt's earlier actions: shake the shock out of my fingers and suck the burn out of them.

Dad gapes. "Where did you learn to do that?"

I smile. "Matt."

"Of course," Dad sighs. "So now what?"

"With both our cuffs now dark, they're going to come after us." I jump to my feet. "We need to go."

Dad scurries around his desk. "Let me grab some stuff."

"We don't have time." I stomp on the cuff until the flashing red light dims to nothing.

Dad jerks toward me. "We're never going to get out of here alive without nanites."

I back toward the main doors. "I don't understand. That's why we're running."

Dad shuffles through the work top, sticks a key in a locked cabinet and pulls out a drawer. Stuffed inside are vials of pills. "Temporary nanites."

I whip around on my heel. "You've been planning on escaping?"

"Not planning, as such. Just preparing." He stuffs pill bottles in his trouser pockets.

We don't have a lot of time, but I want to vanquish as much of this lab as possible from existence. So while Dad's stuffing his pockets, I rip a fire extinguisher off the wall and throw it at a computer monitor. I smash it repeatedly until it's nothing but parts.

Dad grabs my wrist. "What are you doing?"

I snatch a clump of paperwork from Earl's desk. "Destroying stuff. Let's make it as hard as possible for Bear and his nanite junkies to resurrect the program. Without you and all your notes, they'll have to start a few squares back."

Dad nods. "OK, but hang on a sec."

He goes to his computer, where his fingers fly over the keyboard. A file window opens, and a thick green bar appears at the top of the screen. Files downloading. After a minute, he shoves a flash stick from the hard drive into his pocket.

Dad winks at me, piling more pill bottles in his pockets. "Now you can destroy."

When I reach Earl's desk, I scoop up another stack

of papers. On top is a drawing of a beautifully sketched lion. Male. A tumbling, wind-swept mane, its mouth opened in a jaw-stretching roar, teeth dripping with saliva. Or maybe it's blood. With a sudden shiver, I dump the paper in a metal trash can, lion on top, and look around for a lighter. Rummaging along the work surface with the fridges and centrifuges, I find a box of matches. The match strikes a small yellow flame, and I drop it into the trash can. The image of the lion disappears three seconds later, wilted and burnt, its power diminished. But it makes me wonder what Earl was working on.

Dad waves at me. "Come here, I need your help."

He shoves pill bottles into my empty pockets. Once they're secured, I scan the worktop and the flashing computers. Dad and I find more loose papers and feed them to the growing flames. A lick of smoke curls toward the ceiling. It won't be long before the fire alarm goes off.

Dad grabs a vial of something flammable from one of the fridges, opens the lid and squirts it all over the worktops and computers. I throw a chair, and glass shatters behind me. Crushed pills coat the floor like flour after a bake-off. A red light flashes in the corner. An alarm. Although the lab is silent, a siren could be blaring somewhere.

Dad taps my shoulder. "Time to go."

We jog toward the door, pills shaking with each step.

I hold the knife in my hand, bracing myself to deal with the two guards who flank the door, but when we open it, the small hallway is empty. I point to the set of metal stairs that leads to the bowels of the building.

"There's nothing down there," Dad says.

I yank the sleeve of his shirt. "Trust me."

We clatter down the steps. At the bottom of the stairwell, we step into darkness. I fumble along the breezeblock wall for the metal cabinet. When my fingers slide over flaking metal, I stop, feeling for the top edge, and swing the door outwards. Inside are my backpack and my soft guitar case. I sweep my fingers lovingly over the case, realizing I was foolish to think I could take it with me.

Above our heads a door slams. Several pairs of footsteps charge with a heavy tread.

"We need to hurry," I say, keeping an eye on the stairs.

I pull out the backpack. Inside are two changes of clothes for myself and my father, dry food, full water bottles, orienteering equipment, two sleeping bags, a first aid kit, a coil of rope, and a few other essentials. I stashed the backpack down here over a year ago and refresh the water every week, waiting for the right moment.

From a side pocket in the backpack I remove a flashlight and flick it on. A cone of light illuminates a second, bigger door, equally curling with dried paint.

"The sewers?" Dad asks, splaying both hands.

I nod. "The sewers."

Dad turns in a slow circle. "How long have you been planning this?"

I yank the cords of the backpack tight and slip the straps over my shoulders. "A very long time."

There's no going back now. We've slipped out of our cuffs and set the lab on fire. If Bear finds us now, he'll arrest us both and throw us in prison with my mother.

The footsteps grow in volume as I yank open the rusty door. The deep, dark tunnel brings a thread of warm, putrid air that weaves around us. Dad waves a hand in front of his nose.

I step over the threshold into the moldering gloom. By the light of the flashlight, we pull the door shut behind us and try to avoid taking deep breaths. For a moment, the footsteps quiet, but I can hear someone keying in the code to the lab two flights above.

I put the backpack on the floor and pull out a change of clothes for us. Army camouflage trousers, dark T-shirts, and bandanas to conceal our faces. Tied to the backpack's outside strings are two brand new pairs of hiking boots. Armed with my knife, I hand him a flare gun.

"You've thought of everything," Dad says.

"That remains to be seen." I mentally cross my fingers.

The shouts rumbling down the stairs have me pulling on my boots with rapid speed. I can just make out the whooshing sound of a fire extinguisher.

Dad takes all the bottles of pills and tucks them into the backpack pockets. I attach my new knife to the belt loop of my trousers. A flush of confidence warms my skin.

"Let's move," I say once we're both laced up.

I lead the way, jogging along the raised platform that flanks the swirling stench and murky water. I hold the flashlight high, illuminating a few yards ahead.

Dad pants behind me. "Slow down, Silver!"

"We don't have time to slow down!" I call over my shoulder.

"You're running so fast your feet are a blur."

I slow my pace. The stench hits me anew and I gag, wishing I'd sprayed the bandana with Mom's perfume or something. The reek of feces and piss fills my nostrils and forces its way down my throat.

Up ahead, the beam of my flashlight catches a glimpse of something scurrying on the opposite raised walkway.

"What was that?" I tiptoe to the edge of the platform.

I sweep the beam over the far wall. Nothing moves. But twin glints of light appear in the darkness.

"Rats," Dad says when he catches up with me.

"I hate rats." I swing the beam back and forth and count eight sets of gleaming eyes along the tunnel.

Dad shakes his head. "Not just any kind of rats. All the failed nanites we made in the lab"—he looks up at the dripping ceiling—"well, they all ended up down here. Ingested by the rats."

I raise an eyebrow, not taking my eyes off the creatures. "You telling me we might have bulk rats down here?"

Dad nudges my elbow and we start walking. "Maybe, or worse."

"How big do you think they might be?" I shine the flashlight into the distance.

Dad tilts his head. "Unclear." The patch of wall beside him glistens in the cone of light. Green moss seeps down the concrete wall and shimmers with crawling mold.

"Great," I mutter, just as something brushes against my leg. Stifling a scream, I bite down on the inside of my cheek.

A square of light shines in the distance, back the way we've come, followed by the hulking shadow of a bulk. They've opened the door to the sewer. Flashlights flick on.

Something big and hairy winds through my legs and makes me stumble. Dad's fingers brush my arm, but then he's falling. He splashes into the water. The scurrying of several pairs of claws flies down the tunnel, getting louder, and glowing eyes emerge from the water. For all we know, the rats may have turned amphibious.

"Dad! Get out of there!" I hold out a hand to him, teetering on the edge. "The army are here!"

Instead, he wades through the water to the other side of the tunnel. I maintain pace with him, keeping my beam focused on the advancing pupils in the water. They come faster and faster, no longer concealing their own movements.

There are a couple of splashes as dark shadows with glowing teeth jump into the water behind him. A whipping tail stretches all the way across the water and slices through the cuff of my trousers.

"Dad!" My foot skids on something slick and my legs go in different directions. I get my hands in front of me just before I hit the ground, but the flashlight cracks, goes out, and rolls away.

Violent splashing comes from the water. Dad yells. I can barely see in the dim light. I duck as the whipping tail snaps back toward me and rolls into the water. Eyes glare at us from the ledge. Dad and I wade to the side as fast as we can and pull each other out, but there's a welcoming party.

Rats. Giant and mutated. Some of them have teeth longer than my fingers. Others have whipping tails, six legs, two heads, bulk skin. I spot one with seven eyes. The monstrous chimeras are endless, and I shudder at the hidden abilities they may have. They scurry together in streams of sinuous movement. Drool drips from their yellow teeth onto their matted fur. Others stop and stare at us, waiting.

The rats squeal and stretch open their jaws. A great boom deafens my left ear and a flash of red light streaks toward the angry swarm, followed by a cloudy trail. The air fills with smoke, then the rats turn tail and scurry away.

A red light bobs in the water. My father holds the flare gun.

He grabs my hand. "Are you OK?"

"For now."

Bright eyes glare at me from the depths of the tunnel.

I tug Dad's sleeve. "Let's get out of here."

The chatter of walkie-talkies echo. I hope we can outrun them. I've spent hours committing the sewer tunnels to memory, but the bulk guards will hopefully be stumbling blind, lost in a twisting maze of excrement. The thought brings a smile to my lips. Rats might not pierce their armored skin, but they'll be able to slow the guards down, maybe buy us some time.

"This way." I hold out a hand, and Dad leans on me as he sweeps a leg over an iron barrier that extends into the water. Solid lumps cling to the mesh as the grate disappears into the water. The stench intensifies, and I push the bandana against my nose.

"Do you know the way?" Dad asks.

I free the compass from my pocket. "We follow the tunnels south."

For the next half hour, we jog through the humid tunnels. Sometimes the water laps at the sides, and we wait for a moment, breaths held, to see if a new monstrosity will emerge. Other times we hear the scurrying of the enlarged rats on our heels or up ahead. Occasionally their large shadows loom on the far wall and we duck into an alcove to catch our breaths while waiting for them to pass. The odd shout of a guard weaves through the tunnels, sometimes stopping me in my tracks, but every corner we round is mercifully clear. My fingers ache around the hilt of the knife, and my chest is tight from shallow breaths.

A half hour later, as we turn the corner of another tunnel, a gust of wind cools the sweat on the nape of my neck and plucks at the damp strands of hair. Muted sunlight filters in through a huge iron grate. Fresh air creeps under my sodden bandana.

"We made it," I say, slowing down.

Dad and I reach the metal grate. Over eight feet in diameter, water covers the bottom foot, flowing along a channel and down a drain that leads to a nearby treatment center.

I place a hand at the corner of the grate and push. It moves an inch before grinding to a clanging stop.

"What the…?"

"It's padlocked." Dad sweeps his hands around the circumference of the grate. "Several times."

But I've prepared for this. I slide my backpack to the ground and dig around for the bolt cutters. Scurrying feet echo down the tunnel behind us. Numerous pairs.

"Get it off me!" someone shouts, followed by the report of five gunshots.

"Hurry!" Dad hisses.

I open the bolt cutter's jaws and snap one of the padlocks, then a second and third. Within seconds I've cleared a big enough space for us to climb through.

"Quick. The rats." I turn.

Wasting no time, Dad and I push the grate back in place. It might not hold a flurry of them, but it'll give us a head start. And it might fool the bulk guards if we can get out of here without them seeing us.

With the knife in my hand, I turn to face the noonday sun.

The street ahead is littered with ogre soldiers.

CHAPTER FOUR

One of the ogres, tall and green, his facial warts gleaming in the sun, stands at the nearest corner. An assault rifle hangs loose across his chest while his eyes lock on something in the distance. They're similar to trolls, but taller and stronger with a slightly higher IQ. More suited to covert military operations.

Dad stands and scans the edge of the tunnel. "It's ten more blocks to the forest. There's a sentry stationed at each corner. That's ten more ogres or bulks to contend with."

A headache pulses in my temples. "Shit." I take a swig of water and rinse out my mouth. I suck in deep breaths, glad to be away from the stench of the sewers. If I inhale deep enough, I swear I can discern the faint scent of pine needles from the forest. And rain. It must have rained while we were dashing through the sewers.

Dad delves into a pocket in the backpack, yanking it down against my shoulders. "I have pills that will make the journey relatively easy."

"Pills? What kind of pills?"

"Temporary nanites." He removes a bottle and shakes out two round pills.

"Temporary? Is that even possible?"

"Of course. I'd never harm your DNA permanently."

I set down the backpack and circle my shoulders. "What is it?"

"Invisibility. From a cephalopod," he says with some pride. "Extraordinary creatures. The kings of camouflage. Effectively, we will appear to blend in with the background, no matter how fast we move. It's about ninety-five percent effective, so our eyes may be visible. We'll want to keep our heads down. The nanite doesn't last long, so we'll have to be fast and fight the tiredness that the change brings."

"How on earth did you manage that? Actually, I don't want to know." I take the pill and hold it in my palm, hesitating. Then I swallow it dry. It catches in my throat, and I gulp a couple of times to drag it lower.

I've just taken a nanite, the very thing I thought I was running from.

"Do we have to take our clothes off or something?"

"That depends." Dad fingers our new clothing, rubbing the material. "Where did you buy it?"

"Camper's Outlet. Why?" My boots blur out of existence.

Dad grins. "Perfect. They're the primary sellers of bio-tech clothing."

I frown. "Meaning?"

"Everything they make pairs with your DNA. In other words, it will do what your body does."

My mouth drops open.

"Don't you remember that science teacher you had in middle school?" Dad closes the pill bottle and sticks it in the backpack.

"The one with the snake-effect clothing?"

Dad clicks his fingers. "That's the one. She took a snake nanite, and the scales were reflected on her clothes."

"I always thought she just liked snake-patterned blouses." I examine my boots; both have disappeared. A heavy tiredness weighs down my limbs. "How does that even work?"

"There are more things in heaven and earth…" Dad grabs my elbow and nudges me along the drainage channel.

I finish the familiar quote. "…than are dreamt of in your philosophy."

We edge out of the shallow drainage ditch. To my left, suburbia has diminished to nothing more than a few patches of disused land and a crumbling billboard advertising conch-shaped heels. Permanent ones, grown from your own skin and bone, with just one pill and a quick sip of water from the city's finest reservoir. To my right, the city's towering skyscrapers glint under the noonday sun.

I look back at my dad, but he's disappeared. My heart beats faster.

Then something grabs my wrist.

"This way."

"I didn't realize it would work so fast." I look down. All of me is gone now. It feels… weird. Like I've been scrubbed out of existence. Except I can hear my breathing and feel my heartbeat.

A bulk soldier reaches the grate, eyes the padlocks and gives the fence a push. It falls over.

Dad and I run. I will my tired legs to move faster, fighting against the sapped energy the pill's change has brought about.

The earthiness of the recent rainfall weaves into my nostrils. Lungs burning, I gulp the air greedily. The tree line is so close I can almost smell the forest's wildflowers.

We dodge new puddles which reflect nothing more than the punishing sun. Another few blocks and we'll be in the forest. We turn a corner, and I almost smack into an ogre. I take a quick step back, splashing into a puddle. I stand rooted. *Please don't turn around.*

Too late.

As Dad tugs me away from the puddle, my wet footprints leave a trail on the drying asphalt. The ogre swivels toward us. The spikes and horns attached to his skull glint in the sun as he walks the perimeter of the puddle. He raises his gun.

When his finger twitches on the trigger, I know I have to make a move.

I leap toward the menacing soldier, my karate training kicking in. The rifle swivels in an arc, not sure where to aim, and releases a shot that skims past my right calf. Before the ogre can pull the trigger again, I jump-kick the hell out of his brains. He drops the rifle, which swings from its strap around his shoulder. His eyes roll as he falls to both knees then faceplants the asphalt. His stubby neck judders with the impact.

I land in a crouch, catching my breath.

I point to the ogre. "We can't leave him alive." My slick fingers wrap around the hilt of my knife.

"I'll do it." Dad takes the knife from me and kneels by the ogre. In my head, I count to three, then Dad presses the blade to the back of the ogre's neck. After another three seconds, he rams the knife into its spinal cord. It twitches once.

I turn my head and swallow the bile that's risen. A ribbon of blood trickles out of the ogre's neck.

"You OK?" Dad looks a little green himself.

I nod, wiping my mouth with the back of my hand.

Increasing our pace, I'm careful not to step in any more puddles. The darkness and safety of the forest loom before us, but as we near the tree line I notice my boots are visible.

"Dad, my boots." I panic. If an ogre comes this way, we'll be seen.

There's a short pause. "I don't see any more ogres."

The relief pours out of me in a shuddery breath.

We scramble a good twenty yards into the forest and collapse on a fallen tree trunk. I buckle, wishing I'd spent more time on the apartment's dusty exercise machines. I push away damp strands of loose hair from my ponytail, then we change out of our reeking clothes into fresh ones. I eat a protein bar, hoping it will replace the energy the pill sapped away. Dad swigs his water, sweat streaming down his face. Helicopter blades thud in the distance. A siren blares.

"We need to keep moving." Dad holds out his hand. I take one last glance at the distant city—the city I grew up in, the only home I've ever known: its towering, glinting skyscrapers, high-rise apartment buildings, museums, art galleries, theatres, and the green of the park in the center of it all. A helicopter rises from behind a dark rectangle of a building and points its nose toward the forest.

I back into the ferns. "We need to run."

I dash deeper into the forest, the branches whipping my cheeks and roots pulling at my feet as Dad struggles alongside me. I misjudge the height of a large root and land flat on my face. Dirt claws up my nose. Something tickly creeps over my hand.

I push myself to a sitting position, rolling the impact out of my wrist. Through a gap in the trees, the distant red light of the helicopter flashes and banks away from the forest. Dad helps me up and we push our way through the undergrowth.

As I walk, I sip water, but the humid forest evaporates it just as quickly as I drink it. After a while, the light diminishes and the sun falls behind the trees. The moon rises, full and bright, but I still can't see much in the shadows. I stop and drop the backpack on the ground.

"Here." Dad hands me a pill. "Night vision. Should last a few days."

"Another one?"

Dad grabs my shoulder and squeezes. "We need it."

"I'm tired enough as it is." I hold my side, working the kinks out of a stitch.

"Me too," Dad says. "But we'll make much better progress."

As I slip the pill in my mouth and swallow it with a sip of water, Dad tells me it was harnessed from an animal's DNA. It will help us see at night but won't affect our day vision. Nothing as tacky as those night vision cameras that are useless as soon as someone turns a light on.

Within five minutes I can see as well as if it were day. A fox prowls behind a clump of ferns. Bats fly from tree to tree while a raccoon skitters across a well-worn path.

"Well, that makes things easier." I push myself to my feet.

Chuckling, Dad slings the backpack over his shoulders.

Using a compass, we press deeper into the woods. Thick branches block the moonlight, and the rich scent of wet leaves expunges the memory of the sewers. Wolves' howls echo through the forest, creating chills on my spine. I wince as every footfall crunches and rustles, reverberating around the trees.

Then I hear distant howling again, maybe a couple of miles away. The eerie cries carry on the humid night.

I pause to listen, wiping the sweat from my forehead. "Those wolves: are they real or modified?"

Dad pauses too. "Either, both. I don't know."

He turns abruptly and scans the immediate area as another howl pierces the night, this time much closer. Others join in.

I hover by his side. "Do we need to be worried?"

Two types of wolves run in these woods. The real ones don't usually pose a threat, but recently they've found themselves in competition for territory with their altered counterparts. The altered wolves are bigger, stronger, and faster. Originally human, many of them have left their city lives behind. They fancy themselves heroes of their own ridiculous werewolf movies. Their aggression depends purely on the type of human they are or were. With several unarmed unadjusteds fleeing through the woods, we could be easy prey.

Another howl ripples through the forest. A lash of fear grips the back of my neck, an icy contrast to the humidity. I look back the way we came, craving the familiarity of the city.

"Keep your eyes open." Dad's Adam's apple bobs a few times.

Something rustles in a bush nearby, and I startle. Dad clamps a hand over my mouth.

We both wait, turning in a circle. His heart pounds against my back and races my own.

Nothing emerges. But we back away slowly, keeping our eyes on a bush that sways in a different direction from the wind.

After we put a few yards between us and the rustling bush, Dad removes his hand from my mouth.

My legs tremble as we move along a hint of an animal track, pushing the overgrowing ferns out of the way. In the strange glow of the night vision nanite, the trees appear to lean toward me with gnarly, grabbing arms.

My blood rushes in my ears. Anxiety hovers, waiting for a moment to take me down. I try to ignore it; I've no time to coax it away, but I know this approach will backfire eventually.

The pendant swings at my neck, reminding me of my goal, reminding me of Matt and all I stand to lose.

My eyes sting with exhaustion as the hours drag on. Stumbling with fatigue, I feel like a puppet controlled by an unseeing hand, forced to plant one weary foot in front of the other. Dad and I swap the backpack every so often, sharing its burden. Eventually, a gradual shift in the darkness shows dawn approaching, illuminating the shadows and expunging evil from the menacing shapes.

Dad stumbles and cries out in pain, holding his ankle.

I rush to his side. "You OK?" I ask, reaching for the laces of his boot.

Dad shakes his head. "Don't undo it. If it swells, I'll never get it back on again."

I look over my shoulder. We haven't heard a howl in a while, but that doesn't mean the wolves aren't out there. And if they're altered wolves, they could be tracking us.

"I just need a minute." Dad bows his head.

"We should take cover for a while," I say, nodding toward a twisted array of fallen branches that offers some shelter.

"I'm not sure we've gone far enough to stop." Dad tries to scramble to his feet, but as soon as he puts weight on his ankle, he collapses again.

"I don't think we have a choice." I help Dad stand, and he wraps his arm around me. Together, we shuffle to the shelter and duck under the latticed branches, where he drops to the ground again.

Sunlight filters through gaps above our heads. A few

inches of leaves and a few moss-covered pebbles carpet the floor. I spread the sleeping bags, and we sit.

I dig through my backpack and hand Dad some painkillers, then a can of peaches. "These have been weighing me down."

I crack open the tab and gulp the juice, licking at the drips that run down my fingers. Remembering the survival skills I learned with Matt, I allow myself only a few small sips from my canteen. We could be in these woods for a week, and while the rain hasn't evaporated from the leaves, I don't want to become that desperate for water. But the humidity of the early summer weighs heavily between the branches; we'll have to find another water source soon.

I take off my boots and socks, cursing the newness of both. Blisters have formed on my heels, and I rub a drop of antiseptic cream on the reddened skin before wrapping a Band-Aid around them.

Grimacing, I slip the damp socks back over my feet and re-lace my boots. Then I take out my knife, checking the blade is sharp.

"Can I see that knife of yours?" Dad asks as he finishes the last of his can.

I hand it to him. He tests its grip, twiddling it end over end.

"Let's see if I can still do this. Oak tree. Two o'clock."

Then he throws. The knife tumbles through the air

and hits the tree almost dead center, scaring a squirrel farther up the sprawling limbs.

I half-stand. "How did you do that?"

Dad smiles. "In college, I took a circus skills class to impress your mother. She was a sucker for a man on a unicycle."

"Really?" I smirk.

"Oh yeah." He smiles. "One Halloween I dressed up as a clown. White face paint, red lips and big floppy feet. I squirted her with a plastic flower ring. She had a wonderful laugh…"

His shoulders round and he looks away.

Had.

A couple of beats pass. I can't quite work up the saliva to say anything after that.

"I miss her so much." Dad crushes the can in his hands.

I crouch and cover his hand with mine. "Me too."

He turns back to me and plants a weak smile on his lips. "She loved watching me throw knives the best."

"Will you show me?"

When he nods, I retrieve the knife and wait for instructions. Dad sits on the floor, kneading his ankle through the thick material of his boot. He gives me a few tips on stance and position.

The knife whizzes through the air, narrowly missing

the target and taking an inch of bark off the same oak tree. "Damn."

"Not bad," Dad says. "You've got to think about the rotations and how many times it will spin before it hits. Alter your stance accordingly."

I retrieve the knife and throw again. This time it hits the target, but with the hilt, and drops to the ground. For the third throw, I flick my wrist. The blade spins in a blur, sailing into the forest. It takes me a few minutes to find it.

"Keep going," Dad says, applauding.

The fourth throw hits the tree with the hilt again. My frustration growing, I hear Claus in my head and remember to breathe. I plant my feet, step forward and release the knife. It spins, slamming into the edge of the tree.

"Yes!" I jump in the air.

I did it. I hit it. Maybe not where I was aiming exactly, but I hit it. And I will get better. I will make President Bear pay. Maybe not on my own with a single knife, but somehow I'll find a way.

CHAPTER FIVE

The sun filters through the slats in the branches. Something rustles next to my ear. I scan the area. The ferns move and the trees sway, but I can't see what woke me.

Until I see Dad, eyes locked ahead and body rigid, balancing on his good leg.

Not far from us, a wolf sniffs the ground. Between one breath and the next, his ears prick up and he raises his grey head. His glowing eyes meet mine. Glowing in the daylight. It must be some kind of altered. My pulse pounds like a war drum. A bead of sweat trickles down my nose.

The wolf snarls, revealing sharp yellow teeth.

Slowly, I stand and unsheathe my knife, my entire body rigid and ready to run. Or fight.

"Dad…"

The wolf lifts its muzzle and howls. Only a second passes before responding howls blend from all directions. The hair on the back of my neck springs up. Inch by inch, I raise my hand.

The wolf snarls again. There's an uncanny glint in its blue pupils and I realize it has a scaled tail. I've heard of animals in the wild ingesting stray nanites, but I've never seen the effect until now.

Dad takes a step back but crumples as his bad ankle gives out. The wolf steps forward.

I release the knife.

It spins through the air. Too high. Way too high. But then the wolf leaps and the blade makes contact with its shoulder. It doesn't stick, but it's enough. The wolf growls, snapping its jaws. Dad shuffles out of the way.

I bare my teeth and roar at the unsightly animal. It takes a long moment to consider me, its eyes flicking between canine and reptile. I roar again. With one last snarl, the wolf turns and flees.

I rush to Dad's side. "Are you OK?"

His hand trembles. "Yes, just a little shaken."

We sit together, watching the trees and bushes.

Dad kneads his ankle again. "I think you should go on without me."

My head swivels faster than a speedster off a starting block. "What?"

He looks at me. "I can barely walk with this ankle," he says. "I'll just slow you down."

A cold sweat breaks out over my skin. "I'm not going to leave you out here. Don't be ridiculous."

"I don't want to be the reason you're found or hurt, or… worse." He hangs his head.

I launch to my feet and pace in front of him. "Mom's already in prison. You think I want to lose you too?"

"But Silver, I can't walk!" Dad throws his hands up.

"Then we'll wait until you can," I snap.

Dad cranes his neck to follow my pacing. "I could rest here in the shelter until the swelling goes down. Then I'll go back, find your mother—"

"You don't even know here she is!" I smack the back of one hand into the palm of the other to emphasize my point. "And they'll just lock you up too!"

Dad unties the laces of his boot. "That's better than them finding you."

I kneel by his boot and pull back the tongue. Without taking it off, I can just make out the purple of a deep bruise and a puff of swollen skin. I re-tie the laces, pulling them tight.

Gripping Dad by his shoulders, I dig my fingers in. "We will do this together. Do. Not. Leave. Me."

"Silver, I know you'll be OK. I ran because I knew you were right, especially with your missing cuff. But if there's any chance your mother is still alive…" He shakes his head. "I need to try."

I hug my knees to my chest. "If she's not been

66

executed already, it's only a matter of time for her. And for you, too. I don't want you to die. I don't want to be alone."

Dad drops his head into his hands. A sob shakes out of him.

I sigh, then kneel by his side again. Placing my arm around his trembling shoulders, I tilt my head against his. "I need you. Mom would want you to stay with me."

Dad grabs my hand and pulls it near his cheek. Hot tears run down the back of my hand. "I'm sorry," he croaks. "You're right."

"We will find Mom," I say. "Just not right now."

I help him back into the shelter and feed him more painkillers. When his eyes are closed and he appears to be sleeping, I scout the area for a stick. After a few minutes I find what I'm looking for and sit with it in front of the shelter. One end has a large, gnarly knot that Dad can grip and use as a cane. I whittle the other end into a point. It will serve as a weapon and as a tool to find purchase in the earth.

Some time passes before Dad wakes, wiping the sleep out of his eyes. "Any sign of the wolf?"

"No," I say, handing him the cane. "But I'm not sure I can take another six nights of playing chicken with wolves, real or not." I draw patterns in the soil with the tip of my knife.

"In that case, I think we should take these now." Dad

67

takes another two pills from the backpack. "It's animal scent: bear and wolf and other predators. It should mask our human smell. But if the altered wolves see us, they'll realize they've been tricked, so we still have to be careful. And I don't know how long it lasts, maybe two days."

I take the pill but don't pop it in my mouth. They drain my energy, but judging by Dad's ankle, it doesn't look like we're going anywhere for a while.

"Think of it more as perfume." Dad mimes spraying a perfume bottle.

"I can't wait for the day when I no longer need to do this." I dig my heels into the ground and scratch until dark soil is revealed. "When nanites no longer exist."

Dad rests a hand on my shoulder. "Me too. It's something I'm hoping for."

"Hoping for?"

Dad's eyes flick around the forest. Despite the shade of the trees, humidity presses into my lungs and sweat dribbles down my spine.

"Just something I've been thinking about." A ghost of a smile twitches his lips.

I swallow the pill. "It started for good reasons."

"I know."

"I mean, it helped with cancer, AIDS, cerebral palsy…"

"I know, Silver. You don't need to list it all to me." Dad gestures for me to help him up. Leaning on the cane, he takes a step with his bad ankle but cries out and sits back down.

"I guess I just wanted to say…" I start. "I don't think…" *It's not your fault.*

"Somehow, I need to make it right." He looks away. "If only I could turn back time, then we wouldn't be in this mess."

It's another two hours before Dad can put weight on his leg. He uses the cane and shuffles along but needs me to clear the path of the roots and thickest ferns. I pick up the backpack and settle it into the familiar ruts in my shoulders.

With our humanness cloaked, our pace becomes more confident. I want to move faster, but Dad can only manage a fast limp. We push through the undergrowth, tripping over tangles of vines and bulbous roots. Dad falls several times, but he insists on continuing despite how pale he looks.

Sweat drips into my eyes and blurs my vision. Just as my hand slips on the rubber hilt of the knife, we stumble upon a small stream and stop to fill our water bottles. I duck my head in the water but leap away when an altered fish with sharp teeth swims at me with an open jaw. Droplets of water run down my back and cool me. Dad and I share a packet of crackers.

Butterflies the size of my hand flutter from one flower to the next. They remind me of Diana. Well. Not Diana exactly, but her selfish mother who pushed the pills on her.

Fairies. Every single one I've met is selfish and narrow-minded.

It's from butterfly DNA that fairies' wings are made. I follow the path of a common blue, one of the more popular choices for wings, and wonder what it would feel like to fly with those chitinous membranes.

Whop-whop-whop.

The noise penetrates the tree canopy, louder than the sounds of rushing water.

Whop-whop-whop.

Trees thrash from side to side, their leaves swaying in wild bursts.

Dad and I shrink into the bushes as a lone helicopter flies low over the forest.

"I didn't think they'd be on our tail so quickly." He shields his eyes, looking at the sky.

The trees spring back to their normal positions and the whirlwind of leaves comes to a stop. The helicopter retreats and begins a low, lazy circle over another quadrant of the woods.

Dad nudges my arm. "Let's get going. We need to up the pace."

"Can you manage with your ankle?"

Lips compressed, he nods.

The ground is mercifully flat as we weave through the

trees, keeping ourselves camouflaged among the thick undergrowth. We dodge and duck under tree limbs, and I help Dad climb over fallen trees. The sounds of the rotor blades are always present, sometimes right overhead, sometimes exploring a distant corner of the woods.

When we stop for a moment, I ask, "Do you think they know we're in the woods?"

"They've probably got searches in every direction," Dad says.

The hours crawl by. Dad pops more painkillers—a combination of ibuprofen and codeine. He refuses to stop moving. Occasionally he glances back the way we've come and I know he's thinking of my mother.

Eventually, when the path weaves up a calf-shuddering incline, he's not the only one who needs to stop for sips of water and to catch their breath.

As the sunlight begins to fade, so do the sounds of the helicopters.

"Maybe a shift change," Dad says. "They could be gone for a while."

Another hour passes before he rests. Dad sits, hand circling his ankle, and gulps more painkillers. Guilt winds through me every time I look at his pain-pinched face, but I can't leave him to die in the woods alone.

And I need him, goddammit. He's my dad.

We dine on another two cans of peaches and more

crackers. I portion out a chocolate bar, and my jaw aches with its sweetness.

"I think we need to keep moving through the night," Dad says, gazing at the sky. "I want to put as much distance as we can between us and those helicopters when they return tomorrow."

My head swims with fatigue. My body aches, my feet blistering, and my eyes sting. What I want most is sleep, closely followed by a hug from Matt. But I know Dad's right. We need to keep moving.

Again, darkness slows our pace. Even though the night vision nanites help us see clearly, they cast everything in an eerie glow. The glints of nocturnal animals' pupils flash through the forest, making us pause. My hand, wrapped around the hilt of my knife, aches with tension. Any one of those pairs of eyes could be a wolf's.

Broken moonlight skirts through the branches, dancing on tree limbs and insect wings. Dad trails behind me, sometimes standing still for seconds at a time to listen. Other times he chooses to walk over the thinner ferns rather than snap twigs on the more accessible path.

"What's the matter?" I ask when he looks over his shoulder for the fiftieth time.

He turns to face me.

"What are you looking for?"

Dad's lips pucker and his brow wrinkles. "Hellhounds."

I glance left and right. "Hell...*what*?"

"Hellhounds," Dad repeats, then sighs. "Genetically modified dogs. Very top secret. They're used by the army and City Investigation Force to hunt down escaped prisoners and the like. They're huge, powerful, and fast."

I gasp. "Why on earth would you create something like that?"

Dad's shoulders drop. "I didn't. It was Earl's project. When he showed me his first creation I had nightmares for a week." Earl. I flash back to the sketch of the male lion I saw on his worktop. But that was a cat, not a canine.

Cold sweat beads on my upper lip and the small of my back. "Why are you worrying about them?"

"I'm afraid they might be on to our scent. I suspect the helicopters may have dropped off a team of bulks and hellhounds to track us in the woods," Dad admits. "They can smell their prey up to five miles away."

"And what will happen if they find us?" I try to control the tremor in my voice.

Dad blows out a breath and leans against a tree. He scrapes at the bark with his fingernails. An owl hoots, startling us both. "I'm not sure. I think we're too valuable to kill, but hellhounds aren't known for their obedience or restraint."

73

I swallow and try to work saliva into my mouth. "But we've taken those pills to mask our human smell."

"Yes, but I don't know how long that'll last. And I don't know how effective they are against hellhounds." Dad rises to his feet again and turns in a slow circle.

"But you've got more, I saw more in your bag." We can't come this far only to be eviscerated by a freaking dog.

"I do have more pills. There are limitations, though. With each pill the effect of the cloak is less effective."

"Well, that's just great," I mumble.

Thoughts of Matt tumble through my head. And of my mother. I've snuck photos of them both into an inside pocket of the rucksack, and I long to take them out and look at their reassuring faces. I'd give anything to be near them. The stark reality that I might not see either of them again grips painfully at the back of my neck. I've been preparing for five years to fight back, and I trained even harder after my mother's alleged treason.

But deep down, I've hoped for another alternative.

My mother's return.

A better world.

Now, the magnitude of my escape slams into me harder than a bulk's stone fist. So many things in this forest can kill me. A hellhound can end me in a few bloody seconds.

Gritting my teeth, I clamp down on the building fear. I can't let it win. "Let's move."

I lead the way again, walking fast, then jogging through the trees and panting the anxiety out of my lungs.

Somewhere behind me, Dad calls, "Silver, wait, you're going too fast." I ignore him and his loud hobbling through the undergrowth.

After half an hour of scrabbling through the woods, I stumble to my knees, exhausted.

Dad catches up with me and rubs my back with a spectral touch. "You were right to make us run. You were right," he says. I lean against him for comfort.

Then I hear growls. "We need to go, Dad."

I slug a quick gulp of water and jump to my feet.

"They're just animal noises, Silver. Normal animals."

"You sure?"

Dad squints at the shadows. Then we hear it.

Whop-whop-whop.

W I have no energy left to run, but with the sounds of the rotors above our heads, we don't have a choice. I grab Dad's sleeve and tug him through the ferns, faster and faster, wincing at the pain in my tired calves.

A growl at my back spurs me on just as I begin to lag. I don't dare look over my shoulder.

After a few minutes, I don't hear any more helicopter blades, but something crashes through the undergrowth behind us. More than one something. Acorns crunch under my feet and goosegrass pulls at the hem of my trousers. I turn an ankle on a large root but manage to stay upright.

Dad grabs my hand and yanks me forward. When he looks behind us, his eyes widen. "Keep running!"

I don't need to look to know the extent of the threat. The growls turn to piercing howls.

It's an attack call.

Ahead, Dad stumbles and goes down. I grab his arm and try to pull him to his feet, but I don't have the strength.

Then the wolves are surrounding us, baring their fangs, growling their menacing intent. Heads low and jaws drooling, their hackles raise as they inch closer.

Slowly, Dad gets to his feet, and we face the wolves back-to-back.

Seven at least, a mixture of black and gray. Saliva flies from their mouths. I grip my knife, knowing I can't take out seven wolves. My eyes dart to the nearest tree. One of the branches hangs down just above our heads.

I point up. Dad nods.

"On the count of three," I say. "One, two, three."

We both jump and grab the sturdy branch overhead, kicking our legs up and scrabbling as high as we can. I place my next handhold but pull back with a stifled scream, my hand coming away covered in stinging ants. I shake them off and clamp down on the radiating pain. Something jumps at me. A gust of warm, sour breath blows past my face, followed by the sound of snapping teeth and a disappointed grunt.

Then we're up and sitting on the branch. But we're trapped. The wolves circle, and one reaches up, front paws clawing the bark. Panic flares in my gut, an inescapable noose. I can't even pace out the anxiety but have to sit and endure this impossible situation.

"My God!" Dad gasps.

I follow his fearful stare and spot the wolf with the snake tail.

"What is it?"

"These are real wolves and altereds, working together." And the difference between the two is obvious. The real wolves look like, well, real wolves. The altereds have snake tails and patches of reptilian skin, and eyes an unnatural color. "I've never seen anything like it."

I don't want to think about the implications of that statement. Nature and science working together. Evolving. Evolving into what?

"Let's move a bit higher," I suggest.

Dad and I climb another fifteen feet up the tree.

"Here." Dad offers another cloaking pill.

"Will it work? Did it even work before?"

"I'm sure it worked. And we'll need them if we want to stay out of a hellhound's sensory range."

The wolves growl and bicker with each other. Their eyes glow hungrily as the day dims. Some of them lie down to wait.

The clouds clear, and the waxing moon becomes visible. A series of howls rips through the night. Eerie and hauntingly beautiful in equal parts. If I were further removed, I would marvel at their music a little more.

I hold tight to my tree branch. "What do we do now?"

"We wait them out. They'll probably disappear in

the morning." Dad's eyes shine almost as brightly as the wolves'. "And to be brutally honest, I could use the rest."

I dig the blade of my knife into the tree. "We may not have that long. If the helicopters come back. If there are hellhounds in the forest…"

Dad turns to look at me from his higher branch. "Do you have a better idea?"

I yank the knife from the trunk and picture myself throwing it. I've only spent one measly half hour practicing. Even if I could spear one of the wolves, there would still be at least six more, and I'd be without a weapon. As confident as I am in my karate abilities, I don't think I can take down a pack of snarling animals with a couple of jump kicks and swift front punches.

"Hand me the rucksack."

Dad passes me the bag. I rummage inside for a coil of rope. Bringing it out into the open, I slice the cord in two and pass half to Dad. "Lash yourself to the tree. If we can't go anywhere, we might as well get some sleep."

But it's as though my words are a curse. The wolves continue to howl, their mouths raised to the patchy sky. And they don't stop. A headache knocks on my temples, and thirst tightens my throat. If a bulk army or hellhounds are in the forest, will they be drawn to the wolves? Or will they flee in another direction?

I spend a couple of hours in a fitful half-sleep, dreaming of teeth and claws and vicious growls. My stomach cramps with hunger, but the thirst is far worse. At least during the night the humidity can't leach me of every droplet of precious moisture. But oh, how I crave just one drop.

"Silver? You awake?"

"Yeah." I cradle my water bottle in my hand and, after a few minutes of promising myself I won't, I bring the bottle to my lips and allow a drop to slip down my throat. I hand the last mouthful to Dad. "We need water."

"Three minutes, three days, three weeks."

Lazily, I swivel my head toward him. "Huh?"

"We can survive three minutes without air, three days without water, and three weeks without food. We've got a bit of time to play with."

"Not if they're still there in two more days and we're so dehydrated we just fall out the tree and into their jaws."

"In the morning, if they're still here, we'll make a move."

"What move?"

Dad nods at my knife. "The best one we can."

I spend the night staring at my empty water bottle, twiddling the knife in my uninjured hand, practicing the aim in my head but knowing it's hopeless.

Dad takes a look at my hand. He sprays something over the stings and wraps a clean bandage around it, then makes me swallow a pill.

"What nanite am I taking now?"

"It's not a nanite." Dad pats my hand. "Just normal painkillers."

A tingling sensation creeps over my hand. I wiggle my fingers and find they're already less stiff. "Isn't there anything you can take for your ankle?"

Dad shakes his head. "There's no nanite to reduce swelling."

"For all the complicated nanites out there, it's amazing you don't have anything to cure a common sprain," I say. "Or even better, a nanite to cancel out all other nanites. Something to reset your body to its human form. Wish I'd had something like that for Diana."

Dad leans his head against the tree. "Wish I'd had something that would have helped my brother too."

I frown. "Brother? What are you talking about? You never told me I had an uncle."

Dad blows a breath between his parched lips. "I don't like to talk about it. He was my older brother by three years. Died when he was seven. I still remember it. Leukemia. I've hated hospitals ever since. Never wanted to set foot in one again. I swore then I'd never let another person I loved die, if I could help it."

"So you invented the nanite pill." I trace the grooves in the hilt of my knife, looping my fingers along the valleyed grip.

"Exactly. I just wanted to fix all the bad stuff in the

world. I knew I could. And I did. But I didn't foresee the greed." Dad stretches his fingers out and flicks some dirt off his trousers. He sighs, then pulls at the string on a loose hem. "Didn't work out so well, did it?"

I unwrap the bandage around my hand. The wound has scabbed over. Pumping my fingers, the raised stings feel a little tight. I shift to get the blood back into my numb butt, then curse the wolves for their incessant sentry. "I'm angry."

"I know."

"I'm angry all the time." I'm tempted to slam my fist into the tree, but a new injury won't do me any good. "They took Mom away because she tried to do something good. If you guys had just never invented the damn pills…"

"I know," Dad sighs. "But someone else would have."

"Diana might still be alive."

"I know."

We fall silent for a minute.

I lean my head back against the tree. The pendant tickles my neck. "I hope Matt's OK. You know he helped organize some mass unadjusted exodus? Thank God he's on our side."

Dad's gaze drops to the wolves, then the surrounding forest. "We haven't come across any other unadjusted humans in the woods."

I scan the forest but see nothing in the darkness.

"Did you think we might? The forest takes up most of the state."

Dad runs a hand through his graying hair and swings his legs back and forth. "Maybe. If as many are running as you say."

"I don't think it was as organized as Matt was hoping. President Bear's announcement made a lot of them run early, unprepared. The city was a mess." I chip away tree bark with my knife and contemplate digging for sap.

"You're probably right."

I glance at a crack of dark sky and sigh. "I hope he got out OK."

Dad taps my shoulder. "He'll be fine," he says. "He's a smart kid."

Although the wolves remain quiet, they're still there. I hold the water bottle to my lips and suck at the memory of liquid. As the night cools and dew lays a fine mist on the vegetation, I stick my tongue out and lick up as much moisture as I can. But there isn't enough to soothe the dryness of my throat.

"How much longer can we wait in this damn tree?" My legs are twitching to run. "If those helicopters dropped off soldiers or hellhounds, we can't just sit around and wait for them to find us."

"We're caught between a rock and a hard place." Dad glances at the wolves. "We'll go in the morning."

"If the army doesn't find us, President Bear will be

furious." The thought twists a smile onto my face. But then I remember: if he can't find us, he'll take it out on my mom. It could already be too late for her.

I close my eyes. "Do you think he'll use Mom as a bargaining chip, if she's still... you know?"

I can't see Dad's reaction in the dark, his face half-obscured by a thick branch, but there's a tremor in his voice. "I'm sure he will."

"What do we do?" I whisper.

I swallow hard. *Mom.* If she isn't already dead, our actions will condemn her. But if we had stayed? It would have been far worse.

"There's nothing we can do from here." Dad's voice is steadier. "When we get to the cave, maybe then we can see about your mother."

My fingers clench around the pendant, the tip of the note digging into my skin. "If he does anything to her..."

"You can't think like that right now." Dad takes my hand and unfolds my tight fingers. "You have to block it out."

"I can't block Mom out." But isn't that what I've been doing for the last two years? Just to get by, going to school and back, training. But that's why I've been training. She has lived in the back of my mind, and one day, I promised myself, she would be free.

I close my eyes, ignoring the tickly sensation of insects marching across my skin. My mind drifts into sleep. When I wake a few hours later, dawn's bruise lightens the sky and birds twitch above my head.

The wolves are still here. Today, Dad and I will have to make a move.

I untie myself from the tree and coil the rope. Inching along my branch, I climb out until the limb begins to sway. Two of the wolves look up and lock their startling clear eyes on me. I adjust the weight of the knife in my hand. Inhaling, I hold the breath in my chest, narrow my eyes, and throw. The blade spins toward the ground and pins one of the wolf's paws to the earth.

A piercing whimper shatters the forest's silence.

"What's going on?" Dad calls.

"Making a move." The wolves bark at us, a mixture of yelps and howls that chill the back of my neck and would bring any curious attention from all over the forest. And I'm without my knife. With all the branches around me, it only occurs to me now that I could have whittled a spear.

"Shhh!" I put my fingers uselessly to my lips.

Whop-whop-whop.

The sound of the helicopter is right overhead. The branches above our heads spread under the pressure of the wind.

Dad shimmies down to my branch. "We need to move."

The wolves growl, then tear away from the base of the

tree. All except the one I pinned. It glares at me, hatred in its pupils. Pulling back its lips, it snarls, then yanks its paw free. Blood spills and it limps away after its pack.

"Let's move!" I yell, half-falling out of the tree.

I snatch my knife from the ground. Dad lands next to me, and despite my grueling headache and barely being able to pull air past my parched throat, we run.

Whop-whop-whop.

Whop-whop-whop.

More than one helicopter circles the canopy.

Thuds sound in the forest around us.

CHAPTER SEVEN

My head snaps to the left at a new sound. A mass of brown fur streaks toward us. It knocks me backwards and pain rakes across my shoulder. A new agony explodes in my skull as I bang my head.

Stars flood my vision and nausea rises in my stomach. The world sways and a muffled growl rumbles at my side. Bracing myself against the teetering ground, I turn.

The creature snarls and drools. Larger than any of the wolves I've encountered, with short, brown fur, claws three inches long and fangs that can shred through a tortoise shell, it gnaws something next to me. Spittle flies out of its mouth. One insidious eye roves in its socket, settling on me. The reek of death and wrongness fills the air.

Hellhounds.

Its jaws snap against flesh, blood splattering as it chews on my father's leg. He lies beside me, unconscious. I glance at his lower limb, and it takes me a few seconds to put the picture together. Blood and muscle and tendons and bone.

I tighten my grip on the knife. The hellhound pauses and snarls a warning at me, but I bring the knife down anyway. The hellhound squeals as the blade sinks into the soft flesh of its neck. Blood covers my hands. Its teeth snap with a new intensity.

I sweep a leg over its back and push harder. The hellhound's muscles strain under my weight, trying to throw me off. It jerks to the side, but I hold on as we roll together across the knobby ground in a slashing and gnashing somersault of muscle. I slash again at what seems an impossible speed to my adrenaline-fueled brain. Teeth sink into my already flayed shoulder. I scream, but I don't let go of the knife.

We crash into a tree and shudder to a stop. I pull and yank and tear. Finally, the black, inhuman eyes glaze over and the hound falls onto its side.

Trembling, I crawl away and vomit in the bushes.

The helicopter blades overhead come booming back into my awareness. Averting my face from the blood ribboning down my shoulder and the puncture wounds pooling red, I scramble to my feet. The trees sway and something crashes through the undergrowth. I turn back to Dad as shouts echo in the forest, bouncing off trees so I can't tell which direction they're coming from. A fevered sweat washes over my skin.

On the ground, Dad moans. Dropping to my knees, I rummage in the backpack for the regeneration pills. Dad's eyes flicker. I pop the cap, leaving bloody fingerprints on the bottle, and shove two of the tiny pills into his mouth.

A bulk in army combat gear rushes at me, yelling. But I can't make out his words. Even the thunderous sounds of the helicopters pale compared to the high-pitched ringing filling my head. I take a step back, stumbling.

My knees buckle. It is all over. *Mom. Matt.* The bulk reaches me, and the intricate pattern of army camouflage is the last thing I see before darkness descends.

———

I open my eyes drowsily. Shadows play at the edges of my vision as a fire crackles in a crumbling hearth. The enticing aroma of roasting meat sends hunger pangs tightening my empty stomach.

My limbs sink into a moldering couch. My head throbs and my shoulder stings.

Without moving my head, I scan the area. A shaft of light reveals a hole in a roof. Broken wooden planks make up the floor, while the walls are a mixture of stone and log. A bulk in army uniform looms over the fire.

Ten bottles of Dad's nanites are lined up on a rotting crate beside me, along with a flask of water. And my knife.

Dad!

I sit up, reaching for my knife. Nausea slithers through my stomach. "Where's my father?"

The bulk turns. I struggle to my feet, but blackness swarms my vision and I immediately fall back onto the couch. I wince at the pain in my shoulder.

The bulk raises his hands, eyeing the knife in my hand. "I have no idea where your father is."

"What did you do with him?" I demand, my voice hoarse from thirst.

He backs off a step. "Nothing. I swear. I think the army got him."

I frown, but even that effort worsens the headache. "Aren't *you* the army?"

He shakes his head slowly, as if afraid I might pounce. "No. No way." The bulk steps closer, out of the shadows. He points at his trousers. "Lifted these from an unsuspecting soldier a couple days ago."

My head pounds and I can't make any sense of his words. He could be lying.

Hell, of course he's lying. He takes another step. I flinch.

"I'm not going to hurt you." The bulk stands over me. Enlarged muscles. A flop of corn-colored hair. The face of a thousand aftershave commercials. Right down to the cleft in the middle of his chin. But that could be a trick.

My body tenses. I open my mouth but can't think of the words to save myself.

The bulk moves closer and hands me a flask. "Have some water."

I eye the flask as if it might contain a snake, then snatch it out of his hand. I drink it greedily, not caring that half of it dribbles down my chin.

"Easy," he says, a hint of amusement in his tone.

I notice a bandage wrapped around my shoulder. Only then do I realize I am no longer wearing my T-shirt, just my bra. Outrage swells in my chest, but I don't have the energy to do anything about it.

The bulk must've seen the look on my face because he points to my shoulder. "You were injured. I needed to dress your wound." Color rises in his cheeks and he averts his gaze.

"Who are you?" I back into the corner of the couch, which squeaks an irritated protest.

"Name's Rucker. Joe Rucker." The bulk sticks out a hand that I don't shake. "And you, I believe, judging by that nice little array of nanite pills, are Silver Melody."

I frown. "How do you know who I am?"

"Everyone knows who the inventors of the nanite pills are." He picks up a bottle and shakes it. "And their very unadjusted daughter. More so since there's been a price on your head."

Narrowing my eyes, I wobble to my feet. "Is that your

plan? To turn me in? Is that what you did to my dad?" I swish the knife between us, then realize my folly. No blade can pierce a bulk's skin.

"Of course not." Joe cocks his head, his golden eyes shimmering in the firelight. "I couldn't get to you both before the army got there. Your dad looked… pretty bad."

"You should have saved my father!" Lurching forward, I drop the knife and pound my fist against his armored chest, bruising my knuckles. I move to sweep his legs out but only succeed on collapsing to the floor. My teeth smack together. "He's more important than me."

A renegade tear leaks down my cheek.

"Hey, it's OK." Joe's hand finds my arm through the sleeping bag, and I leap away from his touch. He holds up both hands. "I didn't mean any harm."

"We'll see about that." I cower away, cradling my knife.

"What were you and your father doing in the woods?"

I don't look at him but keep my head down and try to ignore his presence. If I could move, I would. I'd kick his face in and run into the forest.

Joe leans against a wall and crosses one ankle over the other. "Do you have more clothes? Can I help you get dressed?"

This time I lift my head and glare at him, then pull the sleeping bag tighter.

"Have it your way." He shrugs and returns to the fire, where he turns the sticks. The tempting aroma of meat wafts closer.

"Where are we now?" I ask, eyeing the food.

Joe reaches for one of the sticks and hands it to me. Cautiously, I grab it and inspect it for poison. Joe laughs, takes another of the sticks and gulps the sliver of meat down in one. I nibble the edge of mine.

"Some kind of abandoned village. A couple of ramshackle houses." Joe smiles; it lights up the hard edges of his face. "Looks at least a hundred years old."

"They are." I remember Matt's instructions. If we really are at the ruined village, then we're halfway to the caves. At least Joe has taken me in the right direction. I finish nibbling on the meat and he passes me another.

"That's not where you attacked me."

Joe rolls his eyes and the gesture irks me. "I didn't attack you. I saved you." He kneels next to the crate. Although his eyes are now at my level, he still looms over me. "I carried you here."

"All this way? And my rucksack?" I ask, glancing at it.

Joe nods. "I saw the hellhound. You managed to kill it?"

It's my turn to nod.

"How? I had a run-in with one. It's one of the few times I've been thankful for my impenetrable skin. It kept coming for me until I managed to break its leg."

"I didn't have a choice. It was eating my father." I fiddle with the empty stick in my hand. "It would have killed us both."

Joe appraises me from his position on the floor. I reach for my rucksack and pull out a new T-shirt. I'm unable to slip my injured arm into the right hole. Joe moves to help me, but I shoot him a glare.

He steps back. "Just trying to help."

"Uh-huh."

With no small amount of pain, I manage to slip the shirt over my head. Then I reach for one of the pill bottles. Regeneration. I swallow two.

The light outside the dirty window dims, and with it, my energy as the nanites take effect. Although the last place I want to be is with a bulk in a ruin of a home, I can't stop my eyelids from drooping.

"What did you say about a price on my head?" I hear myself whisper as I drift into a fitful sleep.

"You and your father are wanted. It's a lot of money…"

His voice trails off as I fall asleep. When I wake again, it's the middle of the night. Joe sleeps stretched out in front of the fire. A new rush of energy fills my limbs. Rotating my shoulder, I find it doesn't hurt at all. I remove the bandage to find the wound healed except for a scar.

Staying as quiet as possible, I repack my rucksack and head toward the door.

A hand circles my boot. "Where do you think you're going?"

I try to kick it off, but it's no use. "So I'm a prisoner?"

He releases me and springs to his feet. "You're injured. You need to rest."

I pull back the collar of my shirt and show him the healed wound.

He looks from my shoulder to my face. Twice. "Well, I never."

"I need to find my dad." I turn toward the door.

"You know," he calls after me, "a lot of people are looking for you out there. President Bear put a million dollars on your head. And your father's. Each. That's a lot of money to a lot of people."

"A million dollars?" I gulp. "That is a lot of money."

"Yeah. I could buy a regeneration pill with that. Several." He stares at me, but I can't read his expression.

I edge a step closer to the door. "Why do you need a regeneration pill?"

"I was recruited for the NFL. I'd only been playing for six months when I tore my ACL. My insurance package didn't cover regeneration pills, so they dropped me."

He stands like he's ready to pounce, which doesn't match the words coming out of his mouth. Can I trust him or not?

Definitely not. I'm on my own in this.

I pause, my hand on the door. "And then what?"

Joe shrugs his massive shoulders. "And then, nothing. I argued my case in court for a few months but didn't get anywhere. Got disillusioned. Then I heard about the cave—"

I freeze. "How do you know about the cave?" *Shit.* I could have just walked into a trap.

"Ran into an old school friend in a similar predicament. She told me about a safe place, and with my parents in a compound…" He shakes his head. "There's really no place else for me to go."

I glance out the window and see a perfectly still night. No wolves. No helicopters. Nothing hiding in the dark shadows. My dad needs me. And Matt. There's no way I want to exist in President Bear's nanite world without either of them.

"What compounds?"

He frowns. "You don't know?"

I look away from the window. "No."

"The army and the City Investigation Force have rounded up all the unadjusteds in the country and detained them in compounds."

"To force the nanites down their throats?"

"To start with, but then they got a little desperate." Joe leans against the wall. "With unadjusteds fleeing all over the city, hell, all over the country, it had an effect on the superbeings."

"*Alts,*" I mutter.

"Whatever you want to call us." His face remains neutral, although the cleft in the middle of his chin bobs a little.

I want to push open the door and escape, but I need to know what's going on out there. "What happened?"

"The adjusteds went a little wild."

"Wild how?"

"No one knows. They started killing each other. Like, rampage bad. There's a whole ton of speculation. Some of the superbeings who've taken just one nanite, like me, seem fine. But any more than that, they went bad. The only thing keeping them in control is the presence of the unadjusteds."

"I don't understand." My mind races back to the day of my escape, but everything happened so fast that it was hard to tell what was going on.

"Neither do I," Joe says. "But my parents are unadjusted. They poured all their money into that one nanite so I could have a career. Now they're in a compound." His voice hardens. "And I, for one, am going to get them the hell out."

"Well, good luck with that." I turn and yank the door open.

Joe steps across the room. "Where are you going?"

"I already told you, I'm going to get my dad."

"You don't even know where he is."

So what? "I'll go to the caves first. Get Matt to help me."

97

Joe's voice softens. "Matt?"

I glance over my shoulder. "He's my best friend."

"I think he's the one I've been hearing about, helping to organize a resistance." Joe closes the gap between us. "We're going to the same place. We might as well go together."

"I'm OK on my own." I let the door slam behind me.

Although it's dark out, the night-vision nanite I took a few days ago still aids my progress. I refill my water bottle in a nearby stream before trudging through the forest, keeping alert for any suspicious noises. Which includes Joe's not very subtle trampling behind me. He mutters curses under his breath, and it brings an unexpected smile to my lips.

The forest around us falls silent as he thunders through bushes and swears at the branches invisible in the shadows. After half an hour, I hold my breath and double back on him. I wait against a tree, using the knife to pick dirt from my fingernails.

"If you're going to follow me, you really need to be quiet."

Joe yelps and trips over my feet.

He pushes himself up. "Damn, Silver. How can you see where you're going? There's no moon tonight."

I remove a bottle of pills from my pack and place one in his palm. He rolls it between his fingertips. "What is it?"

"Night vision."

"I thought you were an unadjusted."

"Of course I am. I'd never… They're temporary. It lasts a few days."

"I'm not sure I want to take this. Superbeings are going murderous because they're taking too many nanites. As irritating as you are, I'm not sure I want to murder you. Yet." His eyes flash.

"Hmm. I'm harder to kill than I look." I toss my hair over my shoulder. "But you don't need to worry, it'll wear off soon enough."

"Thanks." Joe dumps his pack on the ground, pulls his water flask out and swallows the pill. "How long does it take to… oh my!" He cranes his neck around the tree and peers into the darkness of the forest surrounding us. "I'm not sure I want to see what I'm seeing. There are so many animals out here."

"Surely a big, bad bulk like you isn't afraid of a prowling fox?"

Joe re-shoulders his pack. "There are more than foxes out here."

A slice of fear cuts through my shoulder, echoing the memory of pain. Yes, there are a lot of dangerous animals out here.

Checking my compass, I steer us in the right direction. It should be three more days to the caves, and I want to leave as few tracks as possible. Despite the nanite I've given Joe, he continues crashing through the low-growing shrubbery, favoring one of his legs.

When the sky lightens and the nocturnal animals return to their lairs, Joe sits on the ground and gulps from his flask.

"What's the problem?" I ask. Joe is a bulk. Stronger and bigger and almost immortal, yet he's tiring quicker than me.

"It's my knee. All the walking." He presses around the joint.

The weight of the pills in my rucksack nestles against my back. Looking down at him, I appreciate for the first time the machine a bulk can be. The impenetrable skin, the power in his muscles, his towering height. And his speed. With catlike reflexes, they're fast. Not as fast as a speedster like Kyle, but still fast.

I pluck a bottle of pills from my pack and chuck him a regeneration pill. Sure, he could heal and kill me. But he could have killed me countless times by now. He didn't have to rescue me or tend to my wound or feed me roasted squirrel meat. But he's done all those things. And even though he might be pulling me deeper into a trap, it won't be any better or worse with his knee healed.

"Is this going to kill me?" he asks, staring at the pill.

"Maybe." I can't resist the jibe.

He locks his golden eyes on me, glaring, and pierces my soul with his gaze.

I smile. "It's not going to kill you. It'll help your injury. I promise."

Joe's gaze doesn't move from my face. I wriggle under the scrutiny.

He squints at me. "How do I know I can trust you?"

I bark out a laugh. "Take it, or don't take it. Up to you."

He nods, then swallows the pill. I sink next to him, knowing it will take an hour or so for the genetic changes to take effect.

Then he'll be tired.

Joe offers me some squirrel meat from the traps he set around the house. It's starting to run low. "I don't know how I can ever repay you."

I tap my finger against the blade of my knife. "Just don't make me regret my decision."

CHAPTER EIGHT

Joe massages the muscles around his knee, digging his fingers in. It's been over an hour and the regeneration has taken effect. I watch him, alert for any sudden movements. Now that he's healed, he might change his mind about me and that reward.

He must see the way I'm looking at him because he says, "I'm not going to hurt you, Silver. I just want my life back."

I eye his rippling muscles, wondering if he's ever tried to snap a branch between tricep and bicep. Hell, he could probably crush a boulder in the crevice of his elbow.

"We all want our lives back," I say. Living in a penthouse apartment, with an imprisoned mother and an over-worked lapdog of a father. I shake my head. "Scratch that. I want a new life back."

Joe's shoulders slump and he laces his fingers over his knee. "The American dream."

I snort. "Not a dream. I just want what's mine. I want what I deserve." My neck muscles tauten. "I want my freedom."

Joe sighs. "Me too."

I think of all the anthems in the history of our country. The impassioned speeches and hopeful prayers. So many in the past penned heartfelt words, hoping to change the future. New words come to me, the way they always do when I'm composing a new song. But this time verses fly into my mind, a complete package, their message bold and clear. My fingers ache for my guitar.

I look at Joe. "Then maybe you can help get me to the cave safely."

He smiles. "I'll do my best."

Thinking of the cave reminds me of those in my life who are missing. Images of my father tumble through my mind, images of the hellhound attack and the blood pooling under his mangled leg. *Please be alive. Please.*

I blink away the sudden sting of tears and turn my face so Joe won't see. I can't afford to show weakness. I can't swallow around the meat in my mouth, so I spit it into my hand and cough, trying to hide my bursting emotions. Joe either doesn't notice or is decent enough not to say anything. When I get myself under control, I touch a fingertip to the pendant, wishing I could somehow fast forward through the next three days and get to Matt.

We sit under the tree until dawn. I pick acorns from the ground and run my fingers over the smooth shells before shoving them in my pockets. An old habit, one Matt always grumbled about when we went camping and I'd fill his backpack too.

Occasionally I nod off for a few minutes, but my hand never leaves the hilt of my knife and Joe never leaves my side. And he doesn't murder me in my sleep, either. Actually, he snores for a good two hours straight. Nothing about him is stealthy or quiet; maybe he'll be the death of me after all.

Just before dawn, I collect several handfuls of blackberries from bushes and share them with Joe for breakfast. After stretching, he pushes himself to his feet and grabs his knee. He frowns.

"What's wrong?"

"My knee. It doesn't hurt." He bends and flexes his leg a couple of times, performs a few low squats, and dances around the forest, leaping over ferns.

"Well, that's a good thing then." I clap.

He whoops and yells at the trees and thanks Heaven and God above.

"God and Heaven had nothing to do with it," I call after him.

He runs back to me and crouches so we're eye level. "Thank you."

I shrug. "If you could just keep the noise to a

minimum. Dad and I haven't spent a day in this forest without hearing helicopters. Or wolves."

"Wolves?" He looks both ways. "I don't think they'd attack me."

"They aren't normal wolves." I pick up my pack, check my compass, and point the direction to Joe.

"How so?" Joe pushes a thick branch out of his way. It cracks off the tree and falls to the ground. "Oops."

I can't quite suppress a giggle, then admonish myself for laughing when both my parents are at the mercy of the most evil man in the universe. "Altered wolves run in these woods and have mated with the real wolves. It's made for some interesting genetic offspring."

"Ew," Joe replies, and I laugh again. "I mean, that's gross. Why would you want to… Never mind." He swats flies from his face, and ferns cower as he storms by.

"The other day I saw one with a scaled tail instead of fur."

"Like a snake's tail?" A branch whips back on Joe's face. He doesn't even rub his cheek.

"Yeah. It's probably not the only weird thing we're going to see." A sense of foreboding tears through the morning.

For the first time, Joe's voice drops. "Roger that."

The morning drones on. We walk, sipping at our water bottles and slapping at the insects. I use the hem of my shirt to wipe the sweat from my brow, but within only a couple of hours, it is damp with humidity and sweat too.

I throw my knife at a tree and miss. Retrieving it, I try again. As we walk, I throw and collect. Throw and collect. Gradually, my aim improves.

"Did you drop out of school to join the NFL?" I ask as we wade through a particularly dense area of the forest. Although we're mostly in shade, the summer heat closes in around us.

Joe clears his throat. "Nope. Actually, I condensed my diploma and managed to graduate after junior year."

My eyebrows shoot up. "I thought bulks were..."

"A few beers short of a six-pack?" He chuckles. "We're not all brain-dead fools, you know."

"Not after years of playing football. You'd smash all those brain cells out." My foot slips over a moss-covered rock, and Joe grabs my arm to steady me.

"I *like* football, Silver. And I was good at it. If I wanted to take it seriously, I needed the pill." He makes a resigned clicking noise inside his cheek. "Otherwise I would have been killed out there on the field."

"And then your knee."

"Yeah." He sighs. "After only six months of playing."

"Will you go back to it?" I eye him out of my peripheral vision. Sunlight caresses his unblemished skin. Mosquitoes buzz near but quickly fly away when they can't penetrate him. "When this is all over?"

A rabbit scampers over my feet and disappears into a clump of wild jasmine. The rucksack digs into my shoulders and I long to sit down and rest.

"I'm not sure there's going to be anything to go back to," Joe says quietly.

A distant whop of helicopter blades makes me reach for my knife.

Joe pulls a machete from his belt, a glinting mass of metal that catches the filtered sunlight. It makes my knife resemble a toy. He stands, finger on his lips, head cocked to one side.

"What is it?" I whisper.

"I think we're being followed."

A growl rumbles from the undergrowth at my back. Another growl from the left. The bushes rustle. More snarls surround us.

A wolf leaps at me. Completely black, right down to its flashing pupils, except its stained, snarling teeth. I duck low and under its belly, my karate training coming in handy, and slash my knife above my head. Warm blood drips onto my face and the wolf squeals. It lands heavily, but it isn't dead. It turns and prepares to launch itself again.

"No, Silver!" Joe dashes in front of me. With one flick of his wrist, he slices its belly in two. Joe pushes me back, shielding me from the five others. They begin moving in as one, slowly tightening the circle. A blur of fur streaks toward us.

Joe leaps left, then right, slashing at the wolves. Blood coats the animals' fur and they whine and yelp. A white wolf strikes at me. I roll away from Joe, dodging it. I pop onto my feet and lunge as the wolf attacks again, both of us snarling. My blade sinks into its chest. As it dies, I retrieve my knife and turn to face the others.

Joe stands alone in a circle of dead wolves, blood glistening on his arms and face.

My mouth falls open. "You took out five wolves on your own. How?"

Joe surveys the damage he inflicted. "I'm not really sure. I used to go hunting with my dad. Deer, mostly." Joe's hand trembles as he wipes the bloodied blade on his trousers.

Joe sheathes his knife then tears his bloody shirt from his body.

The scent of death hangs in the air. Flies buzz. We look at the black wolf. With its death, I can see it had been a human altered. A hint of blue in its eyes and a human curve to its lips. Its paws are crossed as a person might fold their arms across their chest.

I look up at Joe. "You saved me. Again."

Joe smiles. It lights up his face. "It was the least I could do for you giving me that regeneration pill."

We leave the wolves behind and carry on through the woods.

"I could have helped more. I am a black belt in karate,

you know." As soon as I say the words, a flush of shame heats my cheeks. Claus would be upset. The first thing he ever taught me was humility. That karate is, first and foremost, a form of defense, and you should never be happy about having to use it. But with all the evil in the world, I still wrestle with the idea. There are people out there who need to pay for their sins.

Joe's smile widens. "Oh, is that what you called those little flicks back in the house?"

"I was dehydrated and wounded!" I slam a front punch at his bare chest and yelp. Of course he doesn't feel it. I am no more than an annoying fly, and now my knuckles ache.

Chuckling, Joe rolls his eyes. "Do I really have to protect you from yourself, too?"

Sliding my knife back into its sheath, I turn before the urge to punch him again overcomes me. "It's all right for you, you're immortal."

Joe's eyes dim, the honey color darkening into a burnt almond. "I'm not immortal, Silver. I have my weaknesses."

"Like what?"

Joe stops at the edge of a trickling stream that winds around the tree trunks. A delicate rain falls from the humid sky like glitter. Joe takes a knee and splashes the water over his bloody arms and chest, then points at the hollow of his throat. He points at the nape of his neck.

Then he taps the back of both knees. "Each of those four spots contains a small area that can be penetrated. Bullets, knives, teeth."

"I didn't know that." My father was responsible for inventing the bulk nanite. He must've controlled the imperfections so that nothing immortal will ever exist.

Joe splays his hands, an earnest expression. "And now you know how to kill me."

"I wouldn't do that, Joe," I say, keeping my hand well away from the hilt of my knife. "You just saved me from a pack of wolves. And from the army. Thank you." I kneel next to him and wash the blood from my arms and face.

"Not a problem." His gaze lingers.

I hold his stare. "We're a good team."

Joe smiles. "We are."

He flicks me with water, and I cup my hands and pour some over his head. He laughs, and the sound warms my insides, revealing a wry humor that has been missing in my life for as long as I can remember.

Joe pulls on a new T-shirt and picks up his pack. "Shall we keep moving?"

"Of course." The heat of a slow blush spreads up my neck. As we walk, the pendant sways back and forth in its own rhythm. Sunlight bounces off the metal, throwing dancing reflections into the trees.

The glittering rain stops, leaving behind sparkles that

lend the forest a magical quality. I wouldn't be surprised if a centaur galloped out from behind a tree. I chuckle, realizing such whimsical thoughts aren't so farfetched. Human and horse DNA can be spliced together easily enough. It's more surprising that it hasn't been done before. But with Earl in the lab, new creations won't be anything as benign as a centaur.

I open my mouth to ask Joe a question, but before I can speak, he presents me with a posy of wildflowers.

"Thought it would cheer you up."

Among the flowers, the larger petals of bright yellow asters frame white buttercups. He holds it to my nose and I inhale deeply.

The heady scent brings a lump to my throat. My mother used to put out fresh flowers on the dining table every two weeks. Lilies are her favorites. And often tulips. But in the two years since she was taken, the vases have remained empty, their glass murky and stained from the memories of the flowers that once were. That last bunch lived on the table for over six weeks before either of us had thought to throw them away; the water dry, the vase turned opaque from the moldering stems, and the flowers themselves hard and brittle and leached of color.

"When my father and I went hunting," Joe says, lifting the posy to his own nose, "I always came back with a posy for my mother. It seemed to soften the kill somewhat, or perhaps it masked the blood on our clothes."

Our arms brush, his shirt creating a static electricity against mine. "That's lovely, Joe."

He pulls out one of the yellow asters and places it behind my ear. I tuck it deeper into the strands of my hair. It's been years since I put a flower in them.

His eyes suddenly dart away and he holds a finger close to my lips just as I'm about to say something. "Shhh."

I follow his eyeline. Ahead, a doe lies on the ground, its flank dripping an ugly wound. Joe grips the handle of his machete.

"No, Joe."

"We need to eat," he whispers out the side of his mouth. "Although we'll lose a chunk by cutting around that bite mark. I'm not willing to take my chances with infected meat. Looks like a nasty wound."

I nod but close my eyes. After a sickening *thwak* and a subsequent *thud*, I know it's all over. When I open my eyes, the mournful, brown eyes of the doe stare back up at me. Joe splits the body the length of its belly.

I wrinkle my nose. "I don't know how you can do that."

Arms elbow-deep in intestines, Joe looks up. "You get used to it." Small slicing and hacking noises come from behind. "Nearly done!"

The small little wet sounds continue, and I hunch my shoulders against them. I can't move. All I can think about is the doe behind me, being sliced into an unrecognizable mess. Not a wolf. Not a hellhound. An innocent prey animal.

It didn't deserve to die.

But Joe is right: we need to eat.

"Would you mind grabbing some wood for a fire?" Joe asks.

I nod and push myself to my feet. At least I can avoid the smell of blood for a while. Walking away, I gather a range of twigs and sticks, remembering the summers of camping. Which reminds me of Matt. And then my mother and father. All of it.

I dump the sticks at Joe's feet and remove the pictures of my family from my rucksack, examining their smiling faces. Matt's sandy blond hair, always in need of a haircut, looking as though he's just come from the beach. His depthless blue eyes are piercing even in a one-dimensional photo, and his T-shirt emphasizes the muscular curves of his body. My chest tightens. He should be at the cave by now. Then my gaze shifts to my parents. A photo I took on the last family vacation we were allowed. Mountains in the background. Their faces slightly in shadow but smiling. Bunny ears behind my dad's head.

I cradle one picture in each hand and kiss them both.

Tears fall silently, which I wipe away with the back of my hand.

"Silver?" Joe crouches at my side, his hand on my shoulder.

"Please don't touch me."

His hand falls to his side and the look of sympathy in his eyes almost makes me lose it completely. "I know it's hard."

I nod. "For you too."

His voice is quiet. "For everyone."

"I don't know what I'd do if anything happened to any of them." I sniff up the tears. "I just… It'd break me."

Joe's hand wavers in front of me. "We can't think like that. We just have to keep moving."

"I know." I shove the photos back in my pack.

I sniff a couple more times, wipe my eyes and present Joe with my most cheery smile, which doesn't fool either of us.

"That's the spirit," he says, patting the ground beside him. "Now, come sit by the fire."

I crawl over to a small, flickering fire, sticks of meat already roasting and filling the darkening air with a new aroma. The doe's carcass has disappeared.

"Thanks, Joe." I nudge my arm against his.

He just smiles and hands me a stick. He watches me as I nibble cautiously, his eyes catching the light of the fire. When I don't retch the meat back up, I eat some more.

"So, boyfriend?" Joe asks, licking his fingers.

I splutter. Joe laughs.

"Isn't that a little personal?"

Joe shrugs his massive shoulders. "Reckon if we can talk about incarcerated parents we can talk about boyfriends."

"No!" I throw the empty stick onto the fire. "I do not have a boyfriend. I've been living under armed guard for two years. No guy is going to go near that."

"Ah, don't sell us guys too short, just because we don't always think with our brains." Joe taps his head and offers me a goofy smile.

Laughing, I throw a pinecone at him.

"It's just that, the whole time I've been with you, you keep touching that necklace." He nods at my pendant and wipes a dibble of meat juice gathering in his cleft. "Like someone special gave it to you."

"Matt. Just Matt." But he's so much more than that. "He's my best friend." I finger the necklace as a nagging hope flutters into my chest. *Please be safe.* "I always thought he and Diana would be a couple."

"Diana?"

I sigh. "Our other best friend. Nanite death on her thirteenth birthday. She was a swimmer." I take the acorns out of my pocket and rotate them in my hand like tiny stress balls. "I think it was her fifth pill, and I don't even remember what. Maybe shark something or

115

other, but it killed her at school." I'm so used to telling this story that I hardly even feel it anymore. Except right now. A whole medley of resentment, anger and loss slices through me.

Matt and I sat there holding her in the hallway for over an hour, not letting the ambulance crew near her lifeless body. She hadn't even wanted the pill. Served to her in a cupcake for her thirteenth birthday by her pushy, fairy-winged parents.

I throw my knife and it lands square in the middle of a trunk.

"I'm sorry. I lost a friend that way too." Joe raises his hands to the flames, rubbing them together. "Does the knife stuff help?" He swivels his head from me to the tree.

"Not really." I launch to my feet, stalk to the tree and wrench the knife away. I re-join Joe and flop to the ground, stabbing another piece of meat with the blade. The yellow flower falls out of my hair and drops into the fire, burning out of existence in a few seconds.

Joe rests a hand on my shoulder and squeezes gently. "You OK?" The warmth of his fingers presses into my tense muscles.

"I will be."

"Thatta girl." Joe pauses, then points to the knife. "I'm impressed with how quickly you've picked that up. You're getting really good at throwing."

"I better be," I say. My hands grip the hilt so tightly my fingers ache. "I'm planning on doing that to President Bear's face."

Joe laughs. "I'll be in line right behind you."

CHAPTER NINE

Joe hacks through the ferns with his machete. The sun presses down on us and I realize the gaps in the trees are bigger. Rhododendrons line our route, their large purple flowers adding to the hope in my heart, but trepidation lessens it as I realize how easily we can be seen.

Today, I'm sure we'll reach the edge of the forest and find the cave system. The trees thin as we walk, and wide meadows full of wildflowers and tall grasses offer idyllic resting spots. By mid-afternoon I know I'll have a sunburn. We stop for frequent rests and water but never stay long.

Anticipation pushes us onward. We lose the stream, and our canteens run dangerously low. I'm beginning to worry about our water supply; our path is lined with only bushes and ferns. Joe keeps one eye on the sky and I keep swiveling my gaze, looking for an ambush.

"I think we're almost there." Despite my weariness, my pace quickens.

We trudge up an incline and pause on a ridge to inspect the valley from the cover of the few fern clumps.

"Any idea where now?" Joe asks, parting a gap in the ferns.

I close my eyes and breathe deeply, imagining I can smell freedom. The melody of my new song floats through my head. I'll have to play it for Matt when I can get my hands on a guitar again.

With Matt's instructions in my mind, I scan the valley. The vegetation is thin and doesn't conceal much, but a dense pocket of fir trees a mile or so farther stands out. That must be where the entrance to the cave is concealed.

I point. "There."

Joe and I scramble down a steep descent to the valley floor. There's no cover here. If a helicopter appears, we'll be caught. With my heart thudding in my chest, we scamper down the hill as quickly as we can manage, throwing worried looks back at the cover of the forest. We trip over the uneven ground as pebbles and loose dirt skitter under our feet.

Arriving at the base of the clump of trees, we stand close together, uncertain what to do now or how to find the entrance. The bushes part and we duck. I prepare myself to fight.

"Hello, stranger." The voice from the dense foliage startles me.

A few seconds later Matt appears, smiling.

"Matt!" I throw my arms around him and squeeze hard enough to keep the emotions inside. I've never been so glad to see anyone. He holds me just as tightly and buries his face in my hair. Then he pushes back a little and plants a big kiss on my cheek, catching the corner of my mouth.

"It's so good to see you," I say, examining him for differences. He looks well, even a little tanned.

"And you. I'm so glad you made it. I heard the hellhounds were in the forest and I didn't know what to think." Matt's eyes crinkle at the edges. He glances at my necklace and touches a finger to the pendant.

"Well, we had an up close and personal with one," I say, a wave of pride swelling over me. "I'll tell you all about it later."

Matt's eyes go to Joe next and immediately narrow. He's never been a big fan of football players.

"Matt, this is Joe. We met in the woods and he saved me, more than once." I desperately hope they'll get along. Matt is my best friend in the world and Joe is, well, Joe is Joe.

They shake hands, examining each other from head to foot.

Matt looks at the ridge line. "Where's your dad?"

I don't move, but drop my gaze.

"Shit." Matt runs a hand through his lengthening hair, pulling at the roots. "Is he...?"

I hunch a shoulder. "He was injured in the hellhound attack." I clear my throat, willing the tremble to disappear. Anxiety comes knocking back, threading through my wobbly calf muscles. "Taken by the army."

Whop-whop-whop.

We all glance at the sky. The helicopter isn't visible yet, but it's near.

"Let's get you guys inside," Matt says, parting the branches at his back to reveal a door sunken into the ground.

Whop-whop-whop.

The wind picks up my hair and we all press into the shrubs. Matt pulls the door open and we tumble inside. The sound of the helicopter blades is immediately quieted.

With the door closed behind us, my heart stills. I blink as my eyes adjust to the lighting of a few LED lanterns along the walls. The temperature drops significantly and the smell of damp clay hangs in the air. As we walk, Joe stoops under the occasional stalactite. But he trips, bangs his knee on a rock and hits his head on the ceiling. A mini avalanche crumbles down the wall.

"Oops." Joe tries to catch some of the rolling pebbles. I sneak a glance at Matt, who tries hard to hold back a smile. I step on his foot and wag a finger at him.

We follow Matt for a couple of minutes before we

emerge into an enormous chamber. The edges are ringed with pairs of stalactites and stalagmites stretching toward each other, the center relatively flat and smooth.

"This is our main assembly area," Matt says. The room is as big as the school practice gym. I turn in a circle, surveying the expanse, and spot huddled shapes at the edges of the room. Moans and murmurs filter toward me. Pain-filled pupils catch in the dim light. As my eyes adjust, I wince when I see the blood-stained bandages and several people clammy with fever.

"What's going on?"

Matt surveys the room with his hands on his hips. "People got injured on their way here."

"Your family?" I ask.

Matt taps an erratic rhythm against his thigh. "They're OK, but Lyla's in a compound."

"Damn, I'm sorry, Matt." My hand floats to his and I squeeze his jittering fingers.

Joe opens his mouth to say something, but Matt cuts in. "She's alive, I think. They're not killing anyone yet."

I drop my rucksack and dive into the section holding the bottles of pills. I hand over the regeneration bottle. Matt reads the label, his eyebrows shooting high.

"This will help. Thanks, Silver."

A familiar shape approaches from across the chamber, dragging his left leg. A shape that fills my eyes with tears. A few feet before me, he bows.

"Sensei," I say. "You're here."

Then Claus wraps me in his arms and kisses the top of my head. "I'm so glad you're safe."

I introduce Joe and ask Claus about his leg.

"Shot through the knee," Claus replies, lifting his leg a little.

I nod at the regeneration pills, but Claus shakes his head. "Let's save them for those who really need them."

Matt hands the pills to a girl with long dark hair and skin so pale it's nearly translucent, but what really draws my eye are her enormous wings. The green of jungle leaves, of precious jade jewels, of bioluminescent plankton. The feathers ruffle and sway in all directions, almost whispering. She turns, and her irises sparkle with an emerald beauty. It's a common side effect of nanites: your irises change to reflect the modifications in your body.

"Who *is* that?" I murmur.

Matt turns to look. "Paige. She's been helpful."

She walks around the perimeter of the chamber, handing out the pills to those most in need, her voice soft and warm, her hands alighting on heads, patting shoulders, wrapping bandages tighter. People smile when she approaches, raising their hands to touch her. One kid plucks a green feather right out of her plumage. She smiles and offers him a second. In the distance, I spot another girl with wings—fairy wings—and a taller girl with long red hair who is almost as big as a bulk.

123

"I didn't realize there would be so many alts here," I say.

"It seems it isn't just the unadjusteds who are unhappy with the current government." Matt tucks his thumbs into his belt loops. "We even had someone with telekinesis arrive yesterday. He could be extremely useful."

Beside me, Joe reaches into his backpack and removes the roasted venison he packaged in a plastic bag. "If you don't mind, I'm going to go hand this off. Hopefully it will help in some small way."

"Kitchen is that way." Matt indicates toward the back. "Thank you, Joe."

"Catch you later," I say.

Claus taps Matt on the shoulder and points to a narrow passageway with his cane. "Why don't you show Silver around?"

I bow at Claus, and Matt leads me away.

"So, who's in charge around here?" I crane my neck to see farther down the passage.

"Francesca."

"Francesca?"

"Mrs. Montoya."

"Our social studies teacher?" I grab his arm. "The one with the tight bun and spider brooch?"

"The very same." Matt chuckles. "And that spider brooch is an anti-Bear symbol."

I arch an eyebrow. "She's been wearing that for years."

"Exactly."

On the other side of the chamber, the injured people who were huddled on the floor begin to stretch and move. They reach for me as I walk by, wide-eyed with wonder and muttering thanks for bringing the regeneration pills. My name is whispered from mouth to mouth. I wonder if they also know about the reward.

Matt's elbow brushes against mine as he explains the cave's layout. "Four other passageways lead off this chamber. One goes to the kitchens, one goes to the bedrooms—and I say that loosely—one goes to the underground lake, and another leads to a series of smaller chambers where we're storing weapons and other equipment."

"Kitchens? Lakes? How big is this place?"

"Huge." He winks. "We lost Megan for a couple hours. We've replaced her wheels with thick tire treads and she's been rolling through the cave like it's just an obstacle course. My parents were seriously freaked out."

"Typical Megan."

"Silver!" Kyle runs a blurry circle around me, then throws his skinny arms around my neck.

"Hi, Kyle." I smile, then remember the last time he touched me in the practice gym when I got the worst cramp ever. I gently remove his arms. "If we've got you here, we'll be taking down Bear before we know it."

He grins and punches the air before taking off down the passageway. "Catch you later! Just on an errand!"

I run my fingers along the damp walls, appreciating the cool after the forest humidity. "How many people are here?"

"So far, we've accounted for about two hundred unadjusteds and adjusteds combined. But more arrive every day. We think we can house up to five hundred, and we're in contact with neighboring hideouts."

"Impressive." I examine the sinuous passageways, trying to picture a new life here, wondering how long we'll have to stay.

We visit the lake, then the weapons chamber. A large room, walls lined with a palsy number of weapons. A few knives, an array of whittled spears and a couple of rifles. Homemade crossbows, maces, slingshots, and some things I don't recognize. Not enough for a rescue mission, let alone an entire resistance movement.

Matt shows me some of the other smaller rooms dotted around. Some people seem to be training in combat. No doubt Claus started them all as soon as he arrived. A fairy flies over the head of a knife-throwing unadjusted. Young children score bull's-eyes with handguns, while an elf takes out the legs of a teenager with indiscernible abilities.

"What are they practicing for?" I whisper in Matt's ear so as not to distract the combatants.

"Their lives," Matt replies, knitting his brow. "We won't be able to live here forever. At some point, we'll need to make a stand."

"And rescue my parents."

"Rescue?" Matt kicks at the ground.

"Yeah." I stare at him hard. "Your sister too, and everyone else rounded up in a compound."

Matt strokes his jaw. "Maybe eventually."

"Eventually?" I look back the way we've come, wondering if I can remember how to get out. I'm still wearing my backpack. I have everything I need.

Matt moves his hand to his hip, seeming to read my mind. "There's a price on your head, Silver. It's not safe for you to go anywhere."

"I will not sit around on my ass waiting for something to happen." I push the words through gritted teeth.

Matt puts a hand on my shoulder. I shrug him off. "Silver, I know Francesca really wants your parents here. She thinks they're an important symbol to the resistance, but more than that, they might have some ideas about how to get out of this genetic mess."

I jab a finger in the air between us. "Now you're talking some sense."

"But we don't have the supplies to launch a rescue mission. Yet."

"What do we need?" I ask, heading toward the archway.

Matt follows me. "To start with, food. Then weapons."

"OK, I'm on it." I keep marching. "Where's the nearest town?"

"Silver. Slow down." Matt keeps up with my fast pace, both of us ducking under stalactites. "The nearest town has turned into a warzone. Altereds are killing each other. The bigger cities have unadjusted compounds to keep them all sane, but nothing near here. It's not safe to go anywhere alone. It's going to take time to put scout groups together."

"I don't have time," I snap, but I stop walking. Both my parents could be dead already. But no, President Bear is too sadistic for that. He'll use them to reel me in, and I'll let him if it means I can get close to him.

"Silver." Matt's eyes settle on mine. I guard myself against his pity. "You just got here. Take a breath. Get some rest. We'll figure it out."

I look down at my scuffed boots. His words make sense. Of course they do. I can't go off all half-cocked to fight President Bear. Just me and a knife and an eternal vat of anger.

Blowing out a long breath, I nod.

"Come on." He grabs the upper loop of my backpack. "You've been carrying that backpack around all this time. Let me show you where you can dump it."

The last passageway leads to the bedrooms. I understand why Matt air-quoted the word. The hollowed-out areas that pass for rooms lie the length of a twisting passage, stretching farther than I can see. Numbers and sometimes names are scratched onto the door arches. Sleeping bags and pillows have been thrown on the floors. A few have pictures of loved ones tacked to walls. Some have extra towels and blankets nailed over the entrance, offering a semblance of privacy.

Matt indicates some empty chambers for my use, and I dump what few belongings I have and lay out my sleeping bags. I recognize Joe's backpack in the hollow beside mine.

We both look up as footsteps pad down the passageway. A familiar shape melts from the gloom.

"Mrs. Montoya?"

She steps forward and takes both of my hands in hers. "Please, call me Francesca."

She's swapped the mid-calf-length skirt for more practical hiking trousers, but her severe lower neck bun remains the same. Her dark hair is peppered with gray around her face and her stern nose adds a little attitude to her short stature. The spider brooch gleams brightly on the shirt. "I just heard about your arrival and your parents. I'm so sorry, Silver."

Matt dips his head and I steel myself against demanding an immediate rescue mission.

"Let me know if there's anything I can do," Francesca says.

I'm about to pose a question about food runs or weaponry, but Matt shakes his head and I fall silent. "Thank you," I say, then frown. "I'm worried about this price on my head. A million dollars—"

"Two million," Matt says. "It's gone up."

I push that information down deep. "What do they want me for? They already have my parents."

Francesca's cheeks tighten. "My guess is your parents are unwilling to comply with Bear's requests. If they have you, it will apply some pressure."

I swallow hard. "Do I have to worry about someone here turning me in?"

Francesca doesn't answer right away. She stares at me and her red lips turn pale. "It's always prudent to be careful, but I would never turn you or anyone else away."

Matt grabs my elbow and steers me toward the main chamber. "You can't think like that. You'll drive yourself crazy. Besides, everyone here wants the same thing we do: President Bear gone and their families out of compounds. There's not enough money in the world to change that."

I cross the fingers on both my hands, knowing it's childish but still hoping it will help. "I really hope you're right."

CHAPTER TEN

I hide behind Matt as we enter the chamber. A growing line leads to the kitchen, where people emerge with bowls of soup and fresh rolls. Joe joins us as I inhale the aroma of warm bread and venison. Ahead, a fairy hovers.

I tap the side of Matt's head with my knuckles. "Are you sure we're all on the same side?"

Matt chuckles. "I've talked to quite a few of them. They were being forced into careers pigeon-holed by their nanites. They're unhappy too, Silver."

"But a fairy? Really?" Although I've learned to give Joe the benefit of the doubt, he's still a rarity among the mentality of bulks. I know I should give this fairy the same opportunities, but something about the sight of those shimmering wings sets my teeth on edge. They remind me of someone I don't want to be reminded of. Several someones.

But I can't take my eyes off her either. There's

something about her wings. Although iridescent like most altered butterfly wings, that's where the similarities end. This fairy's wings shimmer and change color, from pearlescent pinks to opal whites to the yellow of sandy beaches. They flutter faster than a hummingbird, allowing her to maintain a distance a few inches off the ground, and shimmer in a pastel rainbow. Silver flecks decorate her long, lavender hair, sparkling in the dim light. She turns, and the most beautiful violet eyes settle on Joe.

"Erica?" Joe says. "Is that you?"

A huge grin spreads across the fairy's face, showing off a daintily pointed chin and a perfect button nose. Her eyes light up. "Joe? Oh my God! It's so good to see you. When did you get here?"

He steps closer to her, smiling. "Just arrived today. You?"

"Last week, with Addison and Naomi. Do you remember them from school?" Her hands cycle a mile a minute, almost as fast as her wings, and they touch Joe's shoulders often.

The cleft in the center of Joe's chin deepens as he smiles. "Sure. Of course. How are you?"

Annoyance flashes through me.

Matt chuckles. "Happy reunions everywhere."

"Mm."

Erica's wings shimmer in different colors, from russet

oranges to the deep reds and purples of an eastern sunset, as they continue talking. For some reason that annoys me even more.

I toe the ground and keep my eyes off Joe and the fairy, their reunion a little too physical for my liking. "I can't believe you let a fairy in here."

Matt raises an eyebrow. "She's not like the ones at school."

One of the few things I enjoyed about my trek through the woods was not having to lay eyes on a single fairy. I left Annabelle and her mean-girl crowd behind. The one time they got their hands on me, years ago, before I started karate training, they stuck my head in the toilet. Not an original form of bullying, but effective. I refused to go to school for a week, and when I finally admitted to Mom what happened, she was the one to suggest karate.

"And didn't you befriend a bulk?" Matt asks, his eyes sparkling with amusement. "Aren't they just as bad?"

"Joe's different." I catch sight of him still talking to Erica, their heads dipped, laughter widening their smiles. The food line edges forward.

Grabbing two plates of bread and a small portion of venison, Matt frowns.

"What's wrong?" I ask.

"I thought we were scheduled for more food than this."

I look at the metal plate. Half a roll and a large

ladleful of steaming soup with chunks of venison. It isn't a lot, but it's enough.

His eyes sweep over the crowd, scanning the serving line. "Food has been going missing."

I follow his gaze as an icy tickle creeps down my neck. "Missing?"

"Or maybe we just have a lot more people here now, plus the healed people eating more." Balancing his plate and cup in one hand, Matt rakes a hand through his hair. "That must be what it is." But he doesn't sound convinced.

Finding a dark corner where I plan to keep my face hidden, we sit cross-legged, facing each other. The fairy flutters around Joe, throwing her head back and clutching her stomach as she laughs at something he says. I can see the amusement in his eyes across the chamber. He loves to make people laugh. Is that what he was doing in the forest?

"The fairy's name is Erica Swiftfield," Matt says, spraying crumbs as he talks. "She's been quite involved in the resistance so far. She's pretty nice once you get to know her."

I groan inwardly. I have no desire to get to know her any better.

"She's also lethal with a bow and arrow," he adds.

"What's with the color-changing wings?" Right now they're a deep maroon.

"Oh, you noticed that?" Matt pulls the crust off his roll. "It's an interesting little quirk of hers; they change color according to her mood."

"That must be... awkward." I wonder what mood the russet oranges, deep reds and purples reflect now that she's talking to Joe.

"I guess, if you can figure out the pattern." Matt uses his roll to spoon soup into his mouth. "I'm so relieved you're finally here." Matt looks up from his meal and wipes his adorable moustache away with a sleeve, then he runs a finger along the back of my hand, gently at first, before prodding harder.

I laugh and swat him away. "I'm real! You don't need to pinch me."

"Good." Matt grins. "Because circumstances have a habit of changing too quickly around here." The grin slips away.

"What is it?" I ask.

"I'm worried about Lyla. She's not strong." His Adam's apple bobs. "Not like you."

"What happened?" I wrap my hands around the warm mug of tea.

"She was at dance camp when we ran. We didn't have a chance to get to her." Matt drums his fingers against his knee. "Now all the unadjusteds have been rounded up and put in compounds."

My thoughts spin back to a conversation between my

parents, both of them tutting over dinner, and I realize why the unadjusteds are being rounded up and kept in compounds.

My parents said if an altered took too many nanites with animal DNA, they would lose their humanity. The animal DNA would take over, and higher thinking would be lost. But Bear had refused them the funds to test the theory.

Clearly they were right.

When the unadjusteds fled, the altereds lost the stabilizing presence of the unadjusteds. So they needed them close, in compounds, where they could control them.

I lean closer. "Do you know where she is?"

The flickering lanterns highlight the frown on his face as he rubs at a patch of stubble. "There are so many compounds. I have no idea how to find her."

"I'm sorry, Matt." I reach for his hand. "I know how it feels." *Mom. Dad.*

His jaw tightens. "Once we're organized, I'm going to go out looking for her."

"I'm with you, and we'll rescue all of them."

A walkie-talkie attached to Matt's belt crackles. He flicks the switch.

Claus' voice comes over the airwaves. "...helicopters still out here. Over."

"How many? Over," Matt asks, glancing at the ceiling as if he can see through it.

"Hard to tell. Maybe three. Over."

"Understood. Over."

Matt stands. He taps a spoon against his own metal mug and clears his throat. "Shhhh."

Everyone quietens.

"Helicopters overhead. We need to keep the noise to a minimum," Matt says in a lowered voice.

Conversations stop. The only noises are the gentle clinks of silverware and the odd cry of a child. Matt sits again beside me.

"Does this happen often?" I whisper.

"It's happened once or twice. We don't really know if sound transmits out of the cave, so we play it safe."

I take a bite of the crust on my roll, but even that small crunching seems too loud.

We finish our meal in silence. Sibilant whispers snake through different groups. Many people dip their heads as if in prayer. I wince when a baby starts to cry. The father picks it up and jiggles it against his shoulder, shushing it and patting its back.

A few minutes later, Matt's walkie-talkie crackles again.

"All clear. Over."

Matt stands and addresses the group. "Immediate danger has passed, but let's keep it on the quiet side for tonight.

"Speaking of noise, that reminds me." Matt reaches

into a crevice in the side of the wall. "I hid this away earlier. This is for you."

Tears spring to my eyes when he presses a guitar into my hands. After I left mine behind at the apartment, I never thought I'd hold one again. The strings vibrate under my fingers, begging to be loved.

Matt wipes a tear from my cheek. "It's supposed to make you happy."

"It does. Thank you." I wrap my hand around the neck of the guitar and cradle it to my body. My fingers pluck quietly at the strings. "Where did it come from?"

Matt's lips twist into a sad grimace. "Someone who didn't make it here."

The guitar weighs heavily in my hands, and I play for the person who lost their life carrying it.

"Thank you," I whisper, my hands forming the chords I've only envisioned in my mind. "Listen to this."

"We are the sun, we are the dawn,
We are the voice that urges you along.
Cast your eyes to the wreckage, the oppression, and the pain,
Lift your sights to the horizon—learn to live again.
We are the pain, we are the tears,
We're the voices that were lost over the years.
But when our hearts burn quiet in the dark of night,

We won't bear to keep this silence—we will stand, and we will fight."

This time it is Matt's eyes that glisten with emotion. He clears his throat. "That's beautiful. And so strong. And so... *everything.*"

"Right?"

"We need something like that." His voice catches. "An anthem. It will unite everyone. Give them hope."

I smile. Matt always thinks of the bigger picture. For me the words are a way to unleash the fury in my heart. The song is a promise to find justice, but he sees how it can be so much more than that.

The fluttering of wings skims across my cheek. Paige, the girl with the beautiful green feathers and emerald eyes, crouches next to us and smiles at me. "Hi."

After Matt makes introductions, Paige says, "I've talked Meg into a supply run tomorrow. We're going to hit that warehouse on the edge of town." She turns to me. "Silver, I hear you can handle yourself with a knife?"

I nod.

Matt pokes my ribs. "When did that happen? Being a black belt wasn't enough for you?"

I flick his knee. "I had lots of practice in the woods."

"Would you like to come with us?" Paige asks.

"Absolutely." My spirits lift at the thought of a supply run tomorrow.

I stay in the main chamber with Matt for another hour, plucking at the guitar. A small crowd gathers around me, and the words of my freedom song pass from mouth to mouth until a few sing along. The passion shines strong from their eyes, and I see I have nothing to fear. They are just as desperate and furious as I am. There is no price for freedom. Not even two million dollars.

CHAPTER ELEVEN

I shake out the nightmares and roll the kinks out of stiff muscles from sleeping on a rock floor. A yellow ball of fur streaks into the room, and a pink tongue licks my face.

"Einstein!" I grab the golden retriever by the collar, pull him closer, and scrunch him behind the ears. He is Matt's, given to him on his tenth birthday. I went to the pet shop with him to pick him out. Amid the freakishly human talking birds and color-changing lizards and fish whose bubbles played music, Matt opted for an unadjusted puppy.

"Morning," Matt says. "You sleep OK?"

I nod, rubbing at a tense spot on my neck. "It's nice to have walls around me again. Even if they are rock."

Matt nods, seeming to understand. "Hey, we're gathering in the main chamber before we go on the supply run."

"Now?"

Matt smiles. "Yes."

I scramble for my boots and lace them on, and soon we're walking toward the main chamber, now empty of injured people. Matt steers me to the kitchen area and dips his hand into one of several baskets, then hands me a granola bar.

I look at the measly offering. "This is it?"

Matt tears open his own. "I'm afraid so."

I scan the kitchen. Half the baskets are empty. "Food run out or missing?"

"Still unclear. I haven't done a stock take, which I'll have to do from now on. But there are things I remember seeing that aren't around any longer."

"Who would steal food?" I look at the people gathered in the chamber, eating the same breakfast. Most of them are thin, probably having lost weight on their way here.

"I have no idea."

A few people are gathered by the cave entrance, and they fall silent as we approach. Joe is there with Kyle, Paige, and Erica, the fairy with lavender hair.

"You're Silver Melody," Erica says, eyeing me. A bow and quiver are slung over one of her petite shoulders.

I nod and curse the granola crumbs stuck at the corners of my mouth.

There are two others I don't recognize. A bulk, a little shorter than Joe, with much darker hair and a permanent frown etched into his forehead. Joe noogies

142

the top of the guy's head, then they high-five and recount some football game where Joe's team beat his. The second is another girl almost as tall as Joe. Flamered hair licks the length of her spine. She wears shorts and some sort of Amazonian getup across her chest. All leather straps and bangles. Intricately woven tattoos decorate her hands and arms. Old-school ones, not the more recent animated versions. Two throwing stars are buried in the leather cuffs at her wrists.

She looks from Matt to me. "Is this a good idea?"

I bristle, and my fingers dance across the hilt of my knife.

"Addison," Matt addresses the tall girl. "Silver is an asset to the team. She's a black belt in karate."

She tightens the straps snaking around her waist, never taking her pale eyes off me. "But still. If she's seen, it could be dangerous for all of us. There's a price on her head."

"I'm aware," I say, raising my chin. "I'm happy to go alone if my presence causes a problem."

Erica's wings flutter an icy blue while Addison takes a step back.

"We need Silver," Matt says, staring at each member of the group. No one disagrees. A flicker of smugness pushes my shoulder back. Claus would not approve.

Matt leads the way up the passageway into the open. I slit my eyes against the rising sun until they adjust.

After we conceal the entrance, we follow Matt up the far side of the valley and through a sparse forest until we reach the edge of a patch of disused farmland. Matt shows us where he's hidden an army jeep. It's requisitioned to fit a bulk, so my head is level with the door handle.

"We stashed this here a while ago," Matt says. "I've been trying to figure out how to re-adjust the pedals so I can drive. But I guess I don't need to now." He hands the keys to Joe, who hops into the driver's seat. When the engine splutters to life, we all clamber in.

Hal, the other bulk, sits in the front with Joe, Kyle wedged between them. Matt sits to my right, Erica and Addison to my left. Paige hangs out in the back, where there's room for her wings, and nudges her chin between the seats. A vibrant green feather floats around my head and I pluck it from the air and hand it back.

"Keep it." Paige smiles all the way to her eyes, which matches the exact shade of her cut-out T-shirt. Large loops in the back allow space for her wings. In Central City, right down the block from my apartment, is the most expensive clothing shop for winged adjusteds. All sorts of garments with sparkling holes, or lit-up hems to emphasize plumage. Of course, I've never been inside, but the fairies at school would always go there first for their prom dresses.

"The last time I was here, it was meltdown city," Erica

says, wrapping her long lavender hair into a perfect bun. Her bow and quiver rest in her lap.

Addison nods. "I barely made it out alive."

Erica pats her knee. "I had you covered."

"You came this way?" Matt asks.

Erica nods. "We're not from Central City. We came from inland, a couple of states over. But they're all the same."

Joe stops the jeep at the edge of a deserted parking lot. A breeze pushes trash across the empty lot, sending it skittering toward the trees. A rust-colored stain mars the white lines of a parking space. Peering closer, I realize it's blood. A huge gray warehouse towers at the other side of the car park. A couple of cars lie at angles to the bays, doors open, spilling bodies onto the tarmac.

"Jesus," Matt mutters, running his hand along the door frame.

"What happened here?" I whisper. The smell of stale blood drifts close, making me gag.

"People went cray-cray." Erica circles her fingers over her ears.

"But not you?" I ask.

Erica's violet eyes stare hard enough to drill holes. "No. Not me. I only took one nanite."

Silence unfolds around the group as we take in the scene. I've been attacked by wolves and a hellhound and trailed by the army, but I haven't seen this much blood. Ever.

"Do we drive a bit closer or leave the jeep here?" Hal asks, dragging a hand over his closely shaven hair.

Matt leans forward. "I reckon we go closer. Leave the doors open like it's another abandoned vehicle."

Slowly, inch by inch, Joe edges the jeep forward until it sits flush with the warehouse wall. He switches off the engine, and silence descends around us.

"Well, we can't sit here all day." I lean over Matt and pull the door handle.

We climb down from the jeep, hands near weapons, eyes scanning the distant trees. Kyle blurs his way to the open warehouse door and disappears inside. He returns a moment later with two thumbs up and a jubilant smile.

"Let's go," Matt says.

We jog toward the door, the only sound the wind ruffling through Paige's feathers. Just as we reach the doorway, Kyle pops back into view with a thick arm wrapped around his neck and a gun pointing at his temple. We all freeze.

"Help me!" Kyle shuffles his feet, struggling against the bulk, who has him in a suffocating grip.

The bulk moves the gun from Kyle's temple and points it at Paige. Then Erica. One by one, we stare down the barrel of the gun.

"Who are you?" he asks, his voice low and guttural.

Joe and Hal exchange a look. Joe still wears his army clothing. He steps forward. "On a recon mission. Heard there were unadjusteds in the area."

"Like this one?" the bulk sneers.

"I'm not an unadjusted!" Kyle coughs.

My fingers twitch, itching to touch my knife.

The bulk juts his chin at Joe and Hal. "Show me your ID."

Joe takes another step. Hal mimics his movements and approaches the bulk's other side.

The bulk waves the gun at them, realizes his folly and points it at Matt instead. My heart freezes and I bite down hard on the inside of my cheek. Matt stays calm, barely even breathing.

"ID," the bulk growls.

Joe raises his hand, but he keeps edging closer. "In my pocket. Just gonna reach for it…"

Quicker than I can follow, Joe and Hal move at the same time. Joe slams the bulk's neck with the side of his hand, and I hope he's hit the sensitive spot. The bulk drops Kyle, whom Hal grabs and shoves out of the way. The gun waves all over the place, and the rest of us duck and dive to avoid its path. Then Joe grabs the bulk's arm, Hal the gun, and they secure him in an arm-lock. The soldier struggles, but he's coughing so hard his cheeks puff out and his face turns red.

Joe and Hal push him inside the warehouse. By the

time the rest of us enter, it's over. The bulk lies dead along the wall, a hole in his throat, a puddle of blood under his neck.

Kyle kicks him in the ribs. He's trembling.

I touch his shoulder. "You're OK now, Kyle."

He turns his head away and swipes at his nose.

The rest of us catch our breaths and let our eyes adjust to the gloomy interior. Dust plumes circle in the shaft of light that bleeds through the door. Hal sneezes and Addison puts a finger to her lips. Paige's wings drift, stirring the thick air.

"OK." Matt looks at us all. "It's a supermarket warehouse. Our priority is flour and other dried goods. As much as we can fit in the jeep."

Kyle refuses to talk or meet anyone's eyes, busying himself instead with collecting pallets of pasta and cans. He leaves the heavy sacks of flour to Joe and Hal. After an hour of stacking goods near the door, we think we have enough food to feed the cave population for at least a week.

Joe stands in the doorway, about to start loading the jeep, when he suddenly ducks inside and pulls everyone around the corner of an aisle. Clopping footsteps and the irritated shriek of a walkie-talkie sound outside.

Without warning, the door slams closed and we're thrust into darkness. Next comes the sickening slam of three deadbolts.

"We're locked inside," I say.

Joe shakes his head. "I can break through the door. But we don't know who or what is on the other side."

"Could be that soldier wasn't alone," Erica says. We all look at the dim outline of the dead bulk that Joe dragged into the warehouse. The smell of blood hovers.

"Let's give it a couple of hours," Matt suggests. "If we wait for nightfall, we'll have the cover of darkness and whoever is out there might have left. I'm hoping it's just a security guard."

"And if they hang around?" Kyle asks.

Erica thwacks the string of her bow. Matt nods at her. "Then we'll have to take them out."

"Let's go up there." Matt points. A gloomy light sucks some of the darkness from a small second story. A few storage boxes stacked haphazardly and dark office windows are behind that. "We'll be out of the way in case someone decides to come in."

Joe leads the way up the metal stairs.

"Shhhh." I poke him as his heavy boots clang against metal. Of course, he doesn't feel a thing.

Once we're gathered upstairs, Kyle performs a quick check of the offices before declaring we're alone. "There's a shotgun and a box of shells in one of the offices."

"Excellent." Matt ducks inside the office and grabs the gun and ammunition.

Paige sits on a box, her wings sending a cool breeze

over my skin. Addison sits on the floor. Erica tightens the strings on her bow and sorts her quiver of arrows. Kyle opens one of the boxes to find it full of chocolate, which he hands out to everyone. Joe and Hal slip down to the concrete floor. Matt touches my shoulder and indicates a quieter area around a stack of boxes.

Around the corner, the light reduces and I let my eyes adjust.

"I could use a moment," Matt says, perching on a box. "I really hope those soldiers don't come back. Not sure how much death I can take in one day."

I slip down next to him. "Did you run into anyone in the woods?"

He tilts his head. "One. I'm still having nightmares."

I push away the image of a deadly hellhound. "I don't think I'll ever stop."

"I never really thought about how I would feel." He runs a hand through his hair, pulling at the roots. "I just wanted to leave the city. Get out from under President Bear. I mean, I knew there'd be death and blood, I'm not stupid, but I didn't realize it would haunt my dreams the way it does. I barely sleep more than an hour at a go anymore."

"Nighttime is the worst when you're alone with your thoughts and you can't get out of your head."

"Exactly."

"Come find me when you feel like that. I don't care if it's the middle of the night."

Matt presses his lips against my hand. "Ditto."

I hold out my hand to him. "We have each other. And it's not just us, but also the whole population of the cave. We're not alone."

A flicker of movement catches my eye. Too late, I notice the footprints in the dust. A whirling blur hurtles toward me. As I leap to my feet, I catch sight of naked skin and reptilian eyes. A heavy pain slams into my shoulder. I buckle to one knee and sweep my other leg toward the attacker. But he's strong. Focused.

Matt calls for help as I swivel on my hands and regain my footing. The shape comes at me again. A series of front punches, roundhouse kicks and a back thrust kick which I barely manage to block. Whoever it is has some serious technique. Adrenaline courses through me.

I dodge the next attack, and the assailant sails into a box before springing up almost immediately.

As I prepare for another attack, Matt asks, "What do I do?" I risk a glance at him. He stands next to a stack of boxes, shuffling his weight from one foot to the other.

"Just stay there."

I sense the others behind me. The small scratching sound of Erica nocking an arrow.

The assailant stands a few feet away, sizing me up with his reptilian eyes. Wearing only underwear, intricate animated tattoos snake around every inch of olive skin, defining his toned muscles.

Sensing him about to pounce, I attack first, dashing forward with a snap punch, then a low sweep that makes him stumble. Before he can catch his footing, I press forward with a series of knee strikes and punches. He trips over a box and falls backward.

Joe and Hal rush forward and grab the attacker's arms, pinning them behind his back.

"Watch his legs," I warn.

Matt turns to me, his blue eyes wide. "What the hell was that?"

"What was what?" I ask, resting my hands on my thighs.

He steps close but doesn't touch me. "What you just did."

"What are you talking about? You've seen me fight before."

Matt shakes his head. "Not like that."

"Yeah, Silver, it was like you'd taken a speed nanite," Kyle pipes up. "You were as fast as me."

The others stare at me, all nodding.

"That's impossible," I say, a smirk ready on my lips.

Joe pushes the attacker onto a box and chains him to a radiator with a couple of cable ties. "I always wondered how you took out that hellhound. Not even I could manage that, but if you had speed…"

My thoughts spin. "But I've never taken a nanite."

Erica's wings turn a deep forest green. "Your parents

are genetic scientists. They didn't have to give you a nanite."

"My parents would never—"

Matt tilts his head. With his hands on his hips, he narrows his gaze at me. "They helped a lot of people in vitro. And corrected mistakes from the earlier nanites."

I try to back away, but I'm pinned between the railing and their damning stares. "Yes, but…"

Then something my father said in the woods comes back to me. About when the modifications started to take a turn for the worse. That he and my mother knew an unadjusted would never survive. But that didn't mean they'd tampered with *my* DNA. Did it?

No. They wouldn't.

"I'm not… one of you." The railing at my back digs deeper, but I push against it, looking for a place to escape to.

Panic flashes through my limbs. My breath catches in my throat. I can't go down this route. I'm not an alt.

After Diana died, I promised myself I'd never take a nanite. And it's not like I haven't been tempted. I can see how much easier it is for the altereds. I would have been a black belt two years ago if I'd taken strength or speed.

But I promised, and that means something to me.

Diana died because of a nanite, and if I… it wouldn't be fair. No. That's not what's happening here. In time, the others will see it's just me, Silver, an unadjusted.

153

I swallow hard and push the thoughts aside, focusing on the person who's just attacked me. "I think it's more important we find out who this is."

His reptilian eyes blink, just once. A forked tongue escapes his wet lips. "I thought you were the army." He points a finger at Joe.

Joe looks down at his camouflage trousers. "Easy mistake to make. But no. We're not army."

The boy's shoulders slump. "Then who?"

I edge closer. The boy gasps, his narrow pupils widening to almost human. "You're Silver Melody."

Matt tenses.

"How do you know who I am?" I snap.

The boy presses back against the wall. "Everyone knows who you are. The reward—"

Joe lunges forward and pushes his arm into the boy's windpipe. "Are we going to be able to let you leave this warehouse?"

The boy nods vehemently. "Not going to turn you in."

"How do I know I can trust you?" I ask.

The boy coughs and Joe eases up a little. His tattoos swirl and snake around his body. "Because there's no place for me out there anymore. I've been hiding in here for a week."

Matt offers the boy a sip of water from a canteen. "Out with it, then. Who are you and where did you come from?"

Recognition kicks in. "You're Jacob Shea," I say.

He nods.

"Jacob who?" Erica flutters closer and inspects the prisoner.

Kyle pumps a fist into the air. "Hell yes you are! Dude, I knew I recognized you. What happened? Last year you got wiped out of the World Championships. Had your legs swept out before you could teleport—"

"Thanks for the reminder," Jacob says bitterly.

Kyle's smile drops. "Sorry, bro. That was some hardcore action. Dude, I have a hologram of you on my wall." He holds out a hand for a knuckle punch. "Well, my old wall."

After a couple of seconds, Jacob obliges. "Thanks for the support."

"So what happened?" I ask. "You dropped out of the circuit after that competition?"

"My dojo master disowned me. When he lost money on a bet, he kicked me out of the apartment he was renting to me and my mom. We left, then Mom and I got separated when all the shit hit the fan."

"Where's your mom now?" Matt asks.

The reptilian eyes narrow, the pupils turning to yellow slits. "I don't know."

"Unadjusted or..."

"Unadjusted," Jacob says.

"She's probably in a compound," I say.

Jacob looks at me, his tongue sweeping between his lips. "Are you all adjusteds?"

"No!" I cross my arms.

Then I look at us all. Two bulks, a fairy, a girl with green bird wings, a speedster. A seven-foot girl with flaming hair who looks like an altered, though her freakish height is just a blip of nature. Matt. And me. What am I, exactly?

Erica bursts out laughing. "We're all altereds."

CHAPTER TWELVE

I look at the group, and they all stare at me like I'm some sort of animal in a cage at a traveling carnival.

"I am not an altered," I snap. "Where the hell would I have gotten speed from anyway?"

Kyle taps my shoulder. "Maybe it was me? Before you ran, I touched your shoulder and you got that cramp."

"Yeah, but…" Kyle had never made direct contact with me before that. Claus has always been careful not to pit us against one another, what with Kyle's speed advantage, and I'd complained every day. How would I learn to beat an altered if I couldn't spar with one? I shake my head. "I've been in contact with other altereds before and nothing's happened." I look at Joe.

"I helped dress your wounds, but that was when you were unconscious," he says, frowning.

"Why don't we try a little experiment?" Erica reaches out to touch me.

I recoil. "Not you!"

Erica laughs. "It's not so bad having a pair of wings, you know."

I hang my head, a flush of shame heating my cheeks. "I'm sorry, it's not that. I just… It's too much."

It's not who I am. It's not who I want to be.

Matt doesn't say anything, just looks at me with the most pitying expression that snatches the breath right out of me.

Paige approaches. "I'll do it." She holds out her hand.

Burying my trembling hands in my chest, I try to breathe. I focus on a regular rhythm, like Claus taught me. The panic still tickles my limbs, but I don't think it will ever go away until I get this over with. Until I prove them all wrong. I killed the hellhound because I trained. I fought this new boy, Jacob, because I trained. Soon, they'll see that.

Matt whispers in my ear. "It's worth a try, Silver. I'm right here. I won't let anything happen to you."

I roll my eyes. "Let's get this over with. A big, fat nothing."

I step close to Paige and grab her outstretched hand. The pain hits immediately in waves. Hunching over, I wrap my hands around the railing and grit my teeth. Someone gasps.

Breathing heavily, I lift my head, easing my grip from the railing.

Everyone stares.

Joe's jaw drops. Matt reaches for my hand. A wide grin splits Kyle's face in half. Hal stumbles backwards until his back presses against the office window. I glance at Paige, looking for reassurance. She smiles, an uncertain twitch at the corner of her lips. Erica gives me a condescending eyebrow, her wings a smug shade of aqua blue.

"Well, I'll be…" Addison mutters.

Above my head, two brilliant blue wings hover. They move when I roll my shoulders, rising magnificently, feathers ruffling as they undulate up and down. A shorter wingspan than Paige's, but impressive all the same.

But they can't be mine. I'm not an altered. I don't amass abilities at the merest of touches. That's impossible.

I don't want this.

"I am not an altered!" I try to stamp my foot on the ground, but I'm no longer standing as my wings lift me into the air. Panicking, I cycle my legs, trying to find a sense of balance. My stomach drops and my wings beat faster.

I reach the ceiling and grab for the light fixture. The wings try to pull me higher, but I hold on to the flimsy cable.

"Let go, Silver!" Matt calls, his hands cupped around his mouth.

159

"I'll fall!"

He leans over the railing. "You have wings. You're not going to fall."

I'm squeezing the light fixture so hard I'm in danger of shattering it. "I don't know how to use them."

Erica laughs. "And yet you're on the ceiling."

I glance down at my friends again and am accosted by a severe dizzy spell. They seem so far away. If I fall… I squeeze my eyes closed and try to ignore the hammering of my heart and the corresponding beating of my wings.

"Deep breaths," Matt says. "Focus."

I will the breath into my aching lungs. Gradually, my heart rate settles, as do my wings.

"Good," Matt says. "Now, try flying down here."

I shake my head.

"I'll help you," Paige says, her green wings gliding close to my blue ones. "Take my hand."

With her eyes locked on mine, I count to ten. Her expression never changes. Her long dark hair shifts around her face. She keeps a reassuring smile on her lips, and her eyes plead with me to trust her.

"You can do it," she says.

Before I can think about it anymore or how many bones I might break if my new wings refuse to work, I reach for her hand. There is no pain this time. I reach for her other hand, and suddenly I'm pulling her down, my wings doing nothing at all.

"Concentrate." Her wings beat furiously. "Feel where your wings are."

There's a twitch at my shoulder blades and a great whoosh as my wings comply with my wishes.

A small smile splits through my anxiety.

"That's it," Paige says. "Now we go down."

Still holding hands, I slow the beating of my wings until we both step over the handrail and stand among our friends once again.

"I'd say that price on your head just got a little higher," Erica says. There's no sarcasm in her voice. Instead I detect a hint of fear.

I ignore her and bite down on my trembling lower lip. "I don't know what this means."

"It means you have abilities," Matt says, grabbing my shoulders and forcing my eyes to stay on his. "That's all."

"That's all?" I goggle at him. "I don't *want* abilities. I will not be taking on any more." I cross my arms over my chest.

How can something like this happen? I blink away the disbelief. Denial blooms, but denying the obvious won't help. Just like dwelling on the past, which never got me anywhere.

Without warning, Erica jumps off the box she's been sitting on and grabs my hand. A new pain ripples along twin tracks next to my spine. The blue wings disappear and the cream wings of a cabbage white butterfly appear in their place. They flutter with a chitinous rustle and feel much lighter than the previous wings. And they're half the size of Erica's.

The amazement at my new wings and what's happening to me is dwarfed by a furious anger. What right does she have to inflict her ability on me? I open my mouth to hurl a few abusive words at her, but Joe gets there first.

"Erica, you shouldn't have just grabbed her like that." Joe glares at her. "Didn't you hear her? She doesn't want any more abilities." He steps toward me, offering a hand.

I step back. "I don't want to be a bulk."

Joe stops. "Sorry, I wasn't trying to…" He backs up.

"No offense," I add.

Joe holds my gaze, his face unreadable, then he turns away. Shit.

"Don't dismiss other abilities so quickly." Hal nudges closer, keeping his hands clear. "You could be useful."

"*Useful*?" The hurt balls in my chest.

Hal grimaces. "Don't take that the wrong way."

Tears prick my eyes. "How am I supposed to take it?"

Before he can respond, I turn my back, ignoring Paige's and Matt's sympathetic looks, then run down the stairs. Which is harder than it seems as my wings keep fluttering and lifting me into the air. I scramble down a long aisle and around a corner, not caring whether other stowaways might be in the vicinity. Footsteps thud after me.

At the far corner of the warehouse, where I can sit in mostly darkness and pretend wings aren't protruding from my back, I hunch into a corner and weep. I don't even try to bite the tears back down.

Diana. I promised her I'd never take a nanite, but now it's been forced on me.

In such a short time, I've become everything I despised. An altered. The worst kind. How can my parents have done this to me? I clench my fists and roar, my yell echoing off the concrete walls.

Matt comes around the corner and slides down the wall next to me. Without talking, I reach for him and bury my face in his chest. Moving around a crumpled wing, he rubs my back, shushing me. The familiar shape of his body curls around me.

"My parents did something to me," I say, wiping the tears from my cheeks.

"It looks that way." Matt absently plays with the ends of my hair. "There's a modification I've heard about, but it's not accessible by a nanite pill. It has to be done in vitro."

I lift my head. "What was it?"

"DNA harnessed from a chameleon. They're able to take on any background they pass through."

"You think I have a modification similar to that?"

"Seems like it."

I shudder. "I'm never going to be able to touch anyone ever again."

"Not true. You're touching me." He hugs me tight, proving his point. "And you can now come in contact with Paige and Erica."

But not Joe. I'll never be able to come in contact with Joe.

I sag against him. "I can't believe she gave me her stupid fairy wings."

"They're not that stupid." He runs a finger over the fluttering membrane. A tickling sensation makes me shiver. "They're actually quite beautiful."

Half-heartedly, I punch his arm. He grabs my fist in his palm and kisses my knuckles. "They are."

"Does this mean I have to join Anabelle's mean girl crew?"

Matt gives a half-grin. "I wouldn't go that far."

"If you'd have told me a week ago that I'd have fairy wings and…" I drop my head into my hands. "Oh, man."

"Life will always throw you curveballs; it's how you react to them that counts." Matt wears a neutral look, but I can see the smile wanting to release.

"You sound like a fortune cookie." I stick my tongue out at him. "That really doesn't help. We can't all be perfectly adjusted to change."

"I know." He takes my hand and rests it on his thigh. "But we need to try. Especially when there's nothing we can do about it."

After those words leave his lips, my wings shrink and fold into my back.

"What just happened?" I whisper.

Matt examines my back. "Did you put them away?"

I shake my head.

"Try and bring them back." He pokes the skin around my shoulder blades.

I grit my teeth in concentration, thinking of Paige's green wings, the mesmerizing quality of color. Straining all my muscles, I will my wings into existence, but nothing happens. A single blue feather floats above my head.

Matt's fingers continue to press around the length of my shoulder blades. "At least you don't have to exhibit an ability permanently."

"But what does that mean?" I spread both hands. "Am I an alt or not?"

Matt digs a finger into my ribs. "Oh, you're an altered all right."

I flick his nose.

"Too soon for jokes?"

"Way too soon."

I rest my head against his shoulder, exhausted as the dwindling anger at what my parents have done to me fades. "I don't want anyone to know."

"There are about ten people up there who do know." Matt points in the direction of the platform, where soft conversations weave toward us.

"Besides them," I say. "I don't think I can deal with everyone looking at me funny."

Matt rests his chin on top of my head. "No one's going to look at you funny."

"You say that," I grumble.

"I know that," he says. "Do you look at Paige or Joe any differently?"

"No…"

"Exactly."

I pull at the hem of his T-shirt. "I need some time."

"Of course you do." He cups his hands around the backs of my elbows. "Take all the time you need."

"Does it make you feel differently about me? Does it change me as a person?" Unable to look at him, I brace myself for the answer.

"A pair of wings doesn't make you an alt, Silver. It's your mentality. You could have all the abilities in the world and still be an unadjusted." Matt ruffles my hair. "Just think of Diana. She didn't ask for any of it and we still loved her."

"You did love her, didn't you?" I keep winding my finger in Matt's shirt until he snatches the misshapen material back and wraps his hands around my twitching fingers.

"Of course I did. We both did."

"No, I mean. Love her, love her."

Matt pulls back for a moment. "What, like, in love with her?"

I nod.

The blue in his eyes brightens. "No! I was never in love with Diana."

"I just thought, the way she looked at you…"

Matt rakes his hand through his hair. "She might have looked at me, but I never saw her like that."

"Oh." I stare at my scuffed boots. "I guess I'm like her now, right? We loved her for who she was, and we looked past the nanites she'd taken."

"Exactly."

I sigh and shift my numb butt away from the hard ground. "It just makes me feel weird. I've always considered myself an unadjusted, when all along, I'm actually an altered."

"But you're not. Your genes were modified before birth, not with a nanite pill. This ability is actually part of you. It always has been, whether you were aware of it or not."

I sigh. So I'm the same in Matt's eyes. Will everyone else share his view?

A lightbulb moment sparks in my head. "Maybe after we rescue my parents, I'll ask them to take it out."

He drums his fingers against his thigh.

"*After*," Matt speaks softly. "I've been thinking, and please don't be mad at me…"

I look up and catch a calculating look in his eyes.

"What?"

He crosses his forefingers like an anti-vampire cross. "Hear me out."

I'm tempted to stick my fingers in my ears.

He seems to read my thoughts, because he rushes on. "If I could take on abilities—abilities I could use at will—it would give us an advantage."

"Us?"

"The unadjusteds. Everyone in the cave." He grabs my arms, pressing his point into me. "I wouldn't think twice. I'd take on more. I'd use them to rescue Lyla."

"But you hate nanites," I say, shuffling back a little. "They're the antithesis of evil, that's what you said."

Matt shakes his head. "Not all of them. Not the ones that help people. We *need* what you have."

My mouth drops open. "I'm not a weapon."

"You're not *just* a weapon."

"Matt…" I hold up a hand. "Stop."

"Do you want your parents back?" he asks. "Because I want my sister, and damned if I'll let anything get in my way."

A shot of loneliness weighs heavy in my chest. I can see what he's saying, but I don't know if I can do what he suggests. The world has changed, and a resistance is blooming. The hopes and dreams and measuring sticks of morality must change with it. But embrace abilities? Can I?

"I don't want to take any more abilities." I cup my face in my hands.

Matt's hand floats to my shoulder. "So we work with what we've got."

"Whatever that is," I snap. "Did you not see the wings just disappear from my back?"

"So you have limitations," he says gently. "We'll figure them out. Please, Silver. Trust me."

"I trust you with my life, Matt. I always have." I look away from his eyes. The blue of them is too piercing. Too pleading. Too hopeful. "But this is different."

Matt tucks my hair behind my ear.

"I need some time to think about it," I say.

Matt nods and drops his hand. "Of course."

"If President Bear finds out…"

Matt's voice turns to steel. "We need to keep it a secret."

"But everyone else has seen." I flick my gaze to the end of the aisle.

"So we swear them to secrecy, and no one else in the cave can know."

I lean my head back against the wall. "If the reward on my head wasn't high enough already…"

"I'm not going to let anything happen to you. President Bear isn't going to find out."

I match his serious gaze, then smile. "I appreciate the sentiment, Matt, but that's something you can't promise."

CHAPTER THIRTEEN

A loud, metallic clang rouses me from where I've fallen asleep on Matt's shoulder. A series of shouts, followed by the unmistakable thwack of one of Erica's arrows sailing through the air.

Matt and I leap to our feet and run back toward the others. Joe and Hal storm down the metal steps. Paige flies overhead, shortly followed by Erica, who releases another arrow through the now open warehouse door. The arrow must have found a target, as it's followed by a groan and a heavy thud.

"What's going on?" Matt asks.

"A troop of trolls," Joe yells over his shoulder, bringing his machete high and charging toward the door.

Trolls. The footmen of Bear's army. Not particularly intelligent, but they're capable of following an order and scaring prisoners into revealing their deepest secrets with just a flash of their murderous eyes. And they don't live under bridges.

Kyle runs in and out the door, holding fingers high to indicate how many enemies are out there. He runs back outside and I catch a blur of a front jump kick in the morning sunshine.

I release my knife from my belt and speed after the others. Jacob is there too, now dressed in Joe's T-shirt, sleeves rolled to fit his arms. His tongue slithers back and forth and his arms punch as fast as Kyle's.

Matt grabs my arm and whirls me toward him. His face drains of color.

"I don't know how to fight," he says, a hint of desperation in his voice. "All I have are my homemade grenades, and I can't use them with all of you out there."

I glance at the door, then lay a hand on his chest. "Stay here. I need to go help them."

Matt nods. "Be careful."

"Always."

I dash outside, faster than I thought possible. The speed ability is back, maybe because I had a chance to rest. Erica's arrows sail by my head. Paige flaps high above, shouting warnings. Bullets speed through the air, one grazing close to my cheek, but there is another element to this speed ability. Not only am I faster, but I can also watch fast things as if they've all been slowed down. I step to the side as a bullet whizzes under my nose and slams into the warehouse wall, creating a small puncture.

Joe hacks with his machete, nearly decapitating a troll with one slice. Hal fires a pistol and marches toward the rain of incoming bullets, his armored skin protecting him. I pray one won't find the weak spot at his throat.

I turn and find myself face-to-face with a snarling troll. Its nostrils flare as it barks a guttural command, my name harsh on his bulging lips.

"Silver Melody." It reaches for a walkie-talkie on its belt.

I slide my knife up into its guts. Warm blood spills over my hand, and the stench of copper rushes up my nose. Bile rises into my mouth.

"Silver, watch out!"

As if by instinct, my wings erupt from my back, taking me up just as one of Erica's arrows streaks through the space my head was seconds ago. The arrow pierces the eye of another troll.

Matt hovers by the warehouse door, using the shotgun we found in the office to take pop shots at the attackers. My wings take me higher. Flapping violently, the scene below shrinks as my friends battle against a handful of trolls. Joe and Hal lead the charge, bullets merely ricocheting off their armored skin. Erica releases three arrows, two of them finding marks before a bullet punctures a small hole through one of her wings. She stumbles in the air, her wings flashing a tangerine orange.

My own wings continue to beat uncontrollably until I

find myself level with the warehouse roof, some fifty feet above the ground. Panic licks through my limbs, muting the noises below.

One of the trolls spots me and raises his gun. I lift my knife, trying to keep my body steady against the buffeting of my feathers, which seem to have a mind of their own. The troll squeezes the trigger. I throw the knife. Bullet and blade spiral toward each other. The hilt glances off the bullet, but it's enough for the bullet to tear off in a new direction. My knife spins to the ground.

I kick my legs as my wings take me over the roof. Turning upside-down, I reach for the corrugated surface, trying to grab hold before my wings take me all the way to space. I strain against the panic.

I have to get control of my wings. My fingers grasp the edge of a metal rail running the length of the roof, and for a few seconds my arms and wings fight against each other.

Everything is so small down below. My friends like dolls. An attack of vertigo threatens the measly breakfast I ate. Then I remember to breathe and not fight against the panic, but let it flow through me.

The strain in my biceps lessens as I finally isolate the muscles that control my wings. With a flash of triumph, I bring them close to my back so that I'm no longer in danger of floating into the clouds. I release the metal bar, and my feet hit the roof.

Now I just have to figure out how to get down.

On the ground, her injured wing bleeding, Erica kills the last troll with another arrow. Ten bodies lie dead on the tarmac.

Paige flies to my side. "Do you need help getting down?"

I'm about to reach for her hand when I shake my head. "I need to learn how to control these abilities on my own."

She smiles. "I'll stay by your side."

I blow out a long breath and step off the side of the warehouse. I plummet. My hair flies upwards as I try to concentrate on my wings and my arms circle, trying to grab at the empty air.

"Silver, no!" Matt screams. He runs into the car park, trying to reach me.

But before I hit the ground, my wings unfurl. I flap them once, twice, and manage to slow my very inelegant landing. At least I manage to stay on my feet.

"Do not scare me like that!" Matt rushes at me and throws his arms around me. A line of blood drips down his cheek. I touch my fingers to the wound, and he winces.

I pull back. "You OK?"

He nods. "Just a graze. Looks like we got them all."

Retrieving my knife from the tarmac, I grasp the warped hilt and join my friends gathering in a loose circle, sheathing weapons and offering fragile smiles. Joe pats peoples' shoulders, but I step out of his reach before he can touch me. No way do I want to be a bulk right now. His lips lift into a sad smile as he walks away and starts loading goods into the jeep.

"Nine assault rifles, six handguns, three grenades, and two knives." Hal makes a pile of weapons requisitioned from the dead trolls.

"Reckon that's enough for a rescue mission?" I ask.

Hal looks at me. "Rescue mission?"

"My parents. They might be able to find a way out of this mess. Genetically speaking."

A couple of mouths drop open. Kyle does a double take.

"Seriously?" Hal asks.

Matt steps in. "It's something Francesca and I have been talking about. We don't have much hope against an army of bulks without the doctors."

Hal grins and cocks the hammer of one of the guns. "I'll be damned. And here I was planning out the rest of my days in a dark cave, with a little sideline in revenge too."

Joe claps him on the back. "Oh, brother, we can do better than that."

I like the way Joe is with Hal. Hell, I like the way he is with everyone, like everyone's big brother. But as soon as I think the word 'brother,' I feel myself blush and my gaze lingers too long.

"Now we just need to figure out where my parents are," I say.

Hal's smile drops and everyone goes quiet.

Addison emerges from the warehouse marching a troll in front of her. Her hair trails down her back like a ribbon of blood as she shoves the troll to its knees and kicks it in the back. Then she slices its neck with one of her throwing stars.

"Make that ten assault rifles," Hal says.

"We really could use that kid with the telekinesis right about now," Joe says, eyeing the towering mountain of food we somehow need to fit in the jeep.

"He didn't want to come," Paige says. "Only just arrived. I think he went through something getting here. Looked scared witless."

Joe picks up a sack of flour, then glances down the street. "Could use a couple of sentries while Hal and I load up."

We agree and take our positions. Matt and Kyle head around the back of the warehouse. Jacob and Erica walk toward the woods. Addison goes across the street and Paige and I join together. Trash billows on the pavement, mostly a series of dissolvable cups made from yucca roots. They're stained in neon colors, typical of keg parties.

"It's like a ghost town," Paige says, keeping her wings close to her body. Public restrooms up ahead have larger entrances that bulks and winged adjusteds can fit through. They're not divided by gender anymore.

Nearby, the door of an empty drug store stands open to my left. Pills are scattered and crushed all over the floor. Looted. Probably the junkies looking for more nanites. I'm briefly wondering if it's worth going in to check for anything useful when Joe whistles. I doubt anything meaningful would be in there anyway. Most of the nanites you can buy from a pharmacy are class one. White teeth and permanent tan kinds of stuff.

Paige and I head back. As we enter the lot of the warehouse, a shorting holographic billboard catches my attention. It's advertising a new car for altereds with headdresses. Anyone with horns or antlers.

When we get back to the jeep, Hal and Joe have it loaded with sacks of flour and dried pasta. Cartons of soup, tinned fruit, crackers, another box of chocolate, pasta sauces and condiments. Kyle adds a box of Twinkies on top, and Hal emerges from the warehouse carrying a couple of bottles of whiskey.

Matt raises an eyebrow. "Not sure that's a necessity."

Hal grins. "People need to let off a little steam."

Matt chuckles. "The drinking age is twenty-one."

"According to what government?" Hal asks. "Looks to me as if the whole country's fallen to pieces. I say we make new laws."

"Hell yeah!" Kyle points both forefingers skyward, celebratory.

Joe wags a finger at him. "Not for you."

"Aw, man." Kyle throws a lightning-quick punch, but Joe catches it in his hand. The whole group bursts out laughing.

Erica's damaged wing hangs askew and crumpled. There's no more blood, but sunlight shines through a quarter-sized hole in the color-changing membrane. Joe offers her a hand to climb back into the jeep. Eyeing that small contact between them reminds me of the fact that Joe and I have never touched. Not skin against skin. Even though I swear we did, in our days in the forest, walking so closely together. But we can't have, or I would have his bulk ability. All those hours trekking through the woods and our only contact had been to yank each other out the way of danger, by backs of shirts and sleeves.

We tumble back into the jeep, and Matt does a quick head count. "Where's Addison?"

We all look around but can't spot her red head or tall frame anywhere.

Joe hops out of the jeep and starts walking back to the warehouse.

"I'll do another circuit round back." Kyle blurs off to the corner of the large building.

"She wasn't with us," I say. Paige shakes her head.

I jog across the road and pass a fancy office block

with tinted windows. I feel eyes watching me, but I'm probably just being paranoid. Behind the office block is a rolling field and then trees beyond that.

There's no sign of her.

Half an hour later we meet back at the jeep. No one has seen her. We widen the circle. After two hours of searching, my heart sinks. She wouldn't just walk off, and she couldn't have gone that far during the fifteen minutes it took the bulks to load the jeep. Something has happened to her.

"I don't want to get stuck out here another night," Matt says. "Especially when someone realizes that troop is missing."

Flies buzz around the reeking bodies of the trolls.

Reluctantly, we climb back into the jeep. Joe starts the engine and we pull out of the lot. No one speaks. Everyone scans the area as we drive.

The trip back seems to take longer. Once we park the jeep and hide it with branches, Matt addresses the group before we hike to the cave. "I know we're all worried about Addison. Maybe we'll be able to go look for her again with the weapons we have."

"I don't think we're going to find her. She's my best friend. She wouldn't have left willingly." Erica's wings turn a depressing sludge color. "I think she's gone."

"I'm sorry, Erica," Paige says.

She nods and the group starts walking. Joe and Hal

carry the sacks of flour while Matt heaves a case of tinned fruit. Paige and Erica carry packets of pasta, and Hal sticks the bottles of whiskey in his pockets. Kyle and I carry granola bars and other boxes.

As we near the cave, I say, "Guys, we're going to keep this ability thing under wraps for now. I don't want anyone to know, not till I figure out what's going on with me."

"Is that all you care about right now?" Erica huffs.

I turn to face her. "We're all worried about Addison, but this needed to be said before we reach the cave. I don't need this news reaching Bear and the price on my head rising again, tempting any number of people in those walls." I jab my hand in the direction of the cave. "So no, I'm not just thinking about myself. I'm thinking about the safety of everyone."

The scowl on Erica's face doesn't change, but she doesn't argue.

Everyone quickly agrees to keep my abilities a secret. Then we all walk in silence to the cave.

———

When we return, the whole cave erupts in a new sense of hope seeing the load of food we carry. A couple of the residents go straight to work kneading dough and baking bread in the ovens. One of them is the guy with telekinesis. He lifts most of the food with his mind and puts it down in an ordered fashion along the back wall of the kitchen. He sets to work unravelling packets and chopping carrots without touching the knife. An unlit cigarette dangles from his lips.

He glances at Paige. "Everything go OK?"

She turns from the amassing hungry crowd and drops her voice to a whisper. "Hey, Sawyer." She pauses. "We lost Addison."

Sawyer pales. "Lost?"

"We looked everywhere."

The cigarette drops out of his mouth and Sawyer stops chopping. "Maybe she just took off?" But even as he says this, it's clear he doesn't believe it himself.

Paige bites her lip. "Maybe."

Einstein appears and winds himself through Matt's legs. He follows Matt and me down the passageway to my little hollow.

"Sit," I say to Matt, pointing at the floor. Einstein lowers his haunches too, making us both laugh.

I rummage through my rucksack until I find the first aid kit and butterfly bandages. I rip open an antiseptic wipe and dab at the cut on his cheek. Matt hisses through his teeth as I pull the skin together and apply the bandage. Einstein lets out a low growl of sympathy.

"You're a brave soldier," I say, wiping the dirt away from the rest of his cheeks.

Matt shakes his head and catches my wrist. "No, you were brave. Getting control of the wings like that. I don't know what I would have done if I'd ended up on that roof."

I chuck his shoulder. "You would have done what you normally do and thought your way out of it."

Matt smiles, his blue eyes darkening in the dim lantern light. Einstein nestles his head into my lap and licks my fingers. Matt slides my warped knife out of my belt. "I know how to fix this."

"That would be great," I say. "Can't throw a wonky knife."

He slides the knife into his own belt loop and picks something up from the floor. "What's this?"

In the soft lighting, I can just make out he's holding the picture of himself. A blush heats my cheeks.

"I was afraid I wouldn't find you again." I wad up the bandage wrapper in my hand, which trembles a little. That always happens after high anxiety. "If something had happened to you, if I had been caught... You're my best friend, Matt. I can't imagine a life without you."

Matt remains quiet, then he takes a deep breath. He's still holding my wrist in his hand, and now he lowers it and circles his thumb over mine. "Silver, do you think... I mean... maybe..."

"What?" I lean closer.

He hesitates again and drops my wrist. "Nothing.

Just, you're important to me too." He smiles, a sweet sad smile with a million emotions twitching at the corners. "I couldn't imagine a world without you either."

Joe sticks his head around the corner of my archway. "Food is ready!"

"Good, I'm starving." I leap to my feet, dragging Matt after me.

"How's Erica?" Matt asks Joe.

"The wings were too delicate for bandages, but I managed to glue the hole. I think she'll be able to fly like that," Joe says.

"I hope she keeps her trap shut about my abilities."

Joe rounds on me, blocking the passageway. "What is your problem with Erica?"

I take a step back. "I don't have a problem with Erica."

Joe's honey eyes light with an angry fire. My stomach churns, unable to bear his judgment. "It sure seems like it to me."

"It's not Erica." Matt steps in front of me, like he's my protector, or something. "It's the fairy wings."

"They're just wings," Joe says. "Which you happen to have now too. Along with the macaw wings and speed."

Matt touches my arm. "Silver and I lost a close friend to a nanite death."

Diana.

Joe frowns. "I thought she was a swimmer. She took a shark nanite or something, for agility."

"She did." My voice turns to steel. "Her mother had the butterfly wings. Her mother forced her to take the nanite."

"And there's a pack of particularly friendly fairy seniors at our school who haven't left Silver alone since we started." Matt slides a sympathetic look my way.

"They stuck my head in a toilet." I can't quite meet Joe's eyes, but I take reassurance from Matt's presence. "Couldn't even come up with something original."

Joe drops his hand from his waist. "Oh."

I hang my head and kick at the uneven ground. "But you're right. I haven't been fair on Erica. I'm sorry about that." My eyes sting as though I haven't slept in days and my legs turn leaden. I'd give anything to curl up with Einstein and sleep for a week.

"I get it," Joe says. "But maybe just try and go easy on her. She's been through a lot."

I've been giving Erica a hard time merely because she reminds me of another altered with the same wings. And aren't I here because of the way I've been treated by the altereds? By President Bear? Being an unadjusted is the lowest rung of the ladder, and here I am doing the same.

But Erica hasn't exactly been welcoming either. Her wings change to that vile acid green or putrid blue whenever she's near me, and the way she narrows those violet eyes. The way she grabbed me back in the warehouse, inflicting her ability on me.

No, it isn't just me.

CHAPTER FOURTEEN

When Joe and Matt and I enter the main chamber, more lights than usual line the uneven walls, casting shadows around the room. The delicious scent of fresh bread and onions fills the large space, quickening my feet to the line where a couple of volunteers hand out food. People talk animatedly and smile wider, and their pupils shine with, if not happiness, something like it. It's amazing what a few sacks of flour and a full belly can do.

I'm distracted by Sawyer standing in the middle of the chamber amidst a group of people congratulating him on his culinary skills. He blushes under the praise, then removes a pack of cards from his pocket. Even though I know he possesses telekinesis, his illusion tricks are no less impressive. His sleight of hand moves at such speed that it's almost impossible to track, even for me. Cards appear in people's pockets, tucked into the collars of shirts and even along the passageways. It takes the kids a while to find them all and their eyes shine with delight.

Erica walks in the line ahead of me, her injured wing folded down. I tap her on the shoulder.

She turns, and when she sees it's me, her eyes glint with coldness and her wings turned an acid green.

"I'm sorry about your wing," I say.

Her elfin chin rises an inch as she looks me up and down over her button nose. "I'm sorry about your new altered status."

"Yeah, you and me both."

After a pause, she laughs. I smile and breathe a sigh of relief.

Joe grins at me and shoves a plate with a warm roll and a bowl of hot soup at me. I eat where I stand, too hungry for etiquette, watching the people of the cave relate their journeys here.

Kyle joins us, licking soup from his fingers. "What happens next?"

I swallow my mouthful. "Next?"

Kyle points a finger at the chimneys. "Dudes, we've got food and weapons. The more serious injuries are healed thanks to your regeneration pills. So, what happens next? We can't live here forever."

Matt plants a hand on his shoulder. "One step at a time. People are still arriving. We need to take stock and understand this murderous craze that's swept through the adjusteds. And rescue Silver's parents."

"Yeah," Kyle says. "They can make a cure."

I stutter. "A cure? It's too late for that."

"True," Matt says. "But they're our best hope in planning a more just future."

"There ain't no cure for this," Joe says, shoving a thumb in his chest.

But Kyle's suggestion has put an idea in my head. Sometimes when a combination of nanites went wrong, Dad would get a visit in his lab. He was able to reduce each problematic alteration back to the original unadjusted form using a specially concocted virus put right into the bloodstream. Maybe the theory could be harnessed on a wider scale.

"So we break them out." Kyle clicks his fingers. "Where are they exactly?"

"I don't know," I say, then chomp on my bread. "First I need to figure out what the hell is going on with these new abilities I've taken on."

"I can help you with the speed, dude," Kyle says, raising his hand for a knuckle punch.

Claus' figure seeps into view. He has a sneaky way of suddenly appearing, even with the cane he uses to support his bad leg. "Who has abilities?"

Out of habit, I bow. "Sensei."

"We were just talking about the abilities present in the cave and what might be useful," Joe says.

Claus nods, pulling on his thin mustache. "My thoughts exactly. We need to be ready to fight."

Kyle looks around the room. "No offense, but I don't think Hal, Joe and I can take on Bear's army on our own."

Claus swivels his dark eyes to him and lets out a soft chuckle. "Which is why we need to train everyone."

"You think we can win?" I ask. Bear's army is an unbeatable force, but I have new abilities now. I could acquire more and test them out, if I'm willing. I'm still not sure how I feel about that.

"Don't forget the other hideouts. I've been in touch with them on the radio." Matt rolls down the sleeves of his shirt. "There are more of us than you think."

"It's not going to be easy," Joe tells us. "We're never going to win a physical fight; there just aren't enough of us to battle the brute strength of the bulk army. Our success is dependent on something stealthy, swift and quiet."

"Stealthy like you were in the woods?" I say, cracking a grin.

Joe laughs and a dribble of soup shakes out of his bowl. "You bet."

Once the laughter fades, somberness seeps in. "I really hope my parents have an answer," I say.

"We all do, Silver." Claus taps his stick on the ground. "But we must prepare for both eventualities. Now if you'll excuse me, I have new arrivals to approach."

We bow at each other, and he limps away. Matt heads off to check on his radio and any communication that may have come in during our absence, and Kyle re-joins the food line in an attempt to get seconds.

It's just Joe and me left in a sea of unfamiliar faces.

"How are you feeling about the abilities?" he asks, careful not to stand too close.

"I really don't know." I chew on my lip for a moment and fiddle with my pendant. "I mean, it's freaky. I'm not who I thought I was, but I don't want to have an existential crisis when I need to be thinking about other things, like finding my parents and getting all the unadjusteds out."

Joe smiles. His fingers float toward me, then fall back to his side. "What happened to you is huge."

"Keep your voice down," I hiss at him.

He gestures to a quieter area and I follow him around a stalagmite. "This is big, Silver. You're allowed a moment to deal."

I run my finger around the tapered tip of the stalagmite. "Matt says I could be useful if I'm willing to take on more abilities. I get that. If you think of all the abilities in this cave." I look at him, his obvious strength an elephant in the room between us. "But I don't even know how it's happening, why it's happening, or how to control any of it." I raise my eyes to meet his.

"So we need to test your limits," Joe says, like it's the simplest thing in the world.

In that moment, I miss my father. I imagine seeing

190

him, and after I've yelled at him for doing this to me, I think of his arms around me. I crave that feeling of protection. Perhaps it's naïve, or childish. I know I can't rely on anyone else. If I can come to grips with these abilities, maybe other people can rely on me.

I scrape at the stalagmite until clay gathers under my fingernail. "I know."

"Claus set up an assault course in the woods. Let's go try it out."

The half roll I've not finished sits on the side of my plate. I'm not hungry anymore. The soup cools and congeals in my stomach. "Now? It's dark out."

"Exactly," Joe says, nudging my boot in the direction of the exit. "You won't be seen."

After Joe and I dump our plates, we head out of the cave and walk through the cool evening up and over the ridge. He matches his stride to mine and every time he nudges a little too close, I take a step to the side. But part of me wants to lean the other way, if I knew it wouldn't turn me bulk.

We reach the crest of the ridge and Joe leads me between the trees to a small clearing. Piles of tires and various obstacles are set up that I don't bother inspecting in the dark. Joe stands in the middle, hands on his hips, and looks at me.

"You're going to have to keep your voice down, you know," I say, speaking not very quietly myself.

"I'll do my best." Joe winks, and he tries really hard to whisper, but it's barely a decibel lower than his usual volume.

I walk up to him until we're a couple of feet apart. "So now what?"

Joe raises three fingers. "So far you have speed, butterfly wings, and macaw wings, that we know of."

I shudder at his last words and attempt to ignore the anxiety building in the pit of my stomach.

Joe looks at the sky. "I think it would be easier to test one of the wings. Something physical we can see."

"Agreed." I rest my hands on my hips.

He waits. I wait. Nothing happens.

"Maybe I don't have abilities after all. Maybe we just had a mass hallucination. Maybe—" Paige's bird wings pop out of my shoulders. It doesn't hurt a bit this time.

Joe claps his hands. "There you go."

The wings beat above my head, raising Joe's hair and rustling the leaves until they sound like they're whispering at us.

I look down the length of my wings. "They're not as long as Paige's."

"When you produced the butterfly wings, they weren't as big as Erica's either." Joe pulls at his chin, deepening the cleft in it. "I wonder if you're as fast as Kyle when you run."

"We can test that easily enough." I flap the wings

192

and lift into the sky. Air filters through my feathers, and moonlight shines through them. "I don't think my plumage is as thick either. God, that's something I never thought I'd say."

"Don't go too high," Joe says as I lift a few feet in the air. "I don't want you falling again."

"I think I'm getting the hang of it now." I fly a small circuit around the perimeter of the meadow. Joe never takes his eyes off me. After a while I come in to land and sit on the trunk of a fallen tree. The scent of honeysuckle fills the air.

Joe joins me on the trunk. As he sits, it creaks under his weight. My wings rise over both of us, just floating in the night breeze, until I don't have to think about it at all. I'm not quite brave enough to fly above the trees, though. I'll have to wait for Paige to do that. Just in case.

"In the warehouse, the wings just disappeared," I say, my head tilted toward the moon. An ache runs the length of both my shoulder blades.

"Let's wait and see what happens." Joe plucks a blade of grass, sticks it between his lips and produces a high whistle. Something in the bushes whistles back. We smile at each other and he does it again. This time there are two whistled responses.

"Which do you prefer?" he asks. "Bird or butterfly?"

"Bird," I reply immediately.

Joe chuckles. "I thought you might say that."

My eyelids droop and I shiver. I know it's not that late, but after the battle this morning and losing Addison, I'm exhausted. I'm tempted to lean my head against Joe's shoulder. I don't know if his one layer of shirt is enough to keep me taking on his ability, but when he slides his arm around my shoulder, I don't resist.

When I don't transition, fatigue rolls at me in waves and I've never felt so comfortable. So in the moment. So far away from everything.

"You still carrying around those acorns?" Joe asks.

I reach a hand into my pocket and pull out half a dozen. Joe takes one from my hand and holds it up to the moon.

"That's a beech nut," I say. "Squirrels go wild for them."

Joe hands it back. "As do Silver Melodys."

I laugh and put them back in my pocket.

"What would you choose?" I ask sleepily. "Bird or butterfly?"

Joe chuckles. "I don't think butterfly wings would look too good on a bulk."

"True," I say, picturing the ridiculous image. "But what if you weren't a bulk? If you could be anything you wanted to be, what nanite would you choose?"

Joe's brow knits together and he pulls at the cleft in his chin again. "Something non-physical, I think. The bulk didn't work out for me so good, so I think I'd go for

194

intelligence, or something. I'd want to be able to think myself out of any situation."

"I get that." I lean back against him, stretching my legs out on the trunk.

"What about you?"

"I like the wings." Then I realize they're gone. I sit up with a start. "How long have they been gone?"

"A few minutes," Joe says. "They lasted about an hour."

I yawn, not bothering to cover my mouth. "I'm so damned tired, feels like I could sleep for a week."

Joe holds out his hand to help me up. "So your energy drains as you use the ability."

"It looks that way," I say, staring at his hand, wondering what will happen if I take it. "I didn't even feel them disappearing."

"I think it's safe to take my hand." His voice is gentle as his eyes lock on mine. Even though his heart is protected by armored skin, I think I can hear it beating. "I don't think you have enough energy to take on another ability right now."

Without pausing to weigh it up anymore, I take his hand and pull myself up. Joe smiles down at me. The moon crowns his head, and a surge of electricity flashes across my skin, but I'm still me.

"This is the first time we've been alone since the woods," Joe says. I can't quite read his expression, but it feels like my butterfly wings have enfolded in my stomach.

"It wasn't that long ago," I say.

"True." Joe tilts his head. "But I miss saving you."

I poke a finger into his hard stomach. "I can save myself."

"I know that."

We stare at each other. Fireflies wink around us and I'm caught in a moment, wishing for things I can't have.

Joe dips his head, leaning closer. My eyes close. Memories of our time together in the woods play in my mind. Waking up and finding Joe. Him saving me from the wolves. The posy of flowers.

My lips part, but then I step away. "I think that might be pushing it a little too much."

We walk back to the cave in silence. Joe keeps looking at me and I keep my eyes on my feet, pretending I need to watch the ground to see where I'm going. It's a flimsy excuse when there's a full moon out. He was going to kiss me. Why didn't I let him?

All I want to do is head to my hollow and sleep for a million hours, but I need to say something to Joe. I need to make this better. Before I have the chance, Matt appears halfway down the passageway and hands me back my repaired knife.

"Francesca is calling a meeting first thing in the morning."

I perk up a bit. "Is she declaring a rescue mission?"

"Not sure. I think she wants to try and make things a little more organized around here," Matt replies. His gaze flicks between Joe and me, then to our adjoining hollows. "Where have you two been?"

Joe ducks his head and creeps along the passage until he can stand without stooping. "We went to test Silver's abilities."

Matt's eyebrows rise and Einstein comes woofing down the passage. "And?"

"Seems I can only hold an ability for an hour, but it's exhausting. I need to rest. Neither of my wings are as powerful as Paige's or Erica's either. I need to test the speed against Kyle."

Matt looks at Joe, a look that says he wants to be alone with me, but Joe doesn't budge.

Matt leans closer. "That's great, Silver. How are you about it all?"

I step into my hollow and turn to face him. "Honestly? I don't know yet. I just want to sleep."

Matt stays there a minute longer, then wishes me goodnight and retreats down the passageway. I snuggle into my sleeping bag and close my eyes. Sleep is only seconds away when Joe's voice comes from his adjoining hollow.

"Silver?"

"Yeah?" I murmur.

"I wanted to ask you about earlier, in the meadow…"
I can't see his face, but I sense something in his tone.
He's actually whispering for once. "Do you think…?"

"Joe?" I roll over onto my side. "Let's talk in the
morning."

There's a long pause, then he says, "OK. G'night,
Silver."

CHAPTER FIFTEEN

After breakfast the following morning, Francesca stands in the middle of the chamber, eyes scanning the crowd as she gestures for quiet.

"As there are so many of us here now, and thanks to a select group of people, we now have enough food to feed you all for a little while." A resounding cheer ripples around the room. "I thought it was time the situation was addressed. You all have many questions. Although I may not hold all the answers, I'm willing to step up and help, if you'll have me."

Murmurs of agreement ebb around the stalagmites, and a generous round of applause reveals support for Francesca.

Francesca smiles and flicks her graying bangs from her forehead. "We've all come here to escape the tyranny of an imposed nanite induction, and many of us were unhappy with the government long before that. I should know; I used to work for President Bear."

A collective gasp follows her words.

"I was a volunteer on his Senate campaign trail, before I knew his position on the nanites. As a result, I feel I am in a unique position to understand his motivations and how he might be defeated."

"War!" someone yells.

Francesca smiles patiently and presses her fingertips together. "We won't win a war. Now that the unadjusteds are held in compounds, the superbeings have become controlled and organized."

"What, then?" someone else calls.

Matt brushes his shoulder against mine, and his blue eyes glimmer.

"It is my belief that the key to defeating President Bear lies with Drs. Melody, but both esteemed doctors are in captivity." Francesca pauses. "I believe we can get them back, but we need to utilize the gifts of the people here to make that happen. There are a few people with talents among us. If they're willing, I think we might gain an advantage."

A thunderous applause rips through the room, and most of the eyes settle on my friends. We have two bulks, an arrow-wielding fairy, a speedster, a girl with beautiful blue wings, my best friend—a bomb-building expert, someone with telekinesis, and me.

But no one knows about me.

As the whispers die down and the crowds disperse,

Francesca approaches our motley crew. She thanks each of us personally, holding our gazes with warm, fiery eyes and making sure she touches each of us; a gentle tap or a handshake or a squeeze on the shoulder. With each serious look, she gives us jobs. Paige and Kyle are in charge of supply runs. Erica will be the liaison to new altereds arriving. Everyone already knows Matt is working on a perimeter surveillance system for outside the cave and adding more lighting inside. Joe and Hal are tasked with assessing people's strengths in combat.

"Silver." Francesca turns to me. "How good are your karate skills? Do you think you could take down an adjusted?"

I grip the knife in my belt. "I put Jacob down yesterday." I don't mention it was because I used Kyle's speed.

"OK, I need you to keep training," she says, her eyes going to my repaired knife. I hope to hell my wings don't suddenly pop out.

"I'll do whatever I have to do," I say, wincing at the idea of being a bulk. It's an obvious ability to add to my list, but the thought of being eight feet tall with muscles that will deform my body—I don't want to be seen like that by Joe. By Matt. By anyone.

Claus limps over, looks us all up and down, and bows. "If you're not busy, let's get started on the assault course."

When the others head outside, I don't follow. I saw the training ground last night, and I'm afraid my wings might emerge when everyone is there. I'm not ready for that.

Instead I walk the passageways. I pick up a lantern and edge past my hollow. My backpack, my cozy sleeping bag and a couple of photographs are all that make the area mine, but it feels more like home than the penthouse apartment did. When my parents were at the top of their careers, the nanites such a success, President Bear bent over backwards to bequest them every tiny luxury. From gym equipment to weekly massages and all the latest technological gadgets, the apartment was obscene in its wealth.

Until my mother was taken away. Then it all stopped.

With my thoughts in the past, I walk until I find myself in the weapons chamber. Joe and Matt have lined up all the weapons we requisitioned from the troop of trolls and catalogued anything else others brought with them on their journey here. A wallpaper table stands in the corner with bits of clipped wires and some kind of powder dirtying the surface. Matt and his bombs. A constant drip plops toward the back of the chamber, a bead of moisture finding its way to the cave floor.

I'm about to leave when a moving shadow catches my eye. Coming toward me with a light attached to her wheelchair is Megan, Matt's youngest sister. Wearing a Disney T-shirt and Crocs, she inches closer with a tentative smile.

"What are you doing here?" I ask.

"Trying to decide what weapon I want to train with." She raises her lantern to meet mine, and the pool of light stretches into the darker shadows.

"How old are you?" I hold the lantern closer to her face.

She sticks out her chest and pushes her blonde hair away from her shoulders. "Twelve."

It was just agreed that the cutoff was twelve, but now I'm wondering if that's too young. I look at her Disney T-shirt, stained with dirt and splashed with food, and her wheels, which are caked in dried clay. "I'm worried about you."

Megan rolls her eyes. "I may be in a chair, but I still need to learn how to defend myself in case something happens to my family. Who knows, maybe I'll find something I'm good at and I can help rescue Lyla."

I'm tempted to hug her, but I know she's far too feisty for that. "Maybe you can."

Smiling, she peels toward the entrance. "Maybe I'll try a knife, like you." Then she disappears.

Crossing the threshold, I notice another faint light from farther down the passageway. I tiptoe over the uneven ground and stick my head around a new archway.

Joe sits in a plastic chair not built for his size, the back of it buckling under his weight. He leans his elbows on another collapsible table and shifts through scraps of paper.

"Thought you'd be with Claus at the training ground," I say, stepping into the room. The smell of damp clay is stronger in here and I spot a ribbon of water along the back wall. A small puddle forms below it, flowing into a crevice.

Joe looks up and smiles. "Francesca asked me to look over the cave population's capabilities. We've had so many new people arrive in the last twenty-four hours. Erica and Claus have tested a few in the weapons room, and I'm making a chart of their strengths and weaknesses, trying to put people into balanced teams. Why aren't you there?"

I shrug.

"Not ready?" He looks at me as if one of my wings might pop out.

I lean in the archway. "Nope."

Joe pats a chair beside him. "Why don't you help me for a bit?" He shifts, causing it to creak in protest.

I take a seat next to Joe, and we examine the lists of names and abilities.

"Jacob showed up earlier. He's got more talents than karate and speed," Joe says. "He can teleport. Not huge distances, but enough to get out of a spot of trouble, or put someone in one."

"Can we trust him?" I'm thinking of how much money I'm worth if President Bear discovers my abilities.

Joe nods. "He's pretty motivated to find his mom. After he fell out of the competition circuit, I'd say he's a full convert."

I tuck my legs up into the chair and wrap my arms around them. "I never realized the altereds had it so bad. I always thought everything just came so easily to you guys."

Joe's eyes fix on me over the light of our lanterns. "Does it feel easy to you? With the wings?"

I think of how hard it is to control my wings. The speed isn't so bad, as it doesn't involve a physical change, but for those who've taken a multitude of pills? Control would definitely be an issue.

"No," I say.

Joe slouches back in his chair and laces his hands together behind his neck. "There are bulk training weekends after you take the nanite to get used to your new body and strength. The bulk change is complicated. I couldn't have done it without that training. It's one of the reasons that pill is so expensive and a class ten. You have to fly off to one of the training facilities."

"They *teach* you how to be all big and powerful and immortal?"

Joe chuckles. "Well, you gotta have a little natural talent too." He blows on his fingers and wipes them on

205

his shoulder in a parody of modesty. "But seriously. It's nice to feel capable and be able to protect people. If I can give people reassurance and protection, that's enough for me."

"You were pretty strong to start with, weren't you?" I shift in my chair so one leg is underneath me. My other boot digs into the clay ground.

"Yeah." Joe's head bobs from side to side, considering. "I managed to avoid the nanite for a while, but I had to take it eventually or I would have been crushed on the field."

I look at the eight-foot bulk sitting beside me, but he's so much more than the muscle and armored skin. So much more than a handsome face. For the first time I notice a small scar above his right eyebrow and I almost reach out to touch it.

A blush rises to my cheeks.

"It wasn't really something I wanted for myself." Joe shuffles some paperwork out of his way. "But when every player on the field towers above you by at least two feet and you start to cringe every time there's a huddle or a tackle, you either join them or get out."

"I get that." I rest my hand on the table. Our fingertips are so close. Just a hair's breadth apart. I could close the gap, see what his skin feels like on mine, but it might also kickstart a new change. A change I'm not ready for.

I pick up some of the papers, not really reading them. "Joe? Last night you were about to ask me something."

Even though I'm not looking at him, I can feel his eyes on me.

Footsteps sound down the passageway. Moments later, Matt sticks his head into the room.

"Don't worry about it," Joe says too quickly.

I glance at Joe, but he's staring down at his hands. I turn to Matt instead. "How's the surveillance stuff going?"

Matt comes in and leans against the wall. "I've been tinkering with the radio, trying to get a location on the army frequency."

"And?" Joe asks.

"There's news about the compounds."

I brace myself. All three of us have people we love stuck in compounds and prisons.

Matt pulls out another plastic chair and slumps into it. "The unadjusteds in the compounds are being harvested for their DNA."

"What?" Joe sits up a little straighter, eyes wide.

"Blood samples are being taken from them every day." Matt mimes a needle pulling out blood. "They think the reason they lost their sanity when the unadjusteds ran is hidden somewhere in our genes."

"They'll need to have a genetic scientist on board for that," I say. "It's probably Earl." The last time I saw him in the lab, he was only too keen to bow to Bear's every request.

"It seems they're being treated reasonably, given food and water, but I don't know what their ultimate plans are." Matt's hands fist at his side. "I really want to get them out. *All* of them."

"We will," I say, leaning across the table. "As soon as we know where they are."

Matt nods. "It should just be a matter of time. All the hideouts have scouts going out to their nearest compounds, trying to gain intel. Hopefully it won't be too long until we know."

———

Later that day, I climb the ridge, giving the training ground a wide berth. I catch sight of people scaling walls of hay and dodging swinging effigies, but I'm not interested in that. I walk farther into the woods, where I can still hear the activity in the meadow, but where I'm alone enough that I know no eyes will be watching me.

This time, I choose butterfly wings. With the merest of wishes, the wings erupt from my back. The sensation of unfolding is actually quite pleasant. I examine the wings. White and almost translucent, they appear thinner than Erica's and three-quarters the size. I beat them harder and lift into the air. It takes more effort than the bird wings and I feel the tension in my cheeks as I grit my teeth. I suspect it's easier for Erica. She always makes it look so effortless when she's in the air.

I fly higher, staying close to thick branches in case I fall. When I reach the top of an oak, I stick my head above the canopy. All I can see is green for miles. A loud hum sounds in my ears and too late, I realize I'm right on top of a bee's nest.

I let out a shriek as I get stung three times on my hand. I lose air and drop a few feet. Scrapping my arm along the trunk, I beat the wings harder and concentrate on not falling to the ground. When I reach the canopy again, I head for a new tree, find a thick branch and sit. I lick the stings, which takes some of the pain out of it.

Once I've got my breath back, I prepare to fly to the ground. I'd rather use the bird wings as they feel stronger and safer, but there isn't room in the tightly-packed trees, so I stick with the smaller butterfly wings. They rustle as I beat them, but there are no mishaps and I land gently on the ground.

I scream when Kyle suddenly appears before me.

"What the hell?" I say, stumbling back.

He holds his hands up. "Was just going for a run."

"You scared the crap out of me!"

"Sorry, dude." He leans against a tree and watches my wings flutter. "You telling people now?"

I shake my head. "Not yet. I want to get used to them first, and as you're here, I want to test a theory."

We mark out a track in the woods. I push the wings into my back and think of running fast. When my calf muscles twitch, I know the speed ability has risen. Two minutes later, when I complete the track, Kyle is already there. He grins and performs a little celebratory jig. I roll my eyes at him.

"I think that proves it," I say.

"Proves what?" Kyle asks, still shuffling his feet around and pointing both index fingers at the sky.

I flop to the ground. "That whatever ability I take on, it's not as powerful as the person I take it from."

"That sucks, dude."

"That's one way of putting it," I say as the exhaustion swims over me. "I'm going to head back to the cave."

Kyle walks to the tree-line with me, chattering away. I can barely concentrate on his words and my feet are almost too leaden to move. I leave him at the training ground, promising Claus I'll be there tomorrow, and stumble over the ridge and down the valley, going down twice. The stings on my hand start to throb again and when I reach the entrance to the cave, I fall to both knees.

Matt catches me before I nose-dive to the limestone. "You OK?"

I lean into him. "Been testing the abilities. They drain me."

He helps me to my feet and wraps an arm around me for support. "Let's get you inside."

He steers me through the main chamber, where Sawyer prepares dinner, throwing food in the air with his telekinesis. He doesn't even need oven gloves when he moves dough in and out of the chimneys.

A few minutes later we arrive at my hollow. I collapse on my sleeping bag. Matt kneels beside me and tugs off my boots. The intruding sound of a zipper cuts into my dreamy thoughts as Matt opens the sleeping bag, lifts my legs inside, and zips me up again.

"Don't go," I whisper.

Matt curls around me and his hands settle in my hair. We fall asleep like that, Matt's arm draped over my waist and his loose curls falling over his face.

CHAPTER SIXTEEN

The next morning, I avoid the training ground again. I plan to get to grips with the wings, and the only person who can make sure I don't fall out of the sky from a great height is Paige.

Matt and I walk to breakfast together. Sawyer is in the kitchen, a pack of smokes creeping out of his pocket. He fries a bunch of eggs and his face is covered in flour. I guess telekinesis doesn't stop you getting messy in the kitchen. "We've definitely got a food problem," Matt says, approaching Sawyer's area.

Sawyer looks up and grimaces. "I catalogued everything you brought back. Half of it's missing."

My stomach rumbles at the thought of going without food. "Half?"

Matt chucks a glance over his shoulder. "A whole sack of flour and a few packets of pasta. One of the bottles of whiskey, too. Hal is pissed about that."

I perch against the ledge where Sawyer flips eggs. "And we don't know who?"

Sawyer shakes his head, making his curls bounce.

"Keep your eyes open." Matt's lips twist to the side as he drums his fingers on the ledge beside me.

"I will."

We leave Sawyer in the kitchen and follow the passage outside. As we trudge up the side of the valley, I collect acorns and shove them in my already bursting pockets. Matt rolls his eyes and digs his hand into my pocket, pulling out about twenty of them.

"You'll never fly with your pockets so full," he teases.

"Ha ha." I tug the front of his shirt and snatch my acorns back.

The feel of the sun on my shoulders eases the tension there. Looking up and down the valley, I can almost believe we're on one of our camping trips.

"Are we safe out here?"

Matt drops to his feet to retie one of his laces. "I've managed to find the army frequency. They're not in the area. "

We hike for twenty minutes along the ridge, through the woods and into training ground. Then Matt leaves to work on his perimeter alarm. Apparently a couple of guys with a bit of tech equipment have arrived from another hideout to help.

Bluebells, knotweed and red clover grow in patches

between the trees, filling the air with sweetness. The breezeless day magnifies the sounds of chirping insects and twittering birds. In the daylight I can see the obstacles better. Joe and Claus have set up targets attached to hay bales, straw-stuffed dummies swinging from trees, an obstacle course of tires to run through, and a wall of stacked hay bales to climb over. Internally, I groan, remembering the very worst of circuit training Claus put me through one year.

Joe greets me and talks me through the course. But when I tell him about my plans, he agrees to square it with Claus. Erica flutters above people's heads, her wing mostly healed and shimmering a pale color that matches her hair. Until she sees me. Then they transform to the now familiar icy blue.

I thought we were over all that.

A feather drifts by my face. A moment later Paige flies down to stand next to me.

"There's Jacob," Paige whispers, pointing to the boy we found in the warehouse. He leaps over the wall of hay bales, barely disturbing a single piece of straw. "He's amazing to watch."

"Uh-huh."

"He's a mighty fine specimen." She wiggles her eyebrows.

"I'm not sure I could get past those reptilian eyes." I circle two acorns in my palm, round and round, their hard shells clunking softly against one another.

One of Paige's wings flutters high. "That's one of the things I like most. They're... disarming." Paige sighs her appreciation. "He's so damned shy. Hasn't said a word since he arrived."

I watch the group start with the tires. Behind Jacob is Sawyer, who's shifting his feet nervously. Leaves and small twigs float around his head. Behind him, a handful of other unadjusteds stand, warily sizing up the obstacles. Paige and I watch them from the shade of the trees. Two stumble at the tires, while three struggle with the wall.

"Paige?" I back into the bushes when Claus looks my way.

"Yeah?"

"I don't want to do the assault course today."

She groans. "Neither do I."

"I need to test my wings. In private. Will you help me?"

She backs into the bush with me, her green wings an excellent camouflage, a conspiratorial smile on her face.

"I'm not sure I'm entirely in control of the wings yet," I say as they rise from my shoulders without asking. It seems controlling my abilities will take a little more effort than just an afternoon in the woods. "See what I mean?"

"You can do it," Paige says. "Just like the warehouse."

I sigh. "I tried practicing and ended up with a bunch of bee stings."

"Come on." Paige takes my hand and lifts herself into the air, tugging at my arm. A pair of binoculars dangles from her neck. "I'll fly with you."

I kiss the pendant at my collarbone, wishing Matt was here to give me some of the confidence he exudes so easily. A shaky feeling flashes through my limbs, so I take a deep breath and try to stay in the moment. I picture a bird rising in the sky.

I press the timer on my watch. My wings lift and my feet leave the ground. I make them flutter, enjoying the way the feathers move. My chest inflates, filling with air like a helium balloon. The urge to rise is undeniable. My aqua wings flap faster, tunneling a breeze through the meadow.

"Follow me," Paige says.

She flies up, higher and higher, beckoning me to come. Clearing my mind of negative thoughts, I follow, pretending I'm still a young child who believes in immortality. In never getting hurt.

I circle higher, looking down at the valley. Everything looks so small. The broccoli-like trees and the felt-like grass are more appropriate on a miniature train enthusiast's board. The training ground is no bigger than a trampoline, the obstacle course like a playset.

When I fly higher, a moment of vertigo consumes me and I panic. I perform a haphazard and accidental loop-de-loop while I regain my balance, spread my wings wide and ascend toward the sun. Cold air rushes over my cheeks.

Paige and I glide over the forest. Our wing tips touch, mine blending with the sky, hers merging with the trees below. We turn toward the coast but stop short when we see an army of trolls gathering on the beach. We fly higher and farther, farther and higher. It's exhilarating. I feel *free*.

Although my wing span isn't as wide as Paige's, my wings beat powerfully and I can keep up with her.

"See if you can fly with speed," Paige says.

I grin, accepting the challenge. I spend a few minutes in the lead, using the speed ability, leaving Paige in my dust. But my aim reduces dramatically and I crash into a bird, windmilling my arms in the air to halt my speed. A wave of nausea rolls through my stomach, like I've just been on a million rollercoasters. The bird, a seagull, drops for a moment, dazed, then flies off again, giving me a scornful look.

Maybe speed and wings aren't such a good combination.

Clutching my stomach, a leaden feeling settles in my limbs and wings. Paige is a small dot coming toward me. The beach is to my right, the forest to my left. A few feathers separate from my wings and I drop ten feet, like a plane hit by lightning.

I scream.

Another twenty feet. My wings shrink. Within moments they'll be gone. I glance at my watch, seeing I have fifteen minutes until the hour is up, but I used the speed ability at the same time. Perhaps that has drained me even more.

My wings continue to shrink. I can barely lift my arms. Paige closes in on me and stretches out her hand, but she's still too far away. I plummet.

With my wings only stretching a four-foot span, I beat them furiously, trying to slow my descent. I snag my arm on a tree branch, scrapping the soft flesh under my arm. The wings shrink again and I fall backwards. I slam into the sand, the air knocked out of me.

Paige lands a moment later. I sit up and cough, trying to steal a breath. Paige dabs at my bleeding scrapes with one of her feathers.

"That was close," she says.

"Too close," I say, shaking the sand off me. "Now I have no idea how to get back. We're miles away from the cave."

Paige covers my shoulders with one of her wings. "So we'll rest here a while, until you get your energy back."

"I don't know how long that's going to take."

"It will take as long as it takes. I'm not going anywhere." She hooks her arm through mine. "Besides, now we have the opportunity to talk about Jacob again."

I laugh. "He seems nice."

Paige clutches her hands to her chest and a dreamy look passes over her face. "He is. Too nice, maybe, but that's not going to stop me."

"You know it takes two, right?"

She winks. "Oh, I know, and I'm pretty sure he likes me too. He touched my arm the other day."

"He touched your arm?!" I exclaim in mock horror, but then I sober, thinking how I wish Joe would touch my arm. He could, if I let him. If I could face being a bulk.

Paige throws an acorn at me and I put it in my pocket. I elbow her ribs. "Did you have a boyfriend before?"

She flops back against the sand and closes her eyes. "No. There wasn't really the opportunity."

I pick up a handful of sand and mold it into a small hill. Foaming waves roll toward us, pushed by an angry ocean. Deserted. No boats. No swimmers. Rocks line the edges of the beach and rise to craggy cliffs. The aroma of salt blows in from the water. A gentle sun presses its caressing fingers into my tired shoulders.

"Thanks for coming with me, Paige." I glance at my watch. "I'll need to know how long I have to rest before I can use the abilities again."

Paige rises to her feet. "In the meantime, I think we should get off the beach. That troll army we saw isn't too far from here."

Even though my legs are quivering, I push myself

up and follow Paige. We scrabble up the rocks until we reach the more secluded cliff top. Able to hide in the foliage, we make a little den for ourselves and watch the beach from a distance. An offshore wind sweeps my hair in all directions and loosens a few of Paige's feathers. She trains a pair of binoculars on the horizon. We sit in silence as the sun arcs across the sky. I think I fall asleep for a bit.

The gentle thunder of the crashing surf reaches my ears, makes me wonder what it'd be like to have gills like many altereds opted for, to swim away and discover underwater worlds. The second underwater hotel has just been completed off the coast of Los Angeles, and an underwater city has been underway for the last ten years.

"Why wings?" I ask eventually, plucking at the grass.

Paige lets the binoculars fall and picks up one of her loose feathers from the ground, staring at her hands as she runs it between her fingers. Twin white spots appear on her cheeks as her lips tighten.

When she speaks, her words are barely more than a hissing whisper. "So I could get away."

"Get away from what? The altereds?" I stick the blade of grass between my lips, producing a plaintive whistle.

"I guess." Paige's wings rise, arcing over her head before she brings them down and folds them around her body like a billowing magician's cloak. "But more my parents. They didn't even know I existed." She presses a finger to the moisture in the corner of her eye.

"I… shit… I'm sorry, I shouldn't have asked." I search my pockets for a tissue, knowing I won't find one, but it's something to do. The acorns tumble out.

Paige's shoulders hunch. "It's OK. It's not a unique story."

"But it's your story." I cover her hand with mine.

"Yeah," she says with a sigh. "It started with Dad's cancer. It's easy enough to get the nanite to cure it, but afterwards he was strutting around the house, claiming he felt so vital again."

I glance at Paige. "That's good, right?"

Paige tilts her head, her gaze still on the horizon. "For a while. He started going to the gym more, then he bought cheaper nanites. You know, white teeth, a permanent tan, even one to speed up his metabolism and rid his excess body fat. My college tuition money dwindled."

"Oh." Cautiously, I ask, "What happened next?"

"He stopped noticing me. When he looked in a mirror, he couldn't see beyond his own reflection. Then he started in on the physical stuff, like the necklace implant that flashes in time with your heartbeat."

"I know the one." It's one of the first nanites people often buy. The natural implanted accessories are cheaper and less harmful than some of the more powerful nanites. So many of them have the chokers that wind round their necks in natural skin modifications. Some sync with your heartbeat, others match the color of your eyes. My science teacher sports natural skin ruffles around his neck like an old frilly collar from the Victorian era.

"Then my mother joined him," Paige continues. "You know the old adage: 'If you can't fight 'em, join 'em.' She was vain to begin with, being an ex-fashion model. She started with the blue shoulder horns and feline eye shape, but when she got a beak for a mouth and Dad grew antlers, I'd had enough." She wraps her arms around her waist. "They went on vacations with rich friends and left me at home for weeks at a time, and they used up the rest of my tuition money. And then some."

I lean my shoulder against hers and pick up the acorns. I squeeze them in my hand, crushing one by accident. "That's awful, Paige."

A shadow falls over her face and wings, darkening the green into the depthless color of pine needles. "So I decided to take a pill. It was a foolish, impulsive decision. I thought if I had an ability, they might notice me."

"Wings would be a good choice for that."

"Ha! I didn't choose the wings, they chose me." Paige flaps her wings and we both look at the green feathers. "I emptied my bank account, which was only a couple hundred dollars, and spent some time hanging out in back alleys until I found the black market trade."

"Eeesh."

"I know. It was dangerous." Paige takes one of my acorns and throws it over the cliff.

For those who can't afford the more complicated nanites, or the more showy ones, people turn to the black markets, where it's pot luck and you never know which ability you might get. I knew of a girl who ended up with hedgehog spikes and impaled herself on the way home.

"The guy who sold it to me had been at my high school. I remembered him. Somehow it made it seem safer." Paige inhales, sucking her cheeks in. "I went to the park that night, swallowed it down, and huddled in a corner, waiting for the change."

I touch her wing. "I can't believe you went through that alone."

She holds her palms skyward. "Then the wings appeared. My parents didn't even notice. I have a twelve-foot wingspan and they. Didn't. Even. Notice." Her emerald eyes sparkle with pain. "I decided it was the best possible choice for me. I could literally fly away from my problems. So I did."

"And you came here."

Paige nods.

I bump my shoulder against hers. "I think you're really brave."

She shakes her head. "I'm not brave. It was foolish, taking a nanite to make someone love you."

"People have taken nanites for lesser reasons than that."

Paige sighs. "Maybe."

"I think you should give yourself a break."

"I think we should all give ourselves breaks. But unfortunately, we're stuck hiding in a cave." Her voice hardens. "We don't have time to grieve what could have been."

A breeze winds around our heads and lifts our hair from our shoulders. "You can't carry it around forever. You need to let it go." I let the acorns tumble from my hands and we both watch them roll down the slope.

She smiles. "Like you, you mean."

I chuckle. "Do what I say, not what I do."

Paige picks up the binoculars again. She fiddles with the magnification, then pats my thigh. "Silver, I think there's something over there. I think it's a compound."

CHAPTER SEVENTEEN

We jog along the narrow clifftop path. I don't use any super speed; my energy has only just returned and I don't want to leach it all away again. Wind buffets my hair and Paige's wings. After a half mile, Paige pulls me into a thicket of bayberry shrubs.

"There." Paige points. "Do you see it?"

Tucked around the edge of the cliff and spilling onto the beach are two grey prefab buildings, their edges lined with razor wire. They sandwich a courtyard fenced with chain link and more razor wire running in strips to make a roof. Nothing will be flying in or out.

"Hand me the binoculars."

I hold the lenses high and scan the building. In the courtyard, I count five armed guards wielding aggressive firepower. Several clumps of people sit around on broken benches or wander aimlessly without shoes. Their clothes are in tatters, and several show bloodstains and bruising.

"It's a compound, right?" Paige asks.

"I think so." I strain to see more. "So much for them being treated all right."

A flash of blonde catches my eye. Combined with the ballet slippers, which are now a shredded mess, the girl is unmistakable.

Lyla.

Matt's sister. Her blonde hair trails loose from a ponytail, and her pink ballet tights are more suggestion than reality. But physically, she looks unharmed.

"That's Matt's sister." I hand Paige the binoculars. "We need to get her out."

"We do, but not today. Who knows when your abilities are going to turn up again and I can't do much with a pair of wings against bullets and trolls."

I peer around the edge of the bush. "I can't just leave her in there."

"We need the others," Paige says, rising to her feet and retreating into the woods. "Come on, let's see if those wings of yours are working again."

It's been five hours. It's worth a try. I jog after her into the trees, leaping over roots, squashing the urge to use my speed and instead concentrating on the feeling of lifting into the air.

My wings rise once more, but they ache with fatigue. Nevertheless, I beat them hard and follow my friend into the sky, hoping I have enough in me to get home again.

Flying straighter than an arrow, it takes us less time to reach the meadow we left hours earlier, but as it comes into view, a tense ache runs from shoulder to wingtip, then my wings abruptly disappear into my back.

I scream as I plummet at an alarming speed. I try to grasp at trees but come away with nothing more than leaves. Small cuts open on my arms and cheeks. I taste blood. "Paige!"

She presses her wings against her side and tunnels after me, her hand reaching. Claus and Joe stand in the meadow, their faces stricken. Joe runs around in circles, his arms out, as if he thinks he can actually catch me. Maybe he can, but it will hurt.

"Paige!" I scream again.

I hit a branch and a sharp pain stabs into my ribs. My vision clouds, and I stop grabbing for branches.

Paige shoots past me, grabs hold of my outstretched fingertips and yanks. Her wings beat furiously over our heads and we slow, just as my feet smack down on hard ground. A new wave of pain judders into my ribs. The momentum pushes me to my side into a haphazard forward roll, but I come up the other side like it was all intentional. I manage a weak smile at Joe and Claus, but inside my heart thunders.

Claus drops his cane. "What was that?"

Before I can answer, Joe steps close and peers down at me. "You OK?"

I cradle my ribs on my right side and sit, a little dizzy. "I'm not sure."

Joe crouches at my side. "Take a deep breath."

I suck in air and moan when the pain intensifies.

"You might have broken a rib," Joe says.

"Silver?" Claus limps closer. "Why do you have wings?"

Paige lands softly next to me. "That was close."

Claus raises his voice, startling a bird. "What *is* going on? Does everyone apart from me know you seem to possess wings?"

The three of us look at him. I've never heard him shout before.

"It looks like my parents might have done something to me in vitro. Matt thinks it's harnessed from a chameleon. So far it seems I can take on the abilities of adjusteds I touch skin-to-skin." I pause, trying to catch my breath around the throbbing in my side. "But my abilities aren't as big or strong or fast. They only last an hour tops if I use one at a time."

"How long does it take you to recover?" Claus asks, pulling at his mustache.

"Not sure," I say. "I just had a five-hour break but I wasn't quite back at full power. Hence the crash."

"Interesting," Claus says, accepting the cane Joe retrieved for him. "Very interesting."

"Understatement of the year." I wince and hold my ribs again.

He takes a step closer. "With great power comes great responsibility."

I smile at the familiar words from my favorite superhero movie, then contemplate their reality. Until now, it has always been just a clever line. Now those words hold a new truth, one I don't know if I want to face.

He taps his cane on the ground. "Francesca will—"

I sit up. "We're not telling anyone."

"It will be hard to hide," Claus says. "There are people who should know. Francesca is only trying to help. She wants to find the strongest team to rescue your parents. You, Silver, just made that team."

I sigh, but even that hurts. "I'm not ready for that."

"Hm." Claus offers me a hand up. "And you wonder why I never pitted you against Kyle."

I frown. "What do you mean? You knew I was an alt?"

"No, not that, but I suspected something. I couldn't put my finger on what. I've never seen an unadjusted so skilled, so agile in karate." He puts a hand on my collarbone and squeezes paternally, then bows.

I automatically mirror his action.

"Do you want a regeneration nanite?" Claus asks.

I look at his injured leg. "My ribs will heal."

His eyes shine. "I'm proud of you."

I shrug, but the small movement causes me to wince. "Enough about me. More importantly, we found Lyla."

"Lyla?" Joe asks.

"Matt's sister. There's a compound near the beach and she was there." I start walking to the cave. "We need to tell him, then we can rescue her."

Matt and Erica appear over the top of the ridge.

"Where have you been? It's way past dinner." Matt draws near.

"Practicing."

Matt looks between me and Claus and makes a little 'o' with his mouth. He leads us back to the cave for food. When we're inside I put my hand on Matt's shoulder, slowing his pace. "Matt, I've got something to tell you." I lead him into a quiet niche. "Paige and I found a compound along the beach. Lyla was there."

Matt pales and his lips twitch. "Is she OK?"

I nod. "A little dirty, but physically unharmed."

Matt bites down on his trembling lip and wraps his arms around me. "I need to go get her."

"I know."

He pulls back. "My parents went off yesterday to look for her, left me in charge of Megan. I don't know what to do, Silver. I can't just leave her here on her own, but I don't want to wait for my parents to get back either. They could be gone a week."

"Megan will be fine here." Her and her kickass Disney team. "There are plenty of people to keep an eye on her. She's twelve, not two. She won't go wandering off."

Matt rakes his fingers into his hair and grips at the

230

roots. "It's not that. If we're all gone and something happens to us, she'll be alone."

A sad smile forms on my lips.

Matt must've realized what he said, because he grimaces. "Oh, Silver. I'm sorry. I didn't mean…"

I hold up a hand. "I know what you meant. It's OK. I get it. She's only twelve. She can't lose her whole family."

Matt paces, knotting his fingers in his hair. "I can't just sit here knowing Lyla is out there. They could be harvesting her DNA." His voice starts to shake. "Damn it, if they harm her…" He turns abruptly and slams his fist into the wall. Wincing, he shakes out his knuckles. They're scraped and bloody.

I take his injured hand in mine and wrap it tight. "For starters, don't go punching walls and injuring yourself. There aren't many regeneration pills left."

A small chuckle tumbles out of Matt's lips. He blows his hair out of his eyes.

"You're not alone, Matt. I'm here. We've been friends as long as I can remember." I stroke the back of his hand. "We're family."

His free hand rests on his stomach as he sags against the wall. "Family?"

I nod and press my cheek against his knuckles. "Yes, and first thing tomorrow, we go get Lyla."

He wraps me in another hug, his breath tickling my ear. "Thanks, Silver."

Late that evening, Joe finds me in my hollow, trailing a long ribbon of cloth bandage.

I point at it. "What's that for?"

"I remember breaking a rib before I took the nanite. Not fun. You need support." He kneels, ready to wrap the bandage around me.

"Where did you get this bandage?"

"I used to wear it around my knee. Should just about be enough for your ribs." Joe unravels it around his wrist. "Lift your shirt."

I hesitate. His bare fingers are only millimeters away from my skin. I'm fully rested, so any contact will set off a change.

"Be careful," I warn.

He locks eyes with me and stretches the bandage out. I lift my shirt and suck in my waist. The soft material of the bandage winds around my torso.

"Hang on." Joe stands and walks around me. Gently, he grips the edges of the bandage. I can feel the warmth from the proximity of his fingers. So close. I brace myself for a change, but he manages to grab the edges and tuck them in without touching my skin. Once it's in place, I let go of my shirt.

I take a couple of trial deep breaths. With the support of the bandage, it doesn't hurt so much.

"That's so much better," I say, bending my waist.

"Don't overdo it," Joe says. "It's still going to take a while to heal."

"We'll see about that." I twist at the waist, bend over and touch my toes. The pain is still there, but bearable. Maybe they're just bruised.

Joe puts a hand on my arm, through my shirt, stopping my movements.

Matt sticks his head around my archway. Deep lines run across his forehead.

I tense as I take in the way he's clicking his finger repeatedly. He only does that when he's really stressed. "What's wrong?"

He steps into the hollow, but he doesn't stand still. He keeps clicking his fingers. "I've been listening to the army channels. Something's going on in the compounds. They're burning bodies."

Joe's skin turns pale. "Why are they burning them?"

Matt looks heavily between the three of us. "They're experimenting on the unadjusteds. Live autopsies."

"Live? What for?" I stumble back until I hit the wall.

"They didn't find the answers they needed when looking at the unadjusteds' blood," Matt says. "Now they're looking deeper."

CHAPTER EIGHTEEN

The next day, Matt and I sneak out of the cave before dawn. Wearing a baseball cap low over his brow, he carries a heavy backpack full of his homemade grenades. I'm armed with a pistol. It's heavier than my knife, and I'm not sure I feel comfortable with it.

"You sure you're OK to go now?" Matt asks, pushing branches out of his way as we jog through the woods. "Your ribs…"

"I'm OK," I say. "I don't think it's broken, just badly bruised."

Dappled sunlight flickers around our feet. I quickly break into a sweat as the humidity winds through the trees.

"I never thought I'd say this," Matt says, stumbling through a dense patch of ferns. "But right about now, I wish I had an ability. Wings or speed would do."

"I totally get that. Never thought I'd want one either." I watch his broad shoulders as I walk behind him. "The wings…" I pull in my bottom lip. "They're amazing. If only they were strong enough to carry you too."

As the forest thickens, we slow, unable to negotiate the sprawling root networks and hanging branches at speed. After an hour, I stop and gulp water from my canteen. My ribs ache and I press a hand to my side.

Matt's eyes twitch with concern. "You sure you're OK to go on? You could just give me directions."

I cock my head. "Then what? I know what you're like. You'll charge the compound by yourself and end up getting locked inside." I don't mention I was ready to do exactly that when I was with Paige. "Or worse."

"I wonder if you should have taken on more abilities before we left." Matt looks to the path ahead, scanning the trees. "Maybe we're rushing this."

I can't deny Matt has acted impulsively, and it's not like him. He's usually so measured and considered. But it's his sister, goddammit. Who knows what the altereds are doing to them. "It's not like we're going to storm the compound," I say, pointing at his bag, which sags under the weight of the grenades. "We're just going to check it out."

Matt readjusts the straps of his backpack. He grits his teeth and I know he's wondering if he can launch all his grenades at the building.

"This isn't about me taking on more abilities. This is about you not going off half-cocked." I narrow my eyes at him. "I think you should leave your backpack here."

"No." He turns his back and stomps through the undergrowth. I run to catch up with him. It'll be up to me to make sure he's safe, whatever it is he plans to do.

I grab his shoulder. He flinches. "It's going to be OK."

Matt looks at me with watery eyes, then down at his feet. "You don't know that."

"I don't, but I have hope. Remember my song?"

Matt nods. "She's so close."

"Two more hours," I say, starting to walk again. I ignore the throb in my side. Matt needs me at my best. Lyla needs us both.

We walk in silence for a while. Then Matt asks, "Are you going to take on other abilities?"

"You want me to?"

He shrugs, but I can't see his face to read his expression. "Imagine if you were Sawyer. You could just create a hole in the fence or wall or whatever. Rescue mission accomplished. How easy would that be?"

"I guess." A wall of expectation forms between us.

Since I discovered my abilities, I've been thinking of little else. I can see the advantages of these abilities, especially now when they're useful, but I don't want to lose myself in them.

I step over a fallen trunk. The bushes and trees are beginning to change. More low-growing, hard-wearing shrubs indicate we're approaching the beach.

"I think I'm OK with taking on the human ones,"

236

I say eventually. "Jacob's teleportation and Sawyer's telekinesis would be valuable. As much as I like the wings, I'm not sure I want to stick out any more than I do already, but if I have to take on something physical, I'll just get my parents to take it out when we find them."

Matt steps on a long bramble branch and holds it down until I'm in the clear. "No armadillo shell for you."

"God, could you imagine?" I shake my head. "I don't understand some people's choices."

"I guess it depends what level they qualified for."

The light brightens and I look up. The trees have thinned to reveal the golden sand of a wide beach and the gray struts of a compound.

I point. "We're here."

We creep around the edge of a bayberry bush like the one Paige and I hid behind. The courtyard where I last saw Lyla is deserted.

"Where is she?" Panic lines Matt's voice. He moves the binoculars back and forth across the width of the building.

Loud trampling noises sound behind us and I turn, bracing myself for a fight. I relax as soon as I hear Joe's booming voice. A moment later his head pops into view and he holds up a hand in greeting. Paige and Sawyer are with him.

"What are you guys doing here?" I ask.

"Figured you might do something stupid," Joe says, looking between Matt and me.

Matt scowls and drops his backpack on the ground. "This is looking more like a rescue mission every minute."

"Just a recon." Sawyer's voice wavers, glancing at Joe. The scent of a recently smoked cigarette rolls toward me. "You promised."

"That's right." Joe steps forward and rummages through Matt's bag. "We're not blowing up any compounds today."

"Do you want my ability now?" Sawyer's hands are tucked up his sleeves despite the heat, revealing the tips of nicotine-stained fingernails. I'm glad he doesn't use his hands to cook.

I take a step away. "No. It'll drain me too much if I take it now."

Sawyer hunches into the shadows. "I don't know how to fight."

"But you lived on the streets," Matt says.

Sawyer shrugs and his blonde curls bounce. "I was good at staying in the shadows. With my ability, I never needed to use my fists. I pickpocketed with my mind."

"The compound is deserted," I say, hitching a thumb at the miserable building. The sun dims, and gray clouds move in. A sprinkling of rain dampens the sand. The ocean churns and turns a wintry color.

Joe examines the beach and compound. "They could have moved them."

"Or they could be inside," Paige says, keeping her wings tight against her body. "Lunch, or something."

No one says anything for a moment. We all stare at the compound.

"Maybe they're being experimented on," Matt says, clicking his fingers.

Paige juts her chin down the beach. "There's a town a mile or so along. I saw it when we were flying. Maybe we can get some info there."

"But there's a price on Silver's head. If she's recognized…" Joe steps between me and the compound, a protective shield. My heartstrings ping a little at his words and I can't help remembering what we almost did. And the way his fingers almost brushed my skin when he helped me with the bandage last night. God, why am I thinking about this now?

I shake my head to clear it. "I need a disguise."

"Your wings," Paige says.

I raise an eyebrow. "That's not a disguise; it's a big, fat neon sign."

"Paige has a point," Matt says, drawing the strings on his backpack and re-shouldering it.

Joe pulls at his chin. "They're looking for Silver Melody the unadjusted, not Silver Melody the altered with bright blue wings."

"She could just stay here," Sawyer says. "With me."

"I want to go," I say. "But you don't have to come if you don't want to, Sawyer."

Sawyer looks at the ground and runs a hand through his curls.

"We'll need ID cards," Paige says.

Matt steps onto the beach. "We can bluff it."

Joe crosses his arms. "You think we can bluff a troop of bulks or trolls?"

Matt continues along the beach, walking backwards to face us. "Or we take them out, but I'm not waiting anymore. I need to find my sister."

The rest of us tumble out of the woods, including Sawyer. I figure he's more afraid of waiting in the bushes on his own than he is of going into town. Joe and Matt bicker about the approach until we arrive at a bar on the beach. The greasy smell of french fries and stale beer competes with the salt of the ocean. The bar has outside tables and chairs full of soldiers in Bear's army uniform, chowing down on burgers and fries and racks of ribs. It makes my own rib hurt.

"Wings, Silver," Paige says in my ear.

I've been waiting until the last moment to use them. I don't want it to run out at the worst possible moment. When the blue wings emerge from my back, I feel like the bright red piece of cloth at a bullfight. My legs tremble a little, but I won't back away.

We skirt around the wooden clapboard bar until we find the front doors. The five of us enter, and the *thwak* of pool balls echoes around the room. Rock music plays from a jukebox in the corner. My boots stick to the linoleum floor. More soldiers are stuffed into booths with dim lighting. There isn't a single unadjusted-sized seating area. Everything is oversized—even the glasses.

A few pairs of eyes turn to look at us as we stand in the doorway. I realize how ridiculous we must look: two girls with bird wings, a bulk, and two seemingly unadjusteds. Maybe we'll need Matt's grenades after all.

Matt marches to the bar and hops onto a tall stool. I quickly follow, using my wings to lift me into the stool beside him. Paige and Joe slink off to one of the pool tables and Joe puts money on a table to indicate he wants a game.

"Three whiskeys on the rocks," Matt says as the barman approaches.

He's a big, bald man, with a belt cinching his trousers an inch too tight. An open collar shirt reveals a forest of thick, dark chest hair and when he exhales, two small insect pinchers emerge from his nostrils. I don't even begin to guess what he uses them for. Maybe pinching people who don't pay their tabs.

"You got ID?" He leans over the polished counter.

I freeze. Our game is going to be given up already.

Then I realize he's asking for proof of age, not altered status.

I don't have that either. And I've never even drunk whiskey before.

Sawyer steps onto the rung of my stool and slaps a photo ID on the counter with his name and details. Except the photo's not of him. It's of a black man at least fifteen years older. The barman doesn't seem to care and pours out three whiskeys. I'm so nervous I actually take a gulp but regret it immediately as it burns down my throat.

"That a compound down there?" Matt jerks his head toward outside.

The barman leans over the bar, drying a glass with a stained white rag.

"Yup. It's brought a truck lot of business to this little seaside town." He nods his head at the soldiers taking up every square inch of available space. "Plus, it's keeping us all level." He winks. "You guys have any problems with those murderous tendencies?"

Matt shakes his head. "I took intelligence. Seems only those with animal DNA are affected." He eyes the barman's pinchers as they emerge another inch out of his nostrils and draws back a little.

"What about you?" the barman asks me, wiping the counter between us. "And what are you doing here? I've only seen soldiers in here up until now."

"I've been spying from above." I nod at Paige over by the pool tables as the lie blurts out at me. "We're on a special recon force."

The barman nods, accepting.

"Doesn't seem to be anyone over at that compound," Matt says, picking up his glass. He eyes the liquid inside with an indifferent air. "They kill 'em off already?" He pushes a conspiratorial smile onto his lips.

I brace myself for the answer. Sawyer stands beside me, a lit cigarette in his mouth, his head just popping over the bar. He twiddles his glass in his hands and keeps pushing his curls off his face. Then a snatch of color from the TV screen mounted behind the barman attracts my attention. It's a video of Matt and me running away from school and hopping the fence on our last day in the city. How the hell did they even get that footage? Then I think of all the drones in the sky that day.

I look around the room, but no one seems to be watching. Or if they are, they're too drunk to care.

"I have no idea what's going on in that compound," the barman says. He tilts his head. "But they couldn't have killed them off. We'd all have gone crazy."

"Ain't that the truth." Matt holds his glass up in a toast.

The barman takes an empty tumbler and pours himself a glass. An upbeat song plays on the jukebox and someone across the room starts singing along with

243

a drunken slur. Joe and Paige take their turns at the pool table. Her wings flutter and keep sweeping against people's faces. Someone curses at her and she sucks her wings tight to her body.

A bulk a couple of stools down looks at me, then at Matt, then the TV. I wince but quickly plaster a smile on my face. I contemplate throwing him a salute or blowing him a kiss, depending on how drunk he might be, but he leans closer and frowns.

I force myself to stay where I am. Subtly, I nudge Matt's foot with my boot. I down the rest of my whiskey and try not to cough. I have to look like I belong here.

A waitress carrying a tray of empty plates stumbles into me. I turn and reach out a hand to help her, holding on to her arm. The stack of dishes shatters on the floor. Suddenly a flash of pain slams between my eyes and I can't breathe. I didn't notice the waitress had a pair of ornate horns. I double over as I feel them form on my head, mimicking hers.

"What the...?" The barman leans over to get a better look.

Matt leaps off the stool. "She hasn't been well." He takes off his baseball cap and tugs it onto my head.

Sawyer is already at the door. The soldier near Matt and me is off his stool. He holds out a hand to help, I think, but there's no way I'm touching him.

He crouches to look closer. My wings disappear as I

try to cope with this new ability. The waitress is on her knees, picking up all the broken china.

The barman ogles. "Where the hell did your wings just go?"

"You look familiar…" The soldier frowns again, teetering toward us. Drunk.

On the TV, the story has moved on to some army recruitment campaign about how your country needs you to stand against the evil but clever unadjusteds.

"Not from around here." Matt tries to wave the soldier away. He tugs me toward the door, where Joe and Paige are heading too.

The change is complete, and the new horns push Matt's cap off my head. I stumble out the door and trip into another soldier. He's dragging a girl with red hair behind him.

I stop dead.

Addison.

A pair of electric cuffs contains her wrists and her right eye is bruised and swollen shut. She gapes. "Silver?"

The five of us are now outside, plus Addison and her captor and a soldier who's followed us out. The rest of the street is deserted.

"Silver… Melody?" The first soldiers reaches for his gun.

Even though I'm exhausted from the change, I swivel out of the way. Paige flies above our heads and Addison twists her arms free, but her wrists are still tied together.

Joe goes for the troll soldier who followed us and grabs him in a headlock. Sawyer uses his telekinesis to hurl the soldier's gun into the ocean.

The bulk grabs me, squeezing his arm around my neck, and I can't reach the pistol tucked in my waistband. "You're worth a lot of money. Dead or alive."

There's no flash of pain as he holds me in place. I'm too exhausted to take on any more changes. Matt whips out a gun and aims it at the bulk, but I don't think his aim is good enough to go for the weak spot. He points it at us, hesitating.

Addison leaps, raising her electric cuffs. She brings them down on the bulk and he twitches as a current of electricity spasms through him. Joe sharply jerks the troll's neck.

Both soldiers drop to the sidewalk.

Panting, I look at Addison. "What happened to you?"

"Not now," Matt says, holstering his gun. "We need to get out of here."

A soldier taps on the window of the door then tries to push it open. I realize Sawyer is using his ability to hold it shut.

The six of us run. I can barely make my legs move, but I know I have to keep going. When I fall behind, Matt grabs my hand and tugs me along. Soldiers burst onto the street.

Matt grabs something from his bag and tosses it to Joe. "Needs a bulk arm."

Joe pulls the pin on the grenade and tosses it behind us. An instant later it explodes, causing a whirlwind of sand and shrapnel to fly toward us. We dive into the tree line as the stench of burnt plastic hits the air. My legs buckle and I collapse in a heap of ferns, but Joe picks me up and throws me over his shoulder.

"We can't leave," Matt says. "My sister is still in that compound."

"So are Silver's parents," Addison says around a split lip.

The words penetrate the fuzzy haze of my exhausted brain, but I can't grasp their meaning.

"We don't have the firepower," Joe says, marching a determined path away from the beach. "We'll come back when we do."

CHAPTER NINETEEN

The trek back to the cave passes by in a blur with Joe carrying me most of the way. My ears ring from the explosion and my mind reels from the information about my parents. Joe plants me on my feet when we reach the cave door and I'm finally able to stand without my knees buckling. Before Matt can open the door, Francesca thrusts it open, wearing a stony expression. She looks like she wants to ground us all.

Francesca leads us to the weapons chamber. Once there, the six of us sit on a ledge along the back wall. Matt sits next to Addison, removes something from his backpack, and disables the electric current on her cuffs. Then he uses a screwdriver to release her arms. Francesca stands before us with her hands on her hips, and Claus comes across the passageway from the small area where Matt keeps his radio equipment.

"We heard about the explosion on the radio," Claus

says, leaning both hands on his cane. His eyes burn with disappointment. Even his mustache looks limp.

"Of all the asinine ideas!" Francesca takes a breath, presses thumb and forefinger to the bridge of her nose, and starts again. "What the hell were you thinking?"

Matt meets her challenging stare. "I wanted to see my sister to make sure she's OK."

"What if someone followed you back?" Francesca wrings her hands. "What if someone had recognized you?" She points at me. "You put everyone in this cave in jeopardy!"

I stand. I'm tired of being told what I can and can't do. Claus flashes me a warning, which I ignore.

"My parents are in the compound too," I say, the calmness of my voice surprising me. I take a breath. "I get that you're an adult. A teacher. You're used to having kids do what you say, but I can make my own decisions." My hands fist as I glare at her.

Francesca blows out a sigh. "I'm not trying to tell you what to do, but people arrive here injured every day. Food is still going missing and we don't have a doctor. Someone must step up. Someone must organize this place and make sure we're safe. I wasn't trying to do it on my own." Her 'r's roll thick and heavy in her Spanish accent. "I thought we were a team."

I swallow hard, thinking over her words.

Matt comes to my side and looks at Francesca. "I

never wanted to put anyone in any jeopardy. I'm sorry for that."

Francesca's shoulders lower a couple of inches.

"We need to launch a rescue mission," I say. "Not just for Lyla and my parents, but also for everyone in that compound."

"How do we know your parents are there?" Francesca asks.

Addison steps forward, her swollen eye no more than a slit. "That's what the soldier said to me."

Before anyone can reply, Erica flies into the room and throws her arms around Addison. "What happened to you?"

"When we were at the warehouse, I thought I saw something in the woods nearby, so I went to check it out. Then someone hit my head and the world went dark." Her hand floats to her swollen eye, prodding gently. "When I woke, I was in a beach hut with a couple of soldiers playing cards on a table."

"What did they want with you?" Erica hovers in the air. Her wing seems all healed and flutters a golden yellow.

"To know who all of you were," Addison says, resting her head on Erica's shoulder. "I think they were planning on following you back to the cave, until I got in their way."

"What did you tell them?" I ask. From the looks of it, Addison went through hell and back. We're not trained soldiers. Anyone would be tempted to spill with the threat of pain and torture.

Addison smirks and points to her eye. "Does it look like I told them anything?"

"Thank goodness for that," Francesca says, rubbing her hands together.

"But they told you about my parents?"

Addison nods. "They thought I was out of it, but I heard them talking. They mentioned 'the famous scientists' being kept at the beach compound."

Matt frowns. "Why there? It doesn't make any sense."

Claus taps his cane for attention. "It makes perfect sense. Everyone will assume they're in the city and any rescue attempt will be focused there. At the beach, they're out of the way. No one would suspect them being there."

"That was my thinking too," Addison says, rubbing her wrists. The electric cuffs have left angry red lines.

"We need to go get them." I'm already moving toward the weapons lining the far wall.

"Slow down, Silver." Francesca walks over to me. "You just set off an explosion in the very place you want to go back to. Security will be tight. They'll be looking for trouble."

I kick at the ground. "We can't just leave them there."

"Give it a couple days," Francesca says. "Let things die down a little."

She's right, but I still don't like it. I know where my parents are. Now I know exactly how Matt feels.

Francesca beckons me back to the group. "Plus, if we're really serious about launching a full-scale attack, you could use all the abilities you can get."

I look from Claus to Francesca. "You told her?"

Claus stares at me for a good five seconds before he says anything. The kind of stare that says if I think about it long enough, I'll see his logic and can't possibly be mad at him.

And it works.

Francesca has stepped up to organize the chaos in the cage. She's just trying to help. And if I didn't have abilities, or the potential to amass more, she might not let me join the mission.

Claus's voice is firm but reassuring. "Of course I told her."

"Does everyone know?" I snap.

"Of course not." Francesca touches my hand, but it gives little comfort. "Though it will be a hard secret to keep. I'm not sure you should."

As I think of everyone learning this secret, the ground teeters, but I can't worry about what people think anymore. I have a rescue mission to plan. "You really think I need more abilities? Wings and speed aren't enough?"

"What do you think?" Francesca splays her hands.

"Your parents are the most protected prisoners in the entire country, guarded by a president with black widow DNA and bulk guards. Look at Joe and Hal. Do you think you could get past them on your own?"

One of them, maybe, but not both. "I won't be on my own."

"I understand you want your parents back, Silver. We all do, but let's make you as strong as possible first."

It makes sense. Of course it does. Matt and I share a look.

She's right. Again. In that moment, I hate her for it. My parents need me, and ironically, it's their very creation that will save them.

Joe steps close and offers me his hand. A twinge of apprehension dries my throat.

Matt steps to my other side. "Want me to be there?"

Erica watches me carefully, as if I've failed some kind of test. Her gaze fixes on Joe's outstretched hand.

I look at Joe's hand then at Matt's earnest expression. The kindness in Matt's blue eyes almost brings tears to mine. "If you don't mind, guys, I think this is something I'd rather do on my own. Without an audience."

Matt nods and steps away, eyes dimming in a way that concerns me, but I can't put my finger on why.

I don't take Joe's hand, but I follow him out of the cave into the moonlit valley and back to the training ground. The sky is clear and stars twinkle. The fact that we're

253

alone together suddenly swims into my consciousness. Nervous, I struggle to keep up with his long strides and end up jogging past him with my speed ability. I've wanted to touch him before, but there will be nothing romantic about this situation.

When we arrive in the meadow, Joe sits on the fallen tree trunk. Moonlight glints on a patch of smooth pebbles. Crickets chirp all around us.

"How're the ribs?" Joe asks as he places his hands on either side of the trunk.

"Better." I pluck at the bandage. "Thank you for the bandage."

"Anytime." Joe's lips lift and he picks up a couple of the stones and clunks them together in his large hand. "How come you're so afraid to touch me?"

I stand in front of him. "I've touched you loads. You carried me back from the compound, remember?"

He looks up at me. "That's hardly the same thing."

I frown. "And yet I didn't turn into a bulk."

Joe's warm eyes settle on mine. Fireflies glow in the forest all around and in the grass at our feet, like someone has lit a million tea-candles.

"I assume it's because you'd already exhausted your abilities. I'm sure now that you're rested, it will happen." He holds out his hand and smiles. A smile so full of warmth that I believe he has faith in me. Idiot.

Instead of taking it, I step up onto a fallen tree and

walk the length of it, then turn around and walk back. At least now we're somewhere near the same height.

"I don't want to be a bulk." To be so big, so masculine, something so unlike who I feel inside.

"It's only for an hour. You get to turn it on and off at will."

"But I won't look the same." I fiddle with my necklace. "I don't want to be so… *big*."

"It's a relative term. Right now, to me, you're tiny." Joe chuckles. "The world has come a long way. There are plenty of shops available for bulk clothing. Ceilings and doorways were raised. New cars made. Although, with the world how it is, maybe not right now."

My toes itch. I want to get this over with, but I also don't want to do it at all. "I'll split my clothing and you'll think I'm really ugly."

Joe waggles his eyebrows and I burst out laughing. There's a glint in his eye that I recognize: longing. I breathe in and realize he shares the same thoughts as me. About us. The realization makes my fingertips tingle with anticipation.

"Why do you care what I think?" Joe asks.

I don't have an answer.

He stands. "You could never be ugly."

The meadow quiets. A gentle breeze cools my body and tickles the nape of my neck. We stand side-by-side, arms almost touching. The hairs on my arms stand to attention, as though they're trying to close the gap between us.

Joe stares at me with a hard intensity. With me on the tree, we're eye level. He leans toward me, closing the distance between us. My eyes close as his head dips. It feels like an eternity before his lips touch mine. Soft and probing, his mouth parts, and I can't think anymore. It's just him and me and this evocative warmth between us. He pulls me against his armored chest, and the kiss loses all hesitancy.

I kiss him back, harder, a hunger taking control of my body. His hands tangle in my hair. He picks me up, and then we're lying on the grass. He leans over me, one hand still caressing my neck, the other setting the skin at my waist on fire as he explores under my T-shirt. I trace the curve of his biceps and the contours of his impenetrable skin.

"I've wanted to do that from the moment I met you," Joe says.

My lips tingle. Then sting. Without warning, pain shoots through my limbs, as though I've been tied to a rack and stretched. I should have expected it. I fight to breathe as my arms and legs spasm. Gasping, I curl into a ball.

"I'm here, Silver. I'm here," Joe says.

I look at my arms. They are as smooth as Joe's, and they're three inches longer. I look at my legs. My knees are not where they used to be. Newly formed muscles strain against the seams of my trousers and my ankles poke awkwardly out the end. My feet throb inside my too-tight boots. The chain of my necklace tightens around my throat and my skin changes to armor.

So this is what it feels like to be a bulk. I struggle to my feet. That's when I feel the itching at the end of my fingertips, in my shoulder sockets, ankles, and hips. An itching that grows into a painful pressure, as though a phantom person has reached their hands into my body and is pulling it apart. I stumble. My center of gravity feels off, as if I'm a toddler learning to take my first steps.

When I catch my breath, I look up to find Joe standing before me, almost eye-level. I'm not as tall as him. As with all the abilities I've gained so far, it seems I don't possess their full power, but it's still enough of a height growth to make me dizzy. Joe's arm supports me and I keep my gaze locked on the point where our skin touches.

"How do you feel?" Joe asks.

"Big," I reply. There's no other word for it. Joe chuckles.

"Let's do the obstacle course," he says.

"In the dark?"

"I think there's enough moonlight to see by."

Taking his hand, I follow him to the start of the course: the tires, which I merely leap over. The wall of hay is a simple hop and a jump. The swing effigies bounce off my armored skin if I miss them with my knife. Nothing hurts. Everything feels alive.

"You feel like this all the time?" I ask, when we stop to rest.

"I'm kind of used to it now," Joe says, the tips of his fingers pressing against mine. "I'm glad you have the ability so I can touch you without you flinching." He kisses me again, and I kiss him back. But something in the back of my mind niggles. A whispered warning that refuses to make itself clear.

I scooch away.

"Silver?" He reaches for me.

I scan his handsome face, wanting to trace the contour of his jaw. I resist. "I don't think I can do this."

"Do you not… I thought… Hell, I don't know what I thought." Joe finds the pebbles again and slaps them together, their grating noise distilling the moment. He won't look at me.

"It's not you…"

Tension appears in his cheeks. "Do not say 'It's me.'"

I sigh. "It's my parents."

"I wasn't expecting that." For once, Joe's voice is a whisper.

I take the pebbles from his hand and put them on the ground. "It's not that I'm not interested, but I can't think about it with my parents in prison. They're so close. Maybe after we get them out…"

Joe smiles, a hint of dimples flashing in his golden cheeks. "I get it."

I sit when a cloudy sensation in my head makes me teeter. "Blame it on President Bear. That's what I do."

"Another reason he should be dethroned." He kicks at the fallen tree and it snaps in half. "He gets in the way of the love lives of horny teenagers."

A giggle bursts out of me, as well as a blush.

Joe looks me up and down. "You're shrinking."

"Shrinking?" I take a step back.

"Losing the bulk power." Joe towers over me once again.

When I examine my body, I've lost the hard, armored skin. My clothes, although with a few holes along the seams, fit me again. I press a thumb against the delicate area in the hollow of my throat and wind the chain of the necklace around my finger.

"What's next?"

"Rest," Joe replies. "You've worn yourself out again and can't take on any more abilities. It's late. Let's get some sleep and we'll find the other altereds in the morning."

The long, wild grass tickles my skin through the holes in my clothing.

"Adjusteds," I say.

Joe rests his hand on the small of my back and guides me out of the meadow. "Huh?"

259

"They're not altereds. At least the ones living in the cave. You're not an alt." I look at him. "I can't believe I ever thought you were."

"You woke up injured in a deserted, dilapidated house with a bulk towering over you. I can see how you thought I was an altered."

I throw one of my acorns at him. It dinks off his hard skin and rolls to the ground. "I guess. I just never understood the different mentalities. There was a line. Unadjusteds on one side and altereds on the other. Now I see that was a rather naïve assessment. There are so many lines."

"True." Joe tucks a few strands of loose hair behind my ear.

I grab his wrist and press my lips against the pad of his thumb. "Thank you."

"For what?"

"For saving me. For being here."

"Always." His eyes shine with the longing for something more.

That night I can't sleep, not with Joe sleeping so close in the next hollow and the memory of our kiss lingering. I pluck at the guitar Matt gave me, playing a melody, singing the freedom song under my breath.

When you hear the lone wolf howling,
When sky comes crashing through.

With all the hellhounds growling,
If it ends, just me and you...
Just close your eyes and breathe in deep,
Look to the new sun's sky.
Because our voice is freedom,
And they will hear us cry.

CHAPTER TWENTY

The days drag by as I wait for something to do and someone to rescue. I walk the passageways, and when I enter the deserted main chamber in the middle of the day, a clang comes from the kitchen, followed by a curse. Then there's a blur of movement as a person flees the area down a passageway I haven't walked before. I use a burst of speed to follow them, but I end up tripping over the uneven ground and losing them in a dark tunnel.

Returning to the kitchen, I discover some of the supplies are open and strewn over the floor. It's best to let Matt know, I decide.

I find him in a small alcove, bent over a wobbly workbench, clipping wires and sweeping up gunpowder.

"Again?" He puts down a pair of pliers.

I nod.

"How will we have enough food to rescue people if it's all going missing?" He pulls at the roots of his hair. "We'll need to start an investigation."

He picks up the cutters again and pounds a few things on the table. "I'll have a word with Francesca."

When Jacob finds me later, I follow him to the training ground, where Joe is waiting. Over the last few days, since our kiss in the meadow, he's helped Claus train the population of the cave. In between taking abilities, he's been testing me. He times how long my abilities last. We realize I need a six-hour rest before I can use them again.

I know he's been true to his word and not told anyone about my abilities, but the secret leaks. I'm angry for a couple of days, looking for someone to blame, but then I realize it's a wasted emotion. I just need to get on with it. If it brings back my parents, who cares if people know?

Claus sometimes pits me and Kyle against each other, and a few people come to watch us spar. My muscles become more toned, my instincts quicker than any animal and my reflexes almost superhuman. But I guess that's the point of abilities. To be beyond human. To evolve into something else.

Jacob stands before me, wearing only a pair of black karate trousers. His chest rises and falls with his breaths. With his tattoos snaking across his olive skin, he looks zebra-like.

According to the nanite code, teleportation is a class nine. Only those in key governmental positions or at the top of their sport qualify. With a black belt in karate, it's one I qualify for, but Bear would never allow me such a powerful nanite with the parents I have. He would give me something in class one. Something demeaning, like an extra row of teeth.

"Silver?" Joe asks, snapping me out of my thoughts. "You ready?" He sits on the fallen trunk and scribbles notes onto a pad of paper for Claus, who is busy testing newcomers in the weapons chamber.

Jacob shoots me a nervous smile. "What do I do?"

"Just hold my hand," I say.

He takes my hand, then immediately teleports a few feet away. His smile turns sheepish. "Sorry; I know it's going to hurt. I hate hurting people."

I chuckle. "Except in competitions."

He teleports back. "Yeah, right. Except in competitions."

I grab his hand again and hold it firmly. The pain centers at the base of my skull and pushes at my temples. For the few seconds it takes to acquire the ability, I can barely breathe. I grit my teeth and pray the nausea rolling in my stomach won't rise any higher.

"You OK?" Jacob asks. His forked tongue flicks between his lips.

I nod. Weirdly, only my rib aches now. "How does it work?"

Jacob flashes his reptilian eyes at me. "You can only ever jump a distance of six feet, but it can get you out of a tricky spot when necessary. Don't over-egg it. Not that you'll be using it in a competition anytime soon, but if you misjudge, you can end up outside the ring and be disqualified."

"Or in a tree, or something," I mutter.

Jacob laughs. "If that happens, the solidity of the object senses you and pushes you right out again. No harm done, but it doesn't feel great."

I roll my eyes, then prepare for my first jump. I aim for a tree six feet to Jacob's left and end up halfway between him and the trunk. I sigh. This one will take time to master. And no doubt it will have its own limitations, just like the others. I'm about to try again when I catch fleeting movement in the trees.

"Someone's here," I say. "Should anyone be here?"

Joe looks up from the tree. "No. Wait here." He darts through the meadow and into the woods. I hear branches moving and twigs snapping, then a cry of alarm.

A couple of minutes later, Joe returns with Sawyer in tow. Both of them carry bags of flour and other food.

"What's going on?" I ask. "Have you been on a food run, Sawyer?"

"That's not what this is," Joe says, scowling.

I look from Joe to Sawyer, to the bright red of his cheeks, to the flour in his arms. He tries to shrink into his mop of corkscrew curls. "*You've* been stealing the food? I've had half a roll for breakfast the last three mornings because of *you*?"

Sawyer drops the sack and backs away. "I'm so sorry." His thumbs circle each other. "I'm used to taking food whenever I see it."

I frown and look him up and down. Although slim, he isn't too thin. "Why?"

"I've been living on the streets for five years. I ran away from the foster system. The streets are better." He pushes the words through gritted teeth. "And if those soldiers at the beach figure out about the cave, it's good to have a second location."

Joe points a finger at him. "Not when you don't share it with anyone else."

I don't have the heart to ask him what happened. Not with his foster parents, anyway. I spot a small scar on his neck running under his collar. It looks like a cigarette burn. More than one. "Where did you get the ability?"

Sawyer tilts his head and looks up at me. "Living on the streets gives you a certain amount of knowledge. There was a particular alley I lived in for a while because it had a huge porch overhang where I could keep dry. Then one of the buildings in it got condemned and was vacant for a whole year. I could sleep inside. Closest I ever got to security." His eyes dim as he drops his gaze again. "Anyway, that same alley is where a lot of the black market nanite distribution took place. One night, I saw one of the dealers drop a pill."

Jacob's thin dark eyebrows rise. "So you took it?"

Sawyer nods. "Figured an ability might get me off the streets."

Joe whistles. "Telekinesis is a class ten nanite. If they found you..."

"I know," Sawyer says, a small shudder running through his shoulders. "I stayed on the streets, using it to help me with magic tricks. I made enough to eat and sometimes rent a room in a motel with a shower. But I knew I had to keep a low profile. I'm always looking over my shoulder."

Pity swallows my anger. "I don't really know what to say."

Jacob's forked tongue sweeps between his lips as his eyes follow Sawyer's every twitch.

"Please don't make me leave. I don't have anywhere else to go." Sawyer looks at his shoes, which are covered in flour.

"Maybe you could come with us on the next supply run," I say.

Sawyer freezes. "Can't I just give the food back to you? I can't go out there again. Not after the beach... I can't. Please don't make me."

"OK. OK." Joe lays a hand on Sawyer's shoulder, making him jump. "We'll talk about this later. Put the food back. If any goes missing again, I know where to look."

Sawyer blows a stray curl out of his eyes. "Thank you."

He raises his head. "But one more thing: please don't tell anyone else about this."

Joe looks at me. I shrug. "I'll have to tell Francesca, but I don't see why anyone else needs to know."

"Thanks," Sawyer replies, then scampers away as quickly as he can.

"Do you think we can trust him?" I ask.

Joe watches his retreating back. "I'm pretty sure he's learned his lesson."

I dig at a bulbous root with my boot. "But there's a price on my head."

"He's not interested in money," Jacob says. "He just doesn't want to be hungry anymore."

———

Over the next few days I take on the abilities of everyone in the cave. People become alive with chatter about my new powers and the upcoming rescue. Claus replaces my obstacle course and knife training with ability tests. Crowds form to watch my trials. The attention embarrasses me, but no matter how private an area I seek to test my abilities, a crowd always follows. After the first day and dozens of well wishes, I cease caring and take some pride in impressing an audience.

I gain all the characteristics of the adjusteds with physical attributes: one boy with the teeth of a shark–

not a transition I want to repeat, as it felt like my jaw was being torn apart with a car jack; the jumping ability of a flea–I find this weird until Matt informs me a flea can jump one hundred times its own body size. One man loans me the characteristic of webbed feet, borrowed from ducks, and the flippers of a seal. There are countless others, some of which I can't understand the point of, including an elderly lady who shows me how to change my skin into the armor of an armadillo.

Once I've acquired and adjusted to all these characteristics, I move on to the less physical ones. There's more intelligence and Sawyer's telekinetic talent, but I refuse the werewolf ability.

It's exhausting. I sleep between trials and make a dent in the food supply. The changes increase my metabolic rate and I'm constantly hungry.

"It's time to go," Matt says when he finds me in my hollow. He holds a crumpled piece of paper. Einstein wanders in with him and wags his tail at me.

"Francesca's worried more soldiers will come scouting after the bar explosion," Matt says. "And as you've taken on all the abilities here, it's time for that rescue mission."

The back of my neck prickles, but the thought of getting my parents back drowns out the anxiety. "Finally."

"Here are the people she wants to come." He hands me the piece of paper.

Joe Rucker (Bulk)
Hal Small (Bulk)
Matt Lawson (Weapons, technology)
Addison Shields (Strength)
Paige Starling (Flight)
Sawyer Watson (Telekinesis)
Kyle Lewis (Speed)
Jacob Shea (Teleportation)
Erica Swiftfield (Flight)
Silver Melody (Ultimate weapon)

CHAPTER TWENTY-ONE

There are ten of us. Ten people to rescue my parents, Matt's sister, and as many of the other unadjusteds in the compound as we can. The weight of responsibility settles into the sore nooks of my shoulders. Seeing the words 'ultimate weapon' next to my name sends a shiver of fear down my spine.

Ultimate weapon. Me. The very thing I didn't want to be is the very thing I now am, but the cause is bigger than me. I see that now. I was naïve to rebel against nanites and abilities like they're all as bad as each other. As the ultimate weapon, I can help. I can save my parents, but it doesn't mean I'm not terrified.

"I can't wait to see Lyla again." Matt's eyes glisten.

I squeeze his hand. "I know."

I crouch on the floor and open the small pouch on my rucksack. I sort through the bottles of temporary nanites Dad and I used when we fled through the woods. That feels like such a long time ago now. Not just a few weeks.

There is a good handful of night-vision and strength, at least two per person. I give them to Matt, who shoves them in his pocket.

Claus has the regeneration pills. Maybe he'll let me bring one in case someone gets injured. When I open the invisibility bottle, I count only five. Not enough for all of us, and they only last half an hour, but they're worth taking. We can decide who will use them when we're a bit further along. Not seeing the need for the predator-masking scents, I leave them behind. With two bulks in our team and no security swipes to let ourselves into the compound, the mission won't be reliant on stealth. It will take surprise and brute force.

"Let's go find the others," Matt says.

"OK," Paige says. "It's time to saddle up."

"It's kick-ass time!" Kyle punches the air and shuffles his feet so fast all I can see is a blur.

"Francesca's put me in charge of packing the food." Sawyer rolls his eyes. "I didn't think I actually had to come with you. I'm not…" His lips twist into a grimace. "I don't think I can do this."

I touch his arm. "You've been training with Claus, right?"

"Yeah, but before two weeks ago I'd never even held a weapon. I can't…" His gaze shifts to the floor.

My voice is firm. "Sawyer, we need you. You can do this. We're a team. We'll protect each other."

He shuts his mouth. His ashen skin looks ghostly in the pale lighting of the occasional lantern.

I move my hand to his shoulder. "You're going to be OK."

His voice turns squeaky. "Promise?"

I can't say the word. As much as I want it to be true, I won't lie about something I'm not sure of. He's right to be afraid. I've been so focused on rescuing my parents, I haven't really stopped to examine the consequences. But right now, looking at Sawyer blanch at my every word, flickers of panic ignite in my limbs and my breathing turns shallow.

I can't show him how afraid I suddenly am. There's no room for fear.

Sawyer gulps. I force out a laugh, ruffle his blond curls and tell him he won't even have time to be scared, hoping it's true. But being brave is acting in the face of fear, even when it grips so strongly you can't hear anything except your own rushing pulse.

The mission is imminent. It's actually happening. Soon, I'll see my parents again. The team gathers in the main chamber, where Francesca imparts a few final words. A thick round of applause thunders through the chamber as the mission team spills down the passageway. When we throw open the door, the day outside is calm, and we charge into the sunshine. I blink against the sun, wishing I'd thought to bring a pair of sunglasses.

"Everyone's relying on me," I say to Matt as we climb the ridge. The panic I felt when I was talking to Sawyer ratchets up a notch. I try to push it down, but it clutches at the back of my knees and makes my mouth turn sour.

"Silver, we're a team." Matt takes my hand, his eyes more vibrant than usual. "And anyhow, I'm the useless one."

"You aren't useless. You got hold of a gun and gave us cover. I didn't know you could shoot, by the way," I say.

Matt weaves through a dense area of foliage, following Joe's machete hacks. "I had to do something while you were chained up in that apartment building of yours. Lost myself to a few video games."

"Now I really wish I'd asked for one for Christmas when things were still good. Do they have a game where you have to shoot President Bear?"

Matt snaps out a laugh. "No. They don't. But there is one where you have to hunt down unadjusteds. You know that whole 'blindfold them and stick them in the middle of nowhere' scenario, then hunt them down."

"Jesus." I gawk at him. "No wonder things got so bad."

Matt sets his jaw and wags a finger. "Not anymore. Now we get to make a stand."

"Damn straight." I reach out for a high-five.

Ahead, Erica, Addison and Paige sing my freedom song, and the melody filters back to me. The whole cave knows it now and it's often sung after dinner, when I pull out a guitar and strum the melody. Once Francesca had to put an end to it, such was the passion in people's hearts adding a little too much volume to their throats.

Young, like a new star shining
Bold, like a lone wolf stalking
Lost, like a child wandering
Scared, like the whole world's falling
But I am free. And I won't back down.

"See?" Matt says, indicating the others singing. "You're not letting anyone down. You've given them hope to hold on to."

I sigh. "These abilities have limitations."

"It's not you against the world." He matches my pace and brushes his elbow against my arm. "It's all of us, too."

"Thanks, Matt." I watch my feet kick through leaves and acorns, hoping he's right.

But his words do little to ease my tension. Soon, I'll find my parents, and they'll give me back my unadjusted state. Once it's all over, that's my wish: to be normal again. Myself. Whatever that is now. But if they made the change in vitro, is there anything to revert to? Am I stuck like this forever? Although my attitude has changed since being at the cave, meeting Joe and the other adjusteds, who aren't really alts at all, I still can't quite reconcile myself as one of their group.

Until I think about flying. The wings are my favorite ability. To soar so high, away from everything else. Paige is right: it's so easy to fly away from your problems, across an ocean to a deserted island where no one has ever heard of a nanite. The wings don't feel abnormal. They feel like the most natural thing in the world, that perhaps in another million years might be part of a human's normal evolution. Our longing to be in the sky, in space, to discover the boundaries of our universe is so much easier with a pair of wings. Although they aren't spaceproof yet because the feathers freeze, unaided space exploration isn't that far away. And none of that will be possible when the nanites stop.

Sure, we can still use them to cure diseases, to help kids with learning difficulties, soldiers with missing limbs, birth defects. The list of therapeutic purposes goes on. But where do you draw the line? There isn't anything oppressive about owning a pair of wings, but that's where some of the problems started. Those in gymnastics and cheerleading who produced wings always perform better, and it leaks into every sport and every profession possible. However, the thought of giving them up sends a slither of unease through my stomach. Am I becoming so attached to them already?

Scattered sunlight filters through the branches over

our heads. Joe and Hal continue to lead, Erica fluttering close behind, Kyle and Sawyer behind them. Addison, her wounds now healed, walks with Jacob and Paige. The undergrowth thickens, slowing our pace until Hal pulls out another machete and joins Joe hacking at the ferns tangling our feet. Heat shimmers and mirages make me crave water. We slap at mosquitoes and blot sweat from our brows.

When the air carries the scent of salt toward us, Paige leads the way to the thicket of bayberry bushes we hid in before. Matt and Joe remind us of the plan, causing Sawyer to audibly gulp.

I shake out two of the invisibility pills into my palm and hand them to Matt and Sawyer. On a count of three, they swallow them and disappear in less than a minute. Only by the rustling of the bayberry bushes can I mark their progress. Then they're on open land and it's impossible to tell where they are until they reach a dirt track. They leave faint shoe impressions all the way up to the corner of the fenced courtyard.

The razor wire fence judders, then nothing for a full minute.

"When do we go?" Paige asks.

A siren tears through the silence.

"I say now." I jump to my feet.

We charge down the slope toward the courtyard. Guards swivel toward us and raise their guns. Joe and

Hal lead the way, shielding us. I'm tempted to turn bulk myself, but I know I only have an hour's worth of ability to use. I need to save it for a more crucial moment, and the guards aren't getting a good aim at us through the chain-link.

When we approach the razor-wire outer fence, half of us tumble through a small hole. Wire flaps in a breeze, then flies in the opposite direction. Sawyer must still be there, holding the loose strands away from us.

Then we're at the chain-link fence surrounding the courtyard. A hole appears in front of us as we dash toward it. Matt and Sawyer. Joe stabs a troll with his machete as soon as he reaches the other side. A crowd of unadjusteds presses toward us when they see the hole and start filing through.

Something yanks my arm. "This way." Matt's voice in my ear. "I see Lyla."

Using a squirt of speed, I duck under a roving bullet and yank a rifle from a troll's hand. I chuck it to Paige, then speed across to the far side of the courtyard, away from the commotion.

A battle commences at our backs. Trolls pour through a metal door, firing. Despite Joe and Hal trying to shield everyone from spewing bullets, they can't cover everyone; unadjusteds go down. Blood colors the dusty ground. Screams echo in my ears, but people make it through the hole in the fence. Joe keeps one hand over his throat as he slices at the trolls with his machete. Paige, close to the razor wire, fires the rifle at the amassing trolls.

"It's Lyla," Matt says, coming back into view. His body shimmers into existence like a ghostly specter and nudges me along the back wall of the courtyard, away from the main commotion. Moments later he is solid and full color once again.

In the far corner, away from everyone else, Lyla sits huddled in the dirt.

Matt crouches before her. "Lyla?"

She raises her eyes. Not as bright as Matt's, but a deeper, more knowing blue. They settle on him and her face lights up. Tears stream down her dirty cheeks. "Matt." She throws her arms around him. Amid the chaos, they hug, until Matt pulls her to her feet.

He shoots a glance over his shoulder. "I need to get her out of here."

I eye the metal door the trolls poured through. My entry into the rest of the complex. "Go. I need to find my parents."

Matt nods, kisses my cheek, then tugs Lyla around the back of the main group and along the fence to the opening.

The battle pushes into the center of the courtyard, both sides using overturned benches and metal trash cans for a scrap of cover. Although we seem to have the upper hand and most of the blood is the enemy's, none of my friends can be spared. Only I can slip away undetected.

I dash to the door and speed over the threshold. Looking up and down the hall, both directions look the same. I whisper a short prayer for courage. The freedom song comes to me and I mutter the words under my breath, finding comfort in their passionate appeal.

> *But when our hearts burn quiet in the darkness of the night,*
> *We won't bear to keep this silence—we will stand, and we will fight.*

Kyle blurs past me and screeches to a sneakered stop at the end of the hall. "Dude! There you are!" He dashes back to me and joins me along the wall.

"What are you doing here?" I flatten my hands against the wall's reassuring solidity.

"I came to help you. You can't go on your own." He slashes a knife in the air, like he's spelling out the letters in his name.

The thud of helicopter blades sounds above our heads and the windows at the end of the hallway shake in their frames.

"Sounds like reinforcements," Kyle says, checking the door at our back.

If that helicopter means more soldiers, I need to find my parents before I come face-to-face with the enemy. Hopefully the chaos in the courtyard will draw their attention first.

"Let's go," I say, gripping my knife.

Together, we run down the hallway and peel around the corner. Shouts and screams float in through the windows, but I block them out. I scan each room for my parents, for anyone at all, but the hallway only reveals an empty chain of basic offices. A chair, a desk, sometimes a computer or a few loose sheets of paper that fly when I breeze inside. Never my parents.

"Up." Kyle points to a staircase at the end of the hallway.

We run down the hall, burst through the staircase door and jump up the steps two at a time. When we emerge on the second floor, we find ourselves in a hallway identical to the one below.

I try the first door on my right; it's locked. I break the lock with my bulk power and push the door open. A lab of some sort. A centrifuge and large refrigerator, a patient bed with an alarming amount of straps to hold someone down. Empty.

Kyle shouts a cry of alarm. I stumble back and find myself nose-to-chest with President Bear.

"Silver." He draws out my name in his deep voice. "How nice to see you here."

His eyes always draw my attention first. Red. Inhuman. Evil. The pupils and the irises. Tall as a bulk, he looms over me, and his shadow fills the hall at his back. His hulking shoulders slope away to arms thicker than both my thighs, and his hairy hands drip something lacey and white. His spider nanite. The one everyone fears.

The combination of grizzly bear and black widow nanites is what makes him unique and terrifying. Both species enhance his ferocity, making his orders unarguable and irrefutable. President Bear can shoot venomous silk from the palms of his hands. If they cut through your skin, you're dead in minutes.

Kyle screams. A scream of pain and surprise. Without warning, a thready white projectile pins him to the ceiling. A giant web. Bear must possess telekinesis too.

"Let him go!"

President Bear narrows his red eyes at me. "I don't think so."

I raise my knife. The president laughs, and before the sound can fill the hall, another projectile of white shoots from his palm and wraps around both my wrists like a macabre pair of handcuffs.

I don't move. Although I have to look up at him, I manage to channel all my pent-up fury in that glare. "Let. Him. Go."

A beat pulses between us.

President Bear snorts. "All right, then."

With one flick of his wrist, the webbing holding Kyle prisoner to the ceiling untangles and falls to the floor. He thumps to the ground and yelps again. Before he gets a chance to sit up, President Bear shoots out his hand once more. The crack of a breaking bone comes from Kyle, followed by a piercing scream. His face pales enough to blend with the white walls.

There's nothing I can do for Kyle with my hands tied, so I push a little bulk strength into my wrists but only succeed in tightening the webbing. It digs into my skin, and I know if I push any harder, its venom will sink into my bloodstream. Kyle will have to wait.

Unintimidated, I glare at the president. "Where are my parents?"

President Bear pulls on the webbing under Kyle and yanks the lead that connects his palm to my wrist. He drags us both down the hall and into an empty room. I try to slow him by anchoring my feet into empty doorways, but his strength is too much for me.

"Why on earth would you think your parents are here?" President Bear shoves me into a chair and uses more webbing to anchor my arms to its legs. Leaving Kyle whimpering in a corner, he sits on the edge of a flimsy fake-wood desk and raps his knuckles on the surface.

"Because Addison..." My indignation peters out. I don't want him to know how I know things.

The president folds his hands behind his back. "Your parents are in the city, Silver, refusing to cooperate with my requests. Now that you'll be joining us, I think they'll realize the proper motivation."

I lean as close as I can to the desk. "If you do anything to them…"

President Bear laughs. The condescension burns in my veins. I want to snap out of my bonds, but I won't risk the venom or reveal my abilities. I need to stay cool. I glance at Kyle. His eyes are closed but his breathing is regular. Passed out from the pain.

"Why are the altereds all losing their shit without the unadjusteds?"

President Bear raises his one massive eyebrow. "Altereds? Now, now, Silver, that's a little prejudiced."

He smiles—a pink slit in the middle of a heavy beard, wet and shining like a newborn earthworm. "To answer your question, thanks to the willing participants of the unadjusteds in the compounds, we've discovered that those who have taken more than one animal modification need to be around unadjusted humans or those with only human modifications. Otherwise they lose their humanity. According to your father, the animal DNA overrides the human DNA and takes over. Those most severely affected revert to more primal, basic urges, but it's a good thing."

Tense muscles ripple along the back of my neck. "A

good thing? How can you say killing sprees are a good thing?"

"Well, yes, that was unfortunate, but now we are on the brink of a massive shift in evolution. A new species. Once we solve this problem, we will grow as a new species."

I frown. "What's wrong with being human?"

Bear's wet lips curl again. "Oh, Silver. Have you really learned nothing?" He stands and walks to the small window. A deep frown forms as he stares outside. Gunfire sounds in the distance. "It seems the extra troop of soldiers hasn't been able to contain the situation you and your friends started. I should have brought the bulks." He sighs. "I'll have to deal with this myself. Then we can talk some more. I've been enjoying our little chat."

Before passing me, President Bear lays a massive paw on my bare shoulder. Pain sizzles through my body. I grit my teeth and hold my breath, trying to appear normal. Fighting against the pain of new abilities, I hold my breath.

President Bear marches to the door. I work up a mouthful of saliva and spit at his back. He merely laughs and slams the door behind him, locking it. His footsteps fade away.

I give in to the pain. Every nerve sings with a new kind of heat. Every muscle twitches uncontrollably and my bones shift as if I'm transforming into another kind of thing altogether. My spine burns with an intense fire. I have to bite the inside of my cheek to keep from passing out. President Bear has taken more than just spider and grizzly bear nanites, and now I have every single one of his abilities. It takes fifteen minutes according to the digital clock on the desk, much longer than I've endured thus far. But those fifteen minutes feel like an eternity. Black spots flood my vision.

Until the pain fades away, I try concentrating on the words of my freedom song to distract me. When I'm ready, I rely on Sawyer's telekinetic power. I haven't yet practiced it fully, but I think I can manage it just enough to release my bonds. I've only used small instances of speed and bulk power, so I should have just enough energy left to get me out of this situation.

Tensing every muscle in my body, I search for the telekinesis ability inside. A pinprick of a sensation forms right in the center of my forehead. I picture my hands tied behind my back, the webbing releasing. Moments later, the venomous white falls to the floor and I leap to my feet.

I dash to Kyle's side. He's still breathing, but how can I move him with a broken arm and a sprained ankle? He'll never be able to run. I can carry him as a bulk, but I won't be able to defend us.

The helicopter blades continue to thud overhead. I

glance out the window and see Matt disappearing into the woods with Lyla. Unadjusteds run in all directions, most of them heading for the forest, but a few, separated by the firing trolls, dash to the ocean instead.

"Silver," Kyle calls.

I crouch by him again.

He props himself up on his good arm. "Go. You need to go."

"I'm not leaving you here." I place a hand on his flushed cheek.

Kyle shakes his head, then grimaces. "It's OK. You don't need me."

"That's not true." Then I remember the regeneration pill in my pocket. I fish it out and shove it between his lips.

The pill works quickly, but I'm not sure it will be quick enough. When color floods his cheeks, Kyle pushes himself to his feet and sags against me, able to put only the slightest weight on his bad ankle. Regeneration pills can't reduce swelling.

"How do we get out of here?" He scans the room. "You can just break the door down, right?"

I eye the solid, wooden door. "That leads to a maze of endless hallways." I point to the window. "The forest is right there."

Transforming into a bulk, I smash the glass out of the window. With my armored skin, I clear the frame of the remaining fragments.

"Get them! Don't let them get away!" President Bear's grizzly roar rushes through the window.

"Now what?" Kyle asks.

I consider using the flea ability to jump down from the window, but we'd still have to run. I'm not sure if Kyle is up to that, plus his speed and the jump's impact might damage his still-repairing bones. Instead, I push part of the bulk ability away and summon my blue wings. I've practiced them for hours. Half bulk, half bird. Using two abilities at once drains my energy much faster, but we only need to reach the cover of the forest.

I help him stagger to the window and balance on the empty frame.

"Please don't drop me."

"I'll do my best." I tuck my wings in close and curl my arms around Kyle, then push him out the window. For a moment, we plummet toward the ground, then my wings unfurl, catch an upward thermal, and slow our descent.

Holding him with bulk arms, I beat my wings until my throat and shoulders strain with the effort. We rise into the air but keep under the blades of the thudding helicopter. President Bear stands atop the building, shooting webbing at the forest and unadjusteds below.

We lock eyes. His jaw drops as he takes in my wings. Raising a hand toward me, a white froth forms on his palm. I fly backwards, a tricky task that's much slower than going forwards, and transfer Kyle to one bulk arm. Raising the other, I sift through all the new abilities, trying to find the one.

As President Bear's webbing shoots toward me, I turn my palm and attack him with his own power. Silky, white thread spins out of my hand to meet the onslaught. But my energy is draining. My altitude dips and Kyle cries out a warning as a bullet whizzes toward us.

The pressure of President Bear's continual stream of webbing pushes me to the ground. A foot from the sand, I drop Kyle, who scrambles to his knees. Hal, armed with a gun and firing at the enemy, dashes by and grabs him. Now able to use both palms, I direct two streams of lacy white skyward. A mass of webbing forms in the sky where our two streams meet. I push the webbing with bulk strength, but my muscles shake with fatigue.

Soon, I'll be out of power.

CHAPTER TWENTY-TWO

"Silver!"

I risk a glance over my shoulder. Matt runs out of the tree line onto the sand, spraying bullets from an assault rifle toward President Bear. Not that they can hurt him. He has the armored skin of a bulk. I felt it when I took his abilities.

From his position on the roof, President Bear skirts a look to the trees. The unadjusteds have fled, some of the remaining trolls on their heels. Joe emerges from the forest and joins Matt in a volley of bullets. President Bear ducks. My knees give way and I sink to the sand, but I push the webbing out of my palms with every ounce of strength I have left. It's all that stands between me and being captured.

The president takes a step back. With one final push, a mass of his webbing tumbles all around me. He steps into the waiting helicopter, which quickly lifts into the sky. I try to follow it with my own webbing, but only little puffs of lace escape my palms. Joe fires his gun and manages to dink the side of the vehicle, but then it's up and away. Gone.

My body shudders. Blackness ebbs at the corners of my eyes. As the ground teeters, I slump onto Matt and pass out.

———

When I wake, the smell of damp clay winds around me. I shiver and roll over. Soft fur surrounds my hand. Einstein. He chuffs and licks my neck, and I push the dog away. Fairy lights twinkle above my head, and I see Matt sitting on a sleeping bag. We're in his hollow.

"Hey," he says, scooching closer. "You're awake."

A severe headache battles inside my skull. "What happened?" I push the words past my dry throat.

Matt hands me a water bottle. "You had an up and personal with President Bear. That's what happened."

"Oh, yeah." Careful not to rock the pain in my head, I push myself up onto an elbow. "How long have I been out?"

"A couple of days. Taking on all those abilities took it out of you." Matt catches the dribble of water running down my chin.

"I don't even know what they all are." Just the memory of the abilities swimming inside my veins exhausts me.

Matt squeezes my hand. "We'll figure it out."

I reach for him. "Lyla? Did we get Lyla?"

"She's safe." Matt's eyes narrow. "And spending far too much time with Sawyer for my liking."

I laugh, but it hurts my head. "What about the others in the compound?"

Matt makes a triumphant fist. "We managed to get most of the unadjusteds out."

"Most?"

Matt's gaze shifts down and he runs his fingers along Einstein's ears. "There were a few casualties."

"My parents?" I ask, even though I know the answer.

Matt looks at me, but I can't read his expression in the dim lighting. "Not there, but I'm working on it."

My eyes prick with gathering tears that immediately add a squeezing pressure to the throbbing in my skull.

"So Addison was wrong." I massage my temples. "How did she get it so wrong?"

"She feels awful about that," Matt says. He rests his hands on my knees. "She was beaten up and probably misheard, or the soldiers lied to her. Maybe they recognized you from the warehouse. Maybe it was all a trap."

My hands drop from my head. "People died in the compound because of me."

"You can't think like that." Matt raises my chin with his finger. "You helped all those people escape. You saved Kyle."

"Who wouldn't have been hurt in the first place if I hadn't dragged everyone there," I mumble, shifting out of his hold.

"Everyone wanted to go."

I stare at his laceless sneakers. I don't have the words to express the depth of my guilt. It's something I'll have to learn to live with. If I survive.

After a pause, he asks, "You hungry?"

I sigh. "Starving."

He gets to his feet. "Wait here."

Matt returns a few minutes later with a bowl of warm stew and a chunk of bread, but he isn't alone. A woman with elfin slenderness stands beside him. Her face is as soft as a ripe peach, and the warmth in her eyes makes up for her angular points. A long, graying braid trails the length of her spine. She smiles maternally.

"This is Joan," Matt says, gesturing the woman into the room. "She's a healer."

"A what?" I ask, risking the headache to sit a little straighter. I rotatecircle my shoulders, rolling out the aches.

"A healer," she says and crouches next to me.

I look between the two of them. Their hesitant smiles make me hopeful. "I don't know what that means."

"It means she's here to make you feel better," Matt says.

Joan touches my arm through my shirt. Within

seconds, a warm, pulsing light surrounds her fingertips. Slowly, it ebbs its way over the rest of my body, bathing me in an invisible blanket of the most peaceful sensation I've experienced in months. The headache lifts. My muscles vibrate with a new energy.

"Woah." I press my fingers to my temples and pat around for the previous bruises, but nothing hurts. "I feel so much better."

Joan smiles and pats my arm. "You're welcome."

Matt sits again and crosses his arms over his knees. "Joan has been helping with the injuries from the compound escape. We have fifty new members here now. All healthy."

"Not quite healthy. There are a few bumps and bruises around," Joan says, fiddling with her braid. "My power only goes so far. The worse the injury, the harder it is, and some are too severe to alleviate."

Matt looks at her. "There are a lot of people in the cave who wouldn't be alive without you."

"Did you come from the compound?" I ask.

Joan nods and sits beside me.

I dig into the plate of food Matt brought. "I've never heard of a healer before."

"Only a few of us were created. It was a secret project and only five or six I know of along the eastern seaboard were given one. I took the pill altruistically, wanting to help the desperate, the poor who couldn't afford medical treatment, but that's not what President Bear had in mind." She cradles her braid and smooths out the rough ends. "Once Bear and the National Medical Board realized we could take money from them, that we could bankrupt the country with our powers and put insurance companies out of business, he ended the program." A glowing aura surrounds Joan as she speaks. Delicate freckles dance on her nose.

"They couldn't allow that. The healer pills had only been available for six months when they realized this. They quickly discontinued them, and anyone found making or buying one afterward was sentenced to death. I know a few who tried; they were all executed. So there are not many of us in the world. If you're willing, I could up our number so it's one bigger." Joan smiles at me.

"One bigger?" I scoop out more stew with a hunk of bread.

Matt taps my newly healed forehead as if there's nothing inside. "You need to take on her ability."

The ability to heal. I'd no longer need to rely on the two remaining regeneration pills. If I'd had this ability when Kyle was hurt, I would have been able to heal him. Maybe. Joan said there are limitations, and no doubt I'll be limited more, but whatever it can do, I'll take it.

This is the first ability I feel excited about taking on.

Without warning, Joan clasps one of my hands in hers. The tingling starts immediately, but the pain doesn't come. A soft light radiates from where Joan touches my hand. A warmth seeps into my skin, then deeper, into my muscles, then bones.

My mind empties of emotional clutter and focuses on the growing light and warmth. It's as though my soul has risen to the surface to make itself known. All that is pure within me connects with Joan, takes her offering and carries it back down into the depths of me.

The glow and warmth vanish from my skin, and we sit in the light of the fairy lights and lanterns. Sadness swells in my chest with the disappearance of the glow and a few unexpected tears roll down my cheeks. Am I even worthy of such a powerful tool? I sense a darkness in me, an immaturity of heart.

Claus' words echo in my mind. *With great power comes great responsibility.*

"We'll need to test it to see if it worked." Joan pats my knee.

Matt plucks my knife from my belt and suddenly and decisively slices a gash across his palm. I gasp at the suddenness of the blood.

"If you can't do it, Joan's still here." Matt waits.

Joan gestures for me to touch Matt. "You don't need to actually touch the wound itself; you can touch any part of his body, but you must concentrate on the body healing itself. You are merely an instrument that can speed up the body's own processes. If it helps, I think about tiny white soldiers marching to repair the wound or disease."

I turn to Matt. The blood flow slows. I hesitate, unsure where the core of this new ability sits within my body. With Paige's wings I felt the pain along my shoulder blades, with Kyle's speed my calves and thighs rippled briefly in pain, with Sawyer's telekinesis it was in the center of my forehead. But with healing I'm at a loss.

I hold Matt's palm in my hand. His hand twitches as he cups the spilt blood in his palm. Matt. *My* Matt. He was my one hesitation during all those hours I planned to escape, pulling me back, making me endure the commands of the president. I didn't want to leave him. But with his hand sliced open before me, hardened and callused from setting up the surveillance equipment and building his grenades, he becomes mortal. To be protected. Love for my best friend swells in my chest, and the fear of ever losing him lashes holes in my core. It takes my breath away.

I look from his face to our joined hands. My palm glows, and I know the key to accessing it is love: love of life, love of people. Pure, unselfish love. Matt's palm knits together and the flesh becomes smooth as the thin ridge of the wound disappears. All that remains is the blood that escaped.

"Well done," Matt says, giving my arm a squeeze.

I look at Joan. "You didn't tell me the key is love."

297

Joan smiles like a proud parent. "You needed to discover that for yourself. I can't feel the emotions for you; you had to find it, Silver, and you did."

"Can you heal yourself?"

"I don't know. I've never needed to."

We repeat the experiment with my palm. I wince as the blade slices across my hand. Holding my injured hand in the other palm, I focus on the wound. After a few minutes, I begin to worry I'll be left with a scar, but then the wound reduces into a thin line before disappearing. It's much harder to perform on myself and I don't fancy trying it on a more serious injury.

"Thank you, Joan," I whisper. I feel drained from the new ability, but it's worth it and it pushes me to make a decision. When I find my parents, I won't ask them to make me unadjusted again. For this ability I will remain an adjusted.

"You're welcome." Joan pulls me into her arms and gives me a hearty hug.

CHAPTER TWENTY-THREE

After Joan leaves, Matt shuffles close and inspects my face. "You can stay here if you want tonight."

I turn back into the room. The fairy lights add a comforting glow.

"If you don't mind." The thought of returning to my empty hollow alone, with just the picture of my parents as company, fills me with loneliness. And Joe next door. Joe, about whom I still haven't figured out how I feel. But I can't deny the flush that blooms on my cheeks when I think about him.

Matt settles down beside me and closes his eyes. He holds my hand. I sit for a while, staring at the twinkling fairy lights. Despite Joan's healing earlier, tension settles at the back of my neck. It seems a permanent fixture now that comes twined with the worry—always wondering where my parents are, how they are, whether I'll be able to save them. Watching Matt sleep peacefully, I feel a stab of envy. He has a family. A complete family. It isn't fair.

A couple of hours later I leave Matt's hollow and wander the passageways, trailing my hand over the cool limestone walls. After sniffing out a granola bar from the kitchen, I wind my way to the main door. I have the sudden, inescapable urge to be outside in the open, away from the enclosing walls.

Pushing open the main door, I emerge into a thicket of bushes. I fight my way through them and step into the valley. Moonlight spills puddles over the valley floor. The snap of cool air snakes around my shoulders and caresses my cheeks. My wings unfold and I step into the open. Owls hoot from the forest. The occasional bat flies overhead. I search for fireflies but can't spot any. Maybe they're all in the meadow where Joe kissed me.

My toes lift until I'm standing on the very tips, like Lyla in her pointe shoes. I flap my wings and rise into the sky, higher and higher until my teeth chatter with the cold. The coldness centers me. I can think clearly up here, away from everyone else.

My parents are in the city somewhere. Maybe not even in a real facility, but locked in an unknown location. I wish one of my abilities was X-ray vision or the ability to sense where my family is. Like that cell phone app my parents installed when I first started walking to school that fed them my location whenever they chose to check in. I thought it was a bit stalker-y at the time. But now, I'd give anything to find them so easily.

I hover, looking at the magical land below. With the trees and valley and nature in its purest form all around me, it looks so untouched, uncorrupted.

When my shoulder blades tremble, I recognize the signs of fatigue; my ability will soon wear itself out. I glide down to the valley floor and land in the largest pool of moonlight I can find. Bathed in the unearthly light, it feels like anything is possible. That whatever world I imagine inside my head, however I want it to be, can be, if I wish it hard enough.

It's after midnight when I shut the cave door behind me, but I'm still not ready to sleep. The cold air has woken me up and instilled in me a more intense longing for my parents. To find President Bear. I want to kill him with my own hands.

With the scent of clay filling my nostrils once more, I wander past the chimneys, where the leftover aroma of bread mutes the cloying limestone, and back to my hollow to grab my guitar.

I follow the trail of lanterns to a more secluded part of the cave system, where a regular drip echoes at my back. I play my song for hours, rolling the words over my tongue until the anger grows and threads through every thought.

Bind me, blind me—beat me black and blue.
In all your power try me,

Let my light shine through.
And when your lies run empty,
When our rights become your wrongs,
You'll see our banner rising,
And you will hear our song.

Claus limps into my small niche, one hand on his cane, the other on his mustache. "That's a beautiful song."

"Thank you." I put the guitar down and rise to meet him. "I have a gift for you."

Claus bows.

"You've done so much for me."

"You've done more for me than you'll ever realize." Claus' eyes glisten as another man appears at his side. "This is Evan."

My mouth falls open. "Evan, Evan? I thought he was dead?"

Claus turns to the man and squeezes his shoulders. "So did I."

"I didn't die at the march. I was arrested and thrown in prison," Evan says, leaning in to Claus. "But they put out a false list of the fallen."

"Took as many protesters as they could to use in their nanite experiments," Claus says.

The two men smile at each other and it's clear they no longer care; they're together again, even if Evan is missing a couple of fingers and an angry burn mark takes up most of his right cheek. I unsheathe the knife from my belt and hold it up to Evan. "I believe this is yours."

Evan's eyes widen and he runs a finger along the blade. "Never thought I'd see that again." He picks it up and tests its weight, then hands it back to me. "I have no use for it anymore. Keep it."

"Thank you." I turn to Claus. "And I have another gift for you."

"I'm intrigued." Claus rests both hands on his cane.

"I'd like to heal your leg." I hold out my hand and the glowing warmth plays over my fingertips.

Claus holds my gaze, smiling proudly, then raises his cane between us. "I've grown rather fond of this."

Together, the three of us watch the golden glow pulse over my palm.

"You don't want to be healed?"

"No." Claus puts his cane down and rests both hands on top. "It's part of who I am, and it reminds me what I've gone through to be who I want to be."

I bow. "You're a better person than me."

"That's not true." Claus lays a hand over my chest. "And besides, Evan was always better at karate than I am. You can spar with him."

Evan winks. "I don't want to hurt you."

His look turns challenging and before he can sweep my legs, I jump kick his shoulder. Evan laughs and Claus praises my focus.

"No abilities now." Evan wags a finger at me. "That wouldn't be fair on an old man."

A smile twitches on my lips. "It's a good thing you're not old."

For the next half hour or so, we spar in the dim lighting. When we're both exhausted and agree to tie, we bow and head our separate ways.

With sweat cooling on my back, I weave a path back to Matt's hollow. There's still a space where I lay earlier in the night, so I tuck my body around his and plummet into sleep.

——

When Matt wakes me the next morning, I can tell by the force of his hand that something's wrong.

"What is it?" I ask before I even open my eyes.

"Can you get up? I need to show you something." His mouth is twisted and he clicks his fingers rapidly.

I pull on my boots and follow him out of the hollow. Einstein trails us, pressing his snout into my side for a pat as we leave the cave. I slit my eyes against the rising sun until they adjust. Matt leads me up the other side of the valley, onto the ridge, and under the legs of a massive electricity pylon. We sit on the grass in the stretching shadow of a mountain ash tree, its limbs dusted with white flowers, and pass a bottle of water between us.

Matt removes a tablet from his backpack. "I come here to access the internet. I have it disabled when I'm inside, but here I'm far enough away to risk using it for a few minutes."

"OK…" I gesture for him to continue.

Matt places the tablet in my lap and leans close so we can share the small screen. He taps in his security code, dissolving the picture of us from his fourteenth birthday. It was a bowling party. We are smiling, both wearing baseball caps backward, and Matt's arm is slung casually around my shoulder. I smile at the memory. It was from a time when life was less complicated, when I was still free to come and go from my penthouse apartment, before I came to think of it as a prison.

Matt pushes his hair on top of his head, smoothing it down with unnecessary force. "From the intel we've gathered, it seems they've halted the enforced nanite program until they can figure out how to stop themselves all going insane without our presence. But they're still doing terrible things…" Matt rises to his feet, hands fisted. "Lyla told me what they did to some of the people in that compound." He paces back and forth, then takes a deep breath. "But that's not why I brought you up here. Silver, there's something else you need to see."

"What is it?"

Matt re-joins me on the grass and pulls up a video. "It's about your parents."

I brace myself. The screen loads with an image of President Bear. If anything, he looks more terrifying, more arachnid, and his eyes are now completely red, even the whites. I pray that doesn't happen to mine. The scar under his eye pulses.

"Silver Melody is wanted for treason. If she is not found by the 15th of June or has not turned herself in, Dr. Margaret Melody and Dr. Rufus Melody will be executed." President Bear's mouth sets into a thin line, lips barely visible. "The reward has risen to three million dollars. Dead or alive."

"It was broadcast two days ago," Matt says. "Right after we got back."

In the top left corner is a smaller clip. I double tap the screen, and an image of my parents fill the tablet. My mother is dressed in a white shapeless dress now gray with age and grime. No more than a bag of bones, skin hangs off her gaunt frame. Her once lustrous, wavy hair is now a muted gray, and her cheeks are bleached of color.

Each arm is held by an eight-foot troll. She stares resolutely at the camera. Pain radiates in her eyes, but so does her resolve to stand strong. My father is less gaunt, but bruises and blood garnish his face. His hair has been shaved.

Shame and anger burn in my chest and I cry, unsure which emotion is most dominant. Matt cradles me, strokes my back, and pulls my tear-soaked hair out of my face.

"I'm so sorry, Silver."

"What's the plan?" I push the words through my clenched teeth. Surely Matt will have a plan. He'll know where they were.

"I'm working on it." He thumbs a corner of the screen to magnify a section of the image. "I need to compare these images with ones of the other prisons in Central City. Give me an hour. Then we'll know where they are."

I twist the hem of my T-shirt into my tight fist. "And we can go get them."

He nods. "But I don't know who will want to come. It'll be a maximum-security facility. Much more protected than the compound we attacked. There will be casualties. People who come need to know what's at risk."

I blot my eyes. Tension races along my jaw. "What if I turn myself in?"

Matt does a double take. "You can't do that."

I kick at the ground. "Matt…"

"Silver, they'll just kill all three of you. You know that, and we could really use your parents' help figuring out what to do next."

I push my hunched shoulders down and lock a determined stare on him. "So what then?"

He holds up a hand. "Give me an hour to figure out their location. Then we'll talk to Francesca and Claus."

I don't know whether to slap his hand away or lace my fingers through his. "It's only three days till the 15th, Matt."

"I know." The haunted look in his blue eyes chills me.

We have to find my parents. And soon.

CHAPTER TWENTY-FOUR

When we get back to the cave, I seek out Francesca, but words fail me. Matt fills her in on my parents' situation while my friends gather around.

I rock on my feet, eyeballing my friends. Paige, Sawyer, Addison, Erica, Joe, Hal, Kyle and Jacob stand in a loose circle in the weapons chamber with Francesca and Claus. Matt's still trying to identify the correct prison.

"I don't know if I like this," Francesca says. "I think it's worth a day's training at the assault course before you leave."

"Did you not hear what I said? They're going to execute them in *three days*." I slam a fist into the other palm.

Francesca's cool gaze doesn't waver. "You're asking a lot from your friends, and I won't stop you, but some of you are still recovering from the attack at the compound. You haven't learned to work as a team yet.

You and Kyle were isolated. You can't go off half-cocked without backup."

I pace before her. "It will take us two days to get there, at the very least. We need to leave *now.*"

Francesca looks at the other eager faces. "You all want to go?"

Kyle's eyebrows turn into a thundery mess. "I want payback for that dick breaking my arm."

"I'm still looking for my family," Addison says. "Maybe they're in the same place."

"Yes. We're all up for it," Joe says. "There's a wider purpose at play here. People have been whispering about some kind of cure. We need Silver's parents to understand if it's even possible. Without them—"

I snap my heels together. "We'll be stuck in this cave forever."

"Not true," Francesca says. "We can take down President Bear, start a coup and elect a new government."

I laugh. "That will take years. Eighty percent of the population has abilities! They won't want sanctions on how many nanites they can take." My finger stabs at empty air. "It's addictive. They want more and more." Hell, even I'm getting to like my abilities. "It needs to be bigger than taking down President Bear. It needs to involve the whole world."

Francesca looks at Joe. "You still have the jeep in the woods?"

Joe nods.

"Can you just do one day at the training ground with Claus and Evan training you as a team?" She looks at all the faces in the room. "Then take the jeep and you can drive all the way there. That will cut down your time. We've got one shot at this; let's make it the best one."

I wring my hands in frustration.

"Silver," Claus cautions, wearing a fiery look. Evan stands next to him, a softer light in his eyes.

I hang my head. He is the one person who can ignite shame in me. "I'm sorry. It's just… I want them back so bad."

Francesca places a hand on my shoulder. "I understand, but we don't even know where they are yet. While Matt is figuring it out, you might as well take that frustration and use it in the meadow."

"Fine."

"Francesca's right," Joe says, lowering his mouth to my ear. His breath does weird things to my skin, but I'm too fed up to think about that right now. "Let's do this right."

I shake off all the pitying glances and charge down the passageway. Only Kyle keeps up with me. We speed to the meadow together, and by the time I get there, some of the anger has leached away.

While I wait for the others, I take out my knife and aim it at the hay bales nearby. There are five of them with bull's-eye targets attached. I try to remember all the advice Dad gave me in the woods and alter my stance. Distracted, I throw too early. The blade misses the target completely.

I stomp past the target and retrieve my knife. This time, I take a moment to regulate my breathing, and when I exhale, I throw again. With a satisfying crunch, the blade connects with the target, dead center.

"That's more like it," I say.

"Awesome," Kyle says, startling me. I didn't realize anyone was watching.

After a few more perfect throws, the rest of the group catches up with us. Claus beckons me over to the start of the assault course, where the others are congregating.

"Silver," Claus says, his mustache twitching. "I'd like you to run this without any abilities. If you get maxed out, you'll have to rely on your normal human skills."

I groan. Paige laughs and tickles me with one of her feathers.

Claus waits with a stopwatch. He presses the start button and Joe takes the lead, closely followed by a flying Erica. Then Addison. Hal is fourth, Jacob fifth, followed by Kyle and Sawyer, then it's me and Paige taking up the last spots.

We start with the tire run—left, right, left, right; I almost stumble at the last one. Then up the ten-foot rope tied to a branch, over the tree limb, and down the

312

other side. Joe and Hal don't struggle much with that one, considering their height. Next is the mobile wall built from hay bales. Paige flaps her wings and flies over it. She disappears over the top of the wall while I just run into it and fall backward. Erica's wings turn a smug shade of scarlet. Paige's head reappears over the top of the wall, and she holds out a hand. I grit my teeth and accept it.

After that, we run through a tunnel of trees. Straw dummies hanging from branches fly at us, some painted with happy faces, some angry, to depict goodies and baddies. I manage to knife a couple in the face before one clunks me on the head and sends me sprawling into a tree on my right.

Paige and I finish the circuit last, only because I held her back. The rest are standing by Claus as he presses the stop button. "Needs some work, Silver."

Really? You think? With my shirt, I wipe the sweat pouring down my face and neck.

Erica hovers by Joe's side with a worried frown, red wings beating a refreshing wind. I storm off to the shade stocked with canteens and pour water over my heated face and damp hair.

"Don't worry about it," Paige says as she bends to pick up her own canteen. "On a real mission, you'll be using your abilities."

"Some people seem to be good at everything."

One wing rises and shields us from the others. "Some people have had a lot more experience. Some people have abilities that don't come with limitations."

"Maybe if I'd had breakfast," I mumble.

Claus approaches, Evan on his heels. "Again."

Evan looks at me. "You can do this, Silver."

I groan. But it goes better this time. Joe and Hal lead the team. The tallest and strongest, they can get around the course fastest. Erica follows behind them. Sawyer struggles a little ahead of me, but Paige stays with us, helping us clamber over the hardest parts, urging us on. Kyle blurs over everything, using his speed as propulsion, and Addison, nearly as tall as bulks, doesn't struggle.

At least the view is good. I get to watch Joe the entire way around. I try to keep my impure thoughts to myself, but Paige winks at me and I know she's caught me staring.

"Better," Claus shoots in my direction. "The important thing is how well you work as a team. Paige, Sawyer, and Silver showed a fantastic sense of teamwork, helping each other. Joe, Hal, and Erica, it would be better if you could concentrate less on speed and more on the whole team getting through the course together."

We take our places again. Kyle blitzes through the tire tracks, up the rope and over the wall. Clearly he needs no help. This time Joe picks me up and throws me to Hal.

314

"Hey, what are you—?" I protest, but then I'm in Joe's arms again as he hurls me over an obstacle, and I clamp down on the complaints.

We dodge the swinging effigies through the tree tunnel. Joe hoists me in the air again and throws me at Hal over a new obstacle—hay bales covered in barbed wire—then picks up Sawyer and does the same with him. When we're finished, we collapse in the grass and drink greedily from water bottles.

"Good," Claus says.

Matt appears from the shade of a tree on the ridge line with Einstein in tow. My stomach lurches as his eyes find mine.

"Have you found them?" The words rush out of me, and my stomach rolls.

He nods. "Francesca's making preparations. We need to get back to the cave."

"Let's go!" Matt calls to everyone else, then turns to me. "I can't believe you let him throw you around like that."

"Huh?" I ask, getting to my feet.

"Joe." His eyes narrow. "He had his hands…" He looks as his feet.

"It was easier than falling off that stupid wall a hundred times," I say, slapping his stomach with the back of my hand. "More importantly, let's go get my parents."

I hear the fluttering before I feel the shove on my

315

right shoulder. I stumble to the ground, then peer into the sun to see what happened. I'm really tired of landing on my butt today.

Erica flutters into view, her wings an acid green. "Oh, Silver. I'm so sorry. I just didn't see you there. The hazards of flying, you know, not looking down too much." Her voice drips with sarcastic cordiality.

"Seriously, Erica?" I explode.

Paige puts a restraining hand on my arm, but I shrug her off. Sawyer stops, hands on hips, looking between the two of us.

"I thought we were over all this? What's your problem?" I shout at her, back on my feet. "And get your goddamn feet on the ground so I don't have to keep looking up at you!"

Joe and Hal stop and turn to watch the altercation.

"Silver, seriously... I didn't mean—" Erica hastily tries to backtrack, hands held helplessly before her. Her wings cycle through all the colors of the rainbow. She plants her feet on the ground and folds her wings into her back. That's better. Her violet eyes settle on mine.

Joe jogs back to us. "Erica, Silver, what's going on?" He frowns at Erica. Her face crumples, a tear wells and she wipes it away.

"I'm sorry, Joe. It was an accident. Really. Silver, I'm sorry..." she stammers, voice devoid of the familiar sarcasm, actually sounding genuine for once.

"If you two are going to go on a mission together, you need to sort out your differences." Claus points at us with his cane. "Do it right now, and don't come back inside until you have."

I stand on the spot, watching everyone file toward the cave to learn the whereabouts of my parents. And I have to stay here. Evan gives me a sympathetic look before he follows Claus. Erica stands next to me. Tension vibrates in the air between us.

"What's your problem, Erica?" I push the question through gritted teeth. Einstein chuffs and settles at my feet.

She bristles. "I thought you were the one with the problem."

Matt's head disappears into a clump of bushes near the cave entrance. I long to be with him.

"My experience with people with butterfly wings has never been good," I say.

She swivels toward me. "That's not my fault."

"I know." I cross my arms. "But my low expectations have always been met in the past. I bet you were a cheerleader, right? Dated the quarterback?"

Twin spots of red heat her cheekbones. "Being a cheerleader and dating the quarterback aren't bad things."

I can't help the snort that comes out. "Wasn't Joe the quarterback at your school?"

The blush on Erica's cheek reaches a new level of red. She shakes her head. "Joe was the quarterback. I dated the linebacker. But Joe…"

The fight leaves me. "I didn't know you liked him—"

Erica holds up a hand. Her wings flutter again, a pale orange. "I don't. He likes you, and there's nothing I can do about that."

My heart quickens. "Has he said something to you?"

Erica rolls her violet eyes. "He doesn't shut up about you."

I sigh, but my heart skips a beat. "So that's what this is about?"

Along the ridge on the other side of the valley, the sun melts into the trees, shafts of orange light blending into the valley floor, making the grass look golden. Like a promised land. Crickets chirp in the bushes around us and a breath of air breezes through the trees.

"Not entirely," Erica says, fiddling with the sting of her bow. "I mean, yes, I got the wings to be in the varsity cheerleading team and to attract a boy. Foolish, but I'm so much more than that now."

I nod and point to the bow. "That's for sure. Not many cheerleaders go around with a bow and arrow."

Her arms circle around her waist and she drops her head. Her voice is barely a whisper. "It's to remember my friend. Because I killed her."

CHAPTER TWENTY-FIVE

The world pauses, holding its breath. As desperate as I am to learn my parent's location, Erica's statement freezes me.

I goggle at her. "You killed your friend?"

She pulls at her lavender hair, then wraps an arm around her waist. Keeping her eyes on the ridge line, she won't look at me. When she speaks, her voice trembles. "It's my penance, being alone without friends, without love. Every time it looks as though I might find happiness, it's taken away. I don't deserve a relationship. I don't deserve friends."

"What about Addison…?"

"She's the only one left." Erica's voice breaks.

"Nobody deserves to be alone." I take a step toward her. "You've done so much for everyone here, and you're even willing to rescue my parents when you hate me."

"I don't hate you." Her smile is unconvincing.

"I don't hate you either." She's different from the other fairies I've known.

Erica laughs, but then her smile drops. "I can never do enough. Silver, I killed my best friend, and my girlfriend left me for it." She chokes out a sob. Reaching for the tree at her back, she leans against it.

"I didn't realize—"

Erica nods her head rapidly. "I'm bisexual. With the current climate, it's not something I advertise."

I'm tempted to touch Erica's shoulder, but we don't have that kind of friendship and she's hunched up so high I don't think I'll be able to comfort her. "What happened?"

"When I was fourteen my parents gave me the nanite pill for my butterfly wings. It was all I ever wanted. You were right about me, Silver. I was an airhead, a cheerleader, and just wanted to date the quarterback of the football team. *Joe*." She lets his name dangle between us for a few seconds. "But Joe came later. After Sarah… after she died and Jess left me." She hangs her head and her wings turn a brilliant white. "I didn't *care* about anything except being popular and adored. Sarah was my best friend for as long as I can remember and was great with Jess when we got together. When she turned fourteen a few months later, I encouraged her to take a nanite pill too. Another one." Pink blotches creep up Erica's neck.

I think of Diana and how angry I was that nanites were forced on her. How angry I still am.

"She'd taken several already for her archery. Speed, reflexes, strength, augmented hearing. Tons of them, but they were all invisible. Nothing *cool*." Erica's shoulders sag.

"I convinced her that taking something physical would only enhance her already near-perfect aim. Really, I wanted us to rule the school together. She refused. She didn't want any part of that. She didn't want to be an adjusted. I refused to listen to her. I bought a nanite pill on the streets, I didn't even know what ability it was. I forced her to take it. I told her we could never be together unless she had an ability like me.

"Jess yelled at me and told Sarah not to, but she did. She took it. Her body didn't take to the change and she died. The last look on her face was one of fear and betrayal. And Jess never spoke to me again. I lost them both. I'll never ever forgive myself, Silver. Never. She died because of me." Erica chokes and takes a moment to calm herself. "That's why I'm here. I need to atone for that. I need to rid the world of that terrible mentality." Tears stream down her face as she hangs her head. Her voice drops an octave. "I fight against people like *me*."

I stare at her. I can't begin to imagine the guilt she lives with every day. Diana died the same way, by nanite pills forced on her by her parents. Erica might have had one of the worst altered mentalities back in the day, but she's come full circle; she's saved countless lives, she's more than made up for it.

"The bow and arrow?" I nod at the weapon she holds by her side.

She raises it a couple inches. "The only way I could think to remember her and to keep her spirit alive. I took up her sport so that she stays with me every day."

"If there's anything I've learned during my time in the cave, it's that the world isn't black and white. It's very, very gray. Charcoal, even." My dad said that to me so many times while we ran through the woods. Now, I understand the shades of gray. The reality. "There is a silver lining here, Erica. Here's *your* gray: the cave needs you. My parents need you." I touch her shoulder. "You can forgive yourself now. You've done enough. You deserve a better life, Erica. You deserve to find love again."

"But not with Joe." Her wings turn a deep scarlet. "Do you even like him?"

"He kissed me…"

"I know."

"Truthfully, I don't know how I feel." Talking about him still makes my pulse quicken. "I never thought I'd be with a bulk." But that's not it either.

"Are we good now?"

I nod. "I'm sorry, Erica."

"Me too."

This time her smile holds a flicker of warmth. We don't hug or join arms or anything, that would be pushing our luck, but we make our way back to the cave together. We find the others assembled in the weapons chamber with Claus and Francesca. Paige shoots me a sympathetic look.

"Everything OK?" Joe whispers in my ear.

I don't look him in the eye. I can't. "Yeah, fine. It was just a misunderstanding."

"Glad to hear it." Joe sits on a rocky ledge and crosses his arms. Francesca and Claus stand at the front, Matt's tablet between them. We all crowd around the small screen showing a prison on the edge of Central City.

"So where are they?" I ask.

"On the edge of the city," Francesca replies.

My knee jigs up and down. "Can we go now?"

"Soon," she replies. "First we need to tell you what you'll be facing."

Claus runs a thumb over the screen. "The approach to the prison should take twenty-four hours. The woods won't cover you all the way there. You'll have three miles of grassland between the trees and the prison to get through."

My stomach quivers at Claus' words. Fear builds in the pit of my stomach. The panic attacks have left me alone for the most part, but I sense the anxiety tingling at my fingertips and lips. I bite the inside of my cheek. I can't afford to lose it now.

"The first obstacle is a ten-foot brick wall covered in barbed wire. We've all trained for this at the obstacle course; some of you found it a little harder than others." Claus directs his gaze at me.

"Ha, ha," I remark. A few seats down, Joe chuckles.

"This one is a little higher, but I think you can all handle it." Claus points to the wall on the screen. Gray and twisted and ugly. "The next obstacle is an electric fence. I don't recommend trying to climb this one."

A few members of the team chuckle. I grimace, remembering the government-issued commercial about the dangers of electricity; some young boy lost his Frisbee in an electricity station, climbed up the massive pylon, almost made it to the Frisbee when he touched a wire. His body spasmed ungracefully in a ballet of death before he fell forty feet to the ground.

"I'm thinking Sawyer or Silver with their telekinetic power can disable the current long enough for everyone to climb over," Claus says.

Sawyer and I exchange a look.

Sawyer gulps. "Um, I've never tried to control electricity before."

"Electricity is still matter," Claus says. "You can focus on it just like a regular object and harness its power. I suggest you practice on the electricity in the cave."

"OK then," Sawyer says to his shoes.

"Next, you'll reach the outer wall of the prison itself.

The structure is a square with one main door and one back entrance. Both heavily guarded and armed. There are laser beams sweeping the space between the fence and the building, so watch out for those." Claus pauses to tap on a faint red beam on the tablet screen.

"Each door is guarded by one bulk and one ogre at all times. President Bear's special guards. Joe and Hal may need to take them out, quietly. All the guards are armed, so speed and stealth are important here. Paige and Silver, you may wish to have a look from the air to get a bigger picture view. But watch those shifting laser beams; they'll zap you to ash if you get too close," Claus warns.

The list of tasks is growing.

Claus continues. "We know there are another four guards who walk the perimeter around the top of the building and another four outside the most external wall. How many are inside we don't know. You'll have to think on your feet, but I suspect once you're through that wall, you'll have more obstacles to face. Prepare yourselves for any eventuality."

I glance at Matt, whose brow is wrinkled in thought. Paige jiggles her leg up and down beside me and I push my heel into the ground to keep mine still. Sawyer kicks at the floor. Kyle paces at the back of the room, his feet blurring. I wish we could go now, before the building anxiety quashes my resolve.

"Remember," Francesca says, smiling at each of us, "each and every one of you has a valuable ability. If you work together, I believe you can do this. Are there any questions?"

"Can we go tonight?" Addison asks.

"Tomorrow is best. It'll be dark soon," Francesca replies. "The army often patrols the woods at night."

Tomorrow. Tomorrow I will rescue my parents. Tomorrow I will feel their arms around me again.

"What do we do if someone gets injured?" Paige asks.

"That's where Silver can help. She's the healer, but if someone is too far gone, you'll have to leave them behind," Claus says.

I look down the line of my fellow team members, wondering how many of us will make it back.

"Leave them behind?" Addison echoes with a stutter.

Francesca nods. "As harsh as it sounds, the end results are more important."

"Joe and Matt will be leading this mission with the maps and information to guide you. They're your superiors for this mission; what they say goes." Claus looks each of us in the eye, making sure we understand.

"I'd come if I could, but I'm needed here," Francesca says. "I also need Claus and a few of the others to guard the cave. I have faith in you. All of you."

"There's one more thing I want to discuss before you go," Claus says, resting a hand on his hip as he loads a final image. An image that fills my nightmares. It's a monster I have experience with.

"Hellhounds. Most of you haven't come across them. They've been very top secret until recently." An expectant hush falls over the room. It's quiet enough to hear the occasional dripping at the back of the chamber. "These are the deadliest creatures on earth. They will kill you in two seconds, ripping your throat out. They. Do. Not. Hesitate." He emphasizes each word.

Joe and I exchange a look. We've fought hellhounds. We're well aware of the size of the threat. If we come across them on this mission, well, I don't want to think too hard about that.

Joe mentions my hellhound attack. At the urging of my friends, I describe the killing moment several times. A new respect shines in peoples' eyes. *She killed a hellhound, she can do anything.* But it was difficult. Close to impossible. There were several moments during that battle, while terror skittered through my brain, that I didn't think I would make it. I don't want to ever feel like that again.

A burst of static erupts from the radio room, followed by a flurry of angry voices. We all dash across the narrow passageway.

"What is it?" I ask.

"The army," Matt says, swiveling to face us. "They're here."

CHAPTER TWENTY-SIX

"It's time to gear up," Francesca says, her somber eyes roving around the room. "You need to go now."

We reenter the weapons chamber, where Claus has laid out camouflage gear and backpacks with everything we'll need. He hands out the assault rifles and pistols we took from the troop of trolls at the warehouse. While I trained with my knife, the others have learned how to shoot. There's little conversation as we change. Everyone listens to the bursts of voices from the radio.

"Five miles out and closing," Claus says.

"I'm not sure I can do this," Sawyer mutters, pulling a black T-shirt over his head.

"I'll help with the fence." I strap my knife to the new trousers. "We'll do it together."

"Thanks, Silver." The haunted look on his face dissolves somewhat.

"I want to come." Lyla stands at the entrance of the

room, one hand on a hip, her long blonde hair fastened in a ponytail.

"Come where?" I ask.

"On the mission," she says, leaning against the archway.

I laugh.

"It's not funny." She gives me a death stare.

I meet her glare. "You're fourteen."

"So is Kyle!"

"No," Matt says, approaching his sister. "Kyle can run, *fast*. He serves a purpose."

"Give me a nanite." She gesticulates wildly with her hands. "Turn me into a bulk. I don't care what it is, I want to go, I want to make them pay for putting me in that compound."

"I don't have those kind of nanites," I say. "My dad only gave me temporary stuff to aid our escape."

She opens her mouth, but Matt interrupts.

"Lyla. *No*."

Lyla's eyes glisten and she wipes her cheek with the back of her hand. "You have no idea what it was like. I just want to fight back. I've been so close to taking a nanite. Did you know that, brother?" Matt shakes his head. "So close." She raises a thumb and forefinger, revealing a minute gap between them. "I didn't know how I would excel in the ballet company unless I took something, and now there is no company. I need to *do* something."

"I know you're angry," Matt says. "But I need you here. If anything happens to me, you need to look after Megan. Mom and Dad."

"That's not fair," Lyla says.

"The world's not fair, Lyla," Matt snaps.

"I'm sorry." I approach her, but she steps back. "But I think Matt's right."

"Of course you do. You two couldn't think differently if your lives depended on it!" She swivels on the ball of her foot and storms out of the room.

"Maybe I should go after her," I say.

"Leave her." Matt fastens his grenade belt around his waist. "She needs some time to cool down."

"I can go," Sawyer pipes up.

Matt's jaw tenses. "That's not a good idea either."

Claus and Evan walk between the chamber and the radio room, giving us updates. "Four and a half miles out."

"What about you guys?" Matt asks. "What will happen if they find this place?"

Francesca levels a serious stare at him. "If you can get Silver's parents out, it won't matter what happens to us."

Matt frowns. "I'm leaving my family here."

My heart sinks.

"I know," Francesca says. "We've got Evan, and a few of the other men are trained in guns. We'll be OK."

"I feel bad about Lyla," I say to Matt.

"Maybe she'd be better with us." He pinches his bottom lip.

I touch his arm. "If the army does storm the cave, they'll only capture them and put them in a compound, but if President Bear captures us, it's a different story. She can't dance herself away from hellhounds and bullets."

Matt sighs. "You're right. She's safer here."

"She'll understand that when she cools down." I finger the pendant just below my collarbone. Then I make sure the bottles of nanites are packed in my backpack. I nestle the two remaining regeneration pills in my pocket. The cave has Joan.

"Four miles out. You need to go now," Claus says.

We jog down the passageway and step out into the night. As we hike to the hidden jeep, I hand out the remaining night-vision nanites. While we trek through the woods, I can't help but think that there's a good chance not all of us will make it back. I look at my hands, wondering if I have enough power to heal the worst kind of injury.

"I don't want anyone to get hurt," I say to Matt as we climb the ridge. He raises a questioning look. "What if it's because of me? What if I can't protect someone?"

"Silver, we're a team. We'll get through this together." Matt takes my hand. "We have to."

"I'll never forgive myself if someone gets hurt because of me." A thick ribbon of anxiety curls around my limbs.

Matt presses his thumb into my palm. "That won't happen."

I walk through the grass, leaving a trail of wet footprints as the blades bend. Dew glistens in the moonlight. I grip my knife.

I will rescue my parents.

Singing my song under my breath, I jog up the ridge, then run, eager to get this over with. The anxiety accompanies me, but I won't let it win.

Something small and scurrying shoots through the undergrowth and dances around Kyle's legs. Twin orbs stare up at him, and a hiss falls from the animal's mouth.

Kyle yelps, his feet moving in a blur.

"It's just a raccoon," Joe says, grabbing Kyle by the back of the neck.

The raccoon runs one more circle around Kyle then speeds away, taking its eerie night eyes with it.

"Shhh," Matt says. "We need to stay quiet."

Kyle presses close to me, as if he might jump into my arms like some scared cartoon character. "It was trying to eat me."

Kyle's words land deep inside and create a flurry of panic. Not about raccoons or other forest animals, but about the very real possibility of death. This time I can't reason the fear away. This time the anxiety grabs me so tightly all I can do is fall to my knees.

I hold up a hand, wishing I had a paper bag to

breathe into. "Just give me a minute." I try to ignore their presence, all the watchful eyes boring into me, and cup my hands over my mouth and nose, trying to restore calm. Jacob touches my shoulder, and Paige tells everyone to back off. The minutes tick by. I can't get my breathing regular. Or the tightness in my chest, or the shakiness in my legs or the double vision. Shit. Everyone is still staring at me. Me. The ultimate weapon. Having a panic attack on the way to kill President Bear.

Matt kneels by my side and sweeps tender strokes up and down my back. He's seen me like this before. So many times. When my mother was taken away, I had daily panic attacks for months. I would be lost without him, and that's when I realize it.

I'm in love with my best friend.

Matt.

I'm in love with Matt. Why didn't I see it before?

Because I was so distracted by Joe and the newness of his friendship.

Matt's touch on my shoulder feels heavy, almost too intimate, and I wonder if he has any idea how I feel. The pendant swings from my neck and I think about how its presence during my flight through the woods was a constant reminder of Matt, of how much I cared for him. Reassuring me I was doing the right thing. Why hadn't I realized then?

After a moment longer, I get to my feet and try to ignore the painful grip of tension at the back of my neck.

"Thatta girl," Matt says, his smile warm.

Joe steps in, takes hold of my hands and peers down at me, his honey eyes melting into the moonlight. "You OK?"

I nod. He leans forward and touches my cheek, pushing a few loose strands of hair away that escaped from my ponytail. Then brushes his lips against mine. Someone whistles. I pull away and look for Matt, but he's already walking on, Erica fluttering close behind him, her wings a sapphire color I've never seen before.

"I'm sorry." Joe's eyebrows gather together and his hands dangle at his sides. "I know you said you needed time. I just thought it would be a good distraction."

My cheeks burn. "Let's just keep going."

Joe and Hal take the lead, Erica flying from one person to the next, Kyle and Sawyer behind them. Addison walks with Jacob and Paige. Matt walks up ahead somewhere and I trail at the back on my own. We trudge through the forest toward the hidden jeep. Fireflies dance among the leaves. A whispering breeze weaves through the trees and cools the sweat on the nape of my neck.

"Two miles from the cave. Radio silence from us for the foreseeable future. Over." Claus' voice on Matt's walkie-talkie.

At first I think the snap echoing through the forest is me chipping a tooth from clenching them so tight. A quick examination with my tongue reveals no broken teeth. Then a scream pierces the air. I flinch, knife ready.

"Silver!" Paige calls. "Over here."

I wince against the noise, wondering if the ambushing army has heard her. Running, I stumble over roots, jump over logs, push ferns out of my way and scan the undergrowth. Jacob lies in a heap on the ground at the base of a large oak tree. Ferns cover part of his torso. His face, whiter than bleached bone, is streaked with dirt.

"Do something!" Face contorted, Paige pulls at a metal mouth of a trap with both hands.

Jacob's ankle is caught in an animal trap, almost completely severed. Thank God he's passed out. I drop to my knees, and Joe removes the trap. The rest of the team hover around me, frowns on all their faces, each giving their own advice.

I take a deep breath and close my eyes. Placing both hands above the wound, I think of the boy we first met in the warehouse, dirty and half-naked but prepared to fight until death. I picture his recovery, his returning strength, and the authority he oozes when he practices his martial arts. Calmness descends on me and all I hear is my own measured breathing.

I open my eyes. Sounds and images assault me, almost flattening me to the ground. The forest becomes alive with insect noises and the chatter of my teammates once again. They're all talking at once; had they ever stopped? Jacob remains on the ground, eyes still closed, but his leg is healed. New skin, devoid of tattoos, covers a wonky bone.

Paige grabs my shoulder. "Thank you, Silver."

Jacob's eyes flutter open. He blinks rapidly a few times and sits up. "What happened?"

Matt hands him a canteen. Paige whispers in Jacob's ear.

Hal and Joe, impervious to the steel teeth of animal traps, along with Erica and Paige, who can fly above the dangers, scout the immediate area for more. They find five more and spring them all. I wonder who or what the hunter is. Some of the werewolf altereds have taken to laying such traps, adopting a lazier attitude to securing their prey.

Keeping quiet, we reach the jeep, hidden by a tangled mess of branches. Joe and Hal uncover it and we all climb inside.

White-lipped, Jacob sits in the back. His usually olive-colored skin is almost as pale as mine, emphasizing his twisting Chinese tattoos. I remember one of them means 'perseverance.' Sweat beads on his forehead and his tongue skims continually across his lips.

"It didn't work, did it?" I ask Jacob. "Joan said there are limitations?"

"I can walk on it, but it hurts like hell." Drops of moisture form across his upper lip. "I thought I could stretch off the kinks, but it's not feeling any better."

He lost so much blood. It will take time to regenerate the missing pints—time we don't have. The group sits in the jeep while we discuss Jacob's situation. We've only been hiking for forty minutes. We aren't far from the cave.

"I'm going to head back. If I continue I'll just slow you down. You can do it without me," Jacob pleads from his sprawled position.

Paige offers him water and wipes the sweat from his brow. "You can barely walk," she mutters.

"Can you make it back to the cave?" Joe asks.

Jacob nods. "I just need to rest for a little while, then I can get going. I'm sure I can make it before dawn."

"What if…?" I shake my head. I don't want to voice that thought, but if the cave has been compromised…

With Paige's help, Jacob climbs out of the jeep. Joe breaks a branch from a tree, shaves off the smaller twigs and leaves, and sharpens one end into a point. "Here, you can lean on this and use it as a weapon if you need to."

Jacob accepts the crutch, gets to his feet, and takes a few steps back toward the cave. He offers us a jolly wave. Paige goes to him and embraces him fiercely, her wings partially shielding them from view. Then she turns, marching away from Jacob. She doesn't look back.

CHAPTER TWENTY-SEVEN

We bump through the forest along a dirt track for six hours without incident before the jeep runs out of fuel. Joe parks it under the thick branches of a hemlock tree and covers it with ferns.

There's a countdown in the back of my mind that pushes forward, shoving other thoughts out of the way. Although I know guillotines haven't been used in centuries, I keep hearing the slice of a blade as I picture my parents' heads rolling. The image pushes speed into me, but I know I shouldn't use my abilities right now. It takes everything in me to keep a normal, unadjusted pace.

"I suggest we get some shut-eye for a couple hours. We're going to need all our strength when we get to that prison," Joe says. It's not yet dawn and we've stopped for a rest and food. "I'll take first watch."

The last thing I want to do is sleep, but the others settle in, so I sit and twiddle my thumbs, hoping we make it in time. The moon glints through the tree canopy, and a cool sweat covers my skin while insects tick an irregular beat. Matt swats at a persistent mosquito. When Erica flutters her wings, I'm grateful for the breeze they create. She hasn't looked at me once since Joe kissed me in front of everyone.

Matt has, though. I felt his gaze as we walked, and when I looked up, I couldn't read his expression. His blue eyes were guarded and his half-smiles tentative.

Joe opens packets of self-cooking noodles and hands them out. Paige stares into the distance. She'll answer when spoken to. That's all. There's no way of knowing whether Jacob made it back safely.

After we eat, we find hidden sleeping spots. Erica ends up in a tree while I choose the crevice between two large roots. Joe leans against a trunk, pistol in one hand, machete tied to his belt, scanning the area.

Despite my urge to keep walking, sleep comes instantly, and I dream of monsters with demonic yellow eyes and fangs as long as a human hand. Hellhounds.

I startle awake. My heart thunders in my chest and I'm sweating more than when I was walking. I lurch to my feet and it takes me a moment to see everyone is still safe.

The weather has turned gloomy. Gray clouds stretch across the sky, draping the forest in a heavy darkness. Distant thunder threatens. Rain isn't far off.

We gather our supplies and continue, this time in twos, talking quietly.

Matt and I take our turn heading the group, walking a little ways in front. In the past few hours, finding nothing more dangerous than a raccoon, a false sense of security has settled around us. So when I spot the ogre, I almost forget to hide. It crouches in a bush nearby, wearing the unmistakable green combat uniform of President Bear's army, and holds a radio poised at its mouth.

"Matt," I whisper, placing a finger across my lips.

He follows my gaze to the ogre and pulls me behind the nearest tree. "Has it seen us?"

"I don't think so." I size up the distance, wondering if I can make it. Trees and foliage lie in the way. Matt rustles in his backpack and produces one of his grenades.

"Too noisy," I whisper, drawing his arm away. "There might be others in the area."

The rest of the group approaches, trampling in the underbrush. We don't have much time. The ogre looks up and locks eyes with me.

Decision made. I unsheathe my knife and aim, then send it somersaulting through the air. It hits the ogre's neck, right above the hollow in his collarbone, cutting off his voice box. The ogre falls backwards into the bushes, dead.

"Wow," Matt says, almost dropping a grenade.

Joe gives me a silent round of applause. I perform a curtsy in return.

Matt stands straighter than one of the stone statues outside Bear's presidential compound and his jaw locks into a jagged position. When his cheeks flush crimson, something in my stomach hollows.

"What? What's your problem?"

Matt pulls me roughly aside, making it clear he wants a private word. He's never been so physical with me before.

"My problem is *you*." He looks at me expectantly, as if he thinks I might know what he's talking about.

"I... what... huh?" I come up blank.

Matt's hands are chest level. "Silver, for someone so intelligent you can be incredibly dense!"

"Excuse me?" I splutter.

"Joe's not the only one who's into you, Silver. *I* love you. Me, Matt Lawson, best friend for as long as I can remember, has loved you for as long as I can remember. Are you seriously trying to tell me you didn't know that?" Matt glares at me, hands on his hips.

I love you too.

But my mouth won't work. It won't speak the words I will. Everyone's eyes drill into me; I can't do this here and now.

Matt looks me up and down. I feel exposed. He takes a breath and blows his hair out of his eyes.

He backs up a few paces. "I'm sorry." His voice is tight. "I shouldn't have said all that."

Tears sting my eyes, but I don't have time to deal with this now. As much as I want to wrap his arms around me and tell him I love him too, I can't afford to be distracted. My parents' lives are on the line.

"We need to keep moving," I say, trying to keep my voice steady.

Matt nods, a curt movement that pulls at my heartstrings, then turns away. Shit.

Hal clears his throat and picks up a pair of binoculars. Erica flies past me, her face a neutral mask. And Joe, I don't dare look at Joe.

"I see a river," Hal calls, the binoculars pressed to his face.

"A river? Claus didn't say anything about a river," Joe says as the rest of us join Hal.

"It looks calm enough. Wide though, and there could be an undercurrent." Hal steps to the edge of the tree line. The prison building rises in the distance. My heart beats a little faster.

"I can just fly across." I take a step.

"It might be better to conserve your energy for when you're inside." Matt's voice hovers at my ear, creating a hum on my skin I've never felt before.

The sky darkens to a miserable gray. The rain starts, just a trickle at first, but it brings the promise of a storm. Lightning strikes in the distance. Joe takes the binoculars from Hal. "Looks about ten feet across. Erica and Paige, you can fly across. Kyle, you can probably run across fast enough. Hal and I will help the rest of you."

Wind whips through the trees and stings my cheeks with an icy touch.

"We should move now, while we have the rain's cover," Matt says.

Joe nods, and on three, we run, the nine of us in a line with Paige and Erica flapping just above our heads. They reach the other side first, shortly followed by Kyle. The rest of us pull up on the edge of the muddy bank. Sawyer's shoes lose their grip and he slides into the swirling water.

"It's cold!" He grabs for Joe's outstretched hand as his teeth smack together. His blond curls flatten under the burgeoning rain.

Joe drags Sawyer up the bank and he collapses on the sodden grass, trousers caked with mud.

"I'll go to the other side of the river," Hal says. "If Joe gets in the middle, we can pass you across. Just like the obstacle course." He gestures for Joe to climb into our side of the river.

Both the bulks slink into the cold water. Hal wades to the far side and Joe stays close to us. Addison lowers herself down the bank first. As lightning strikes in the distance, she extends a hand to Joe and pulls herself into the middle. Then she grabs onto Hal, who pushes her up the other side. Sawyer is next.

"I just got out," he mumbles, but the next crack of lightning sends him scurrying into the water again. He hangs onto the grassy clumps at the edge of the bank until Joe moves closer and picks him up. He passes him to Hal, who then walks him to the other side.

"Your turn, Matt," Joe says, waving him over.

Matt spends a few seconds repositioning his grenade belt. "I really hope the seal on these is tight." He edges into the water. Joe holds him around his waist. Both of them look anywhere but at each other. Then Matt reaches for Hal, but he loses his slippery grip with Joe, and the current yanks him downstream. Joe tries to go after him, but he loses his footing and has to claw at a rock in the middle to prevent being washed away.

My heart lurches. Without thinking, I use my wings and go after Matt. I skim the surface, both arms reaching, until my fingertips grasp his. I pull.

He's heavy with his clothes drenched, and I have to use a pinch of bulk power to drag him out. We collapse on the bank just as Hal and Joe climb out of the river.

Thunder booms above us and rain runs down my cheeks.

"Thanks, Silver," Matt says, climbing off me.

"Matt, wait," I call after him. We're not far from the prison. One or both of us could die in there.

He turns, his hair dripping, his soaked T-shirt clinging tight. "What?"

Thunder booms again. The rest of the group stand huddled, waiting for us. Erica stands on the ground, her wings too wet to fly, and lavender swirls of hair stick to her neck. I climb out of the mud and face him. I lose my nerve. "Nothing."

"Let's go," he says, and holds out his hand.

My heart soars a little as I grab it and we run to the others. Then we take off toward the prison.

CHAPTER TWENTY-EIGHT

As our group nears the prison, light suddenly spills around us. The heavy rain glints under the floodlights.

"Shit!" Matt yells, dashing with the rest of us toward the brick wall.

"Remember, the guards are on regular perimeter walks. We just have to time our approach," Joe says, crouching by the wall.

"Hey! What are you doing?" A shout comes from the wall. Two guards appear with their weapons swinging up.

In unison, Joe and Hal leap to their feet and dash alongside the brick wall. The razor wire gleams. Hal puts a bullet in the ogre's brain. Joe takes out the bulk. Both bodies collapse on the ground.

"We need to hurry," Matt says, grabbing the fallen guards' walkie-talkies and weapons. "The guards march this wall every thirty minutes. When these guys don't report in…"

"Over the wall, just like we've practiced," Joe says.

Joe launches himself at the wall. As he's almost the same height, he merely places his hands along the top and pulls himself up. Sitting on the razor wire, he cuts into it and drops a section at our feet. A red laser beam angles toward him.

"Joe!" I call.

He ducks out of the way just in time. I count to five until the beam comes back again. We each have five seconds to get over the wall. That's it.

Joe jumps down to the other side. One by one, Hal and Erica help us onto the wall. No one wastes any time up there, leaping down as soon as we can, away from the searing beams.

When it's Paige's turn, she hisses as the beam singes a few of her feathers. An acrid scent mingles with the earthy rain. I raise my hand to her, but she shakes her head. "I'll be OK. Save it for someone who needs it."

Reassembled along the inside of the wall, and now out of the danger of the external laser beams, we huddle in the shadowy corner. Sawyer eyes the electric fence two yards ahead. It buzzes with activity, whispering warnings of death. Vertical concrete struts, six feet apart, separate the wires. Beyond the fence lies the inner brick wall, as tall and thick as the outer wall.

There's a foot gap between each electrified wire, a space we can all pass through if Sawyer can turn it off.

Sawyer takes two steps forward. I narrow my eyes at the glow of cigarette butts farther down the inner wall—guards smoking in the recess of the doorway. *Please don't look this way.*

Sawyer takes another step into a triangle of light. A wire fizzles. It turns white with heat, then short-circuits. Sawyer inches closer. Another wire turns white-hot, but only for an instant before it leaps back to its insistent buzzing.

Sawyer gulps and shakes water out of his hair. "Silver, I need your help."

I tiptoe over to Sawyer, one foot from the fence. I glance at the guards. Laughter floats toward us. A match is struck. Another glowing ember.

"What I'd give for a cigarette right now," Sawyer mumbles.

"It's a good time to quit," I say.

Sawyer gestures to the fence. "I can't turn it all off."

"I need to save my abilities for inside." I place my hands on his shoulders. "You can do this."

I stand with him as he refocuses his concentration on the remaining five wires in the six-foot section of the fence immediately before us. He blocks the electricity in the middle of each wire and reverses its direction. He grips my hand as he holds it there, each of the wires temporarily inactive. I beckon the group to start climbing through. Paige throws a coin at the fence. It bounces off harmlessly.

"Hurry," Sawyer says to the group. "I don't know how long I can keep this up."

Paige sucks in a breath before ducking through the wires. One by one, the rest follow, each holding their breath in turn.

Then it's Sawyer's turn. As he approaches, a burst of electricity surges across one of the lower wires. He steps back and looks at me.

I give him a thumbs-up. "Take it easy, you can do it."

With the electricity held at bay once more, Sawyer crouches, passes one leg over a wire, then his body, then the other leg. He pulls the remaining foot through just as another surge comes flooding across one of the higher wires. Sawyer turns to me. He clenches his jaw and stands near the fence, ready to help me through.

Pushing my abilities away, I creep through two wires and score a shock to my ankle, but it's not serious, and I stumble away from the electricity. With a last glance at the smoking guards, I join the group at the corner of the inner wall. Addison, Joe and Hal are already making their way toward them. Rain drips from the roof, over-spilling the gutters and splattering onto the ground, forming muddy puddles. Lightning flashes.

Addison walks casually along the wall. Joe trails her, hugging the bricks. She draws level with the guards. Low voices engage in conversation. A burst of laughter. Hal follows Joe. The rest of us stay at the wall, out of view. Joe reaches for his machete.

"Joe Rucker! As I live and breathe!" A grin stretches across the bulk guard's face.

Joe stumbles back a step. The group freezes.

"How the hell are you? I didn't realize you'd joined the army," the bulk guard says. He flicks a cigarette on the ground and steps forward. "Don't tell the boss I've been smoking." He lays a finger across his lips.

"I... Mark... Well, it's been a long time." Joe's hand drops to his side, the machete hidden behind his back.

"How do you two know each other, then?" the other guard asks.

"Ah, back in the glory days, before I traded football for a rifle." The bulk skims his hand over the barrel of his gun.

"What are you doing here?" The bulk guard turns his attention to Addison. "I can't remember the last time we had a girl bulk in the army." He pauses. "Wait a minute, you're not a bulk..."

Addison steps close, her eyes flashing and her fingers stretching for her throwing stars.

"I know you." The troll guard narrows his eyes. "You're that pretty thing Mack took from the woods. Saw you talking to that scientist guy a few nights ago."

"And you sold me a bunch of misinformation about my family," Addison snarls.

"Wasn't sure if you were coming back or not." The troll splits a grin. "You unadjusteds are so unpredictable."

Addison curls her lips into an ugly sneer. Both Hal and Joe turn toward her.

"Scientist guy?" Joe asks. "Addison? What is he talking about?"

Earl, he's talking about Earl. This is bad. I edge out from behind the wall. Matt hisses at me, but I wave him away.

"Earl!" the troll guard says. "That's his name!"

"Hang on," Joe butts in. "I thought you were captured?"

"I was," Addison retorts.

"Care to explain?" Hal snaps.

"They have my family." Addison holds out her hands. "When I ran out of things to negotiate with, they promised me they'd release them if I… if I…." She hangs her head.

Paige follows me along the wall. So far, we haven't been spotted, and I'm sensing Joe and Hal might need my help.

"Did you turn us in?" Joe steps up into her face.

"They wanted Silver alive." Addison looks at the wall and spots me creeping along. "It was a lot of money. We were promised our freedom. I'm so sorry, Silver."

Paige and I join the group.

"Three million dollars is worth everyone's lives, is it?" Anger blurs my vision.

The bulk guard coughs. "Silver... Melody?"

The troll guard holds his finger against the trigger of his gun. Addison fingers one of her throwing stars, and the bulk guard raises his weapon at her. Tears stream down her face. "I never wanted it to be like this."

"Silver Melody?" The bulk guard says again with a satisfied smirk. "We've been expecting you."

My body tenses and I face the guard.

"Addison…" Hal glances from the guards to Addison and gestures for her to lower her weapon.

With his eyes on me, the bulk guard pulls the trigger. Addison's head explodes. Paige ducks out of the way of a swinging arm. Hal catches it on the chin, but it barely registers on his iron-like jaw. Joe and Hal turn to face our adversaries.

Dodging bullets from the bulk, Hal attacks. He stabs a knife into the weak spot on the bulk's neck, cutting off his air and vocal chords. The gun makes an arc of bullets in the sky. Feathers burst into the air; Paige collapses to the floor. At the same time, Joe leaps at the remaining guard and drives his machete into his heart. The guard, too, falls to the ground, gurgling briefly before he bleeds out.

I turn to Paige. Her emerald eyes are wide and staring. She blinks. Not dead. Thank God.

The rest of the group rush forward to meet us. Erica huddles over Addison's lifeless body and sobs into her hair, then she slams a fist into the wet ground and pushes to her feet.

Joe checks Paige for injuries. "It's her wing."

"I just need a minute," Paige says, her voice barely more than a rasping whisper.

Joe puts pressure on a ragged hole in her wing. "She might not be able to fly."

I lay my hands on her chest, but she shakes her head. "Save your energy."

I give her my hand and haul her to her feet. Her wing hangs askew, but the bleeding has stopped. She'll be OK.

I stare at the puddle of Addison's red hair. "That was close," I say quietly. "Too close."

"We have a mole." Matt stares sadly at Addison.

Hal crouches and throws a scrap of cloth over Addison's head. "But she's dead now, she can't do us any more harm."

Shoulder shaking, Erica turns her back. I walk up to her and touch her shoulder.

"I'm sorry." Her voice cracks.

"It's not your fault. You didn't know." I drop my hand. "We've got to go. We don't have time to stand around here. I'm sure President Bear knows we're here."

Erica clears her throat and flicks her lavender ponytail over her shoulder. "I'm ready."

"Let's get going, guys," Joe says. "All that gunfire won't go unnoticed."

A deafening siren splits the night in two.

CHAPTER TWENTY-NINE

We stand outside the main door to the prison complex, leaning close to the walls to get away from the rain and any unwanted eyes that might suddenly appear. A red light flashes from the windows of the building.

"We need to get inside," Matt says over the piercing siren. "They know we're here."

Not waiting for further instructions, Joe pummels one strong fist at the door. It crumples, spilling strobing red light around the edges. Hal shoves the door off its hinges and we all tumble inside.

I take a moment to orient myself. Our labored breathing fills the hall we find ourselves in, and we drip rainwater all over the floor. Echoing footsteps dash down unseen areas of the building.

"We need to split up," Joe says, dividing us with a quick flick of his finger. "Two teams. Silver's parents are the priority."

"Paige, Erica, and Kyle with me," Hal says, jerking a thumb.

That leaves me, Matt, Joe, and Sawyer. We nod at each other and distribute the weapons more evenly. Paige offers me a fragile smile, then the two groups peel off in opposite directions.

The red light casts an eerie glow on the white walls like some sinking submarine in a disaster movie. Rain and wind slam at the windows and shake the glass. Hoping to stay hidden as long as possible, we run away from the voices around a couple of corners. We reach a staircase leading up.

"Split again," I say.

Joe nods, grabbing Sawyer's arm and pulling him down the hall. That leaves me and Matt to go up. We race up the stairs and into a dark hallway. The light continues to pulse, fragmenting our movements, until we almost skid into a group of guards. They shout and raise their weapons.

"Down here!" I tug Matt around a corner into a shallow alcove, realizing too late it has no escape route.

Matt yanks a grenade from his belt and pulls the pin. He sticks his head around the corner. A volley of gunfire streams toward us, but he hurls the grenade and ducks back around the corner.

"One, two, three…" An eruption booms and I stick

my fingers in my ears. Plaster crumbles and cascades to the floor.

I know I can't stay in this alcove forever, but I don't really want to venture out into gunfire either. "Do you think they're dead?"

"No idea," Matt says. "Let's keep going." We leave the warped hallway behind and follow a new route through winding white walls. The thundering footsteps of dozens of guards pursue us, slamming doors a few seconds after us, but not quite in view.

We dash through another empty hallway. This one has doors with small windows, like the compound. We peer in the windows, discovering empty offices instead of cells. The administrators obviously aren't part of Bear's welcome party.

"Where are they?"

Matt's eyes find mine. "We'll find them."

Another staircase leads higher. The white walls change to concrete breezeblock, and we come face-to-face with an electronic door.

At least the entry point is deserted.

Matt's lips bunch together. "I could blow it up?"

I walk to the transparent gateway. "Let me try something first."

I examine the thick door. A swipe card is the only thing that will allow access, and neither of us possesses that. I short-circuit the wires with my telekinesis. The door clicks open. In my head I keep a running tally of how much time I've spent using abilities. Five minutes saving Matt, ten seconds on the lock.

Matt raises an eyebrow and grins. We creep through the door and close it quietly behind us, but it won't engage its locking mechanism again. It seems we've lost the guards for now.

We sneak around a corner and emerge on a balcony overlooking a deserted prison yard. Basketball hoops without chains stand sentry at either end, and a pair of worn bleachers sags toward the sodden ground. Along one side of the fence stand a couple of metal posts. The same posts my parents were tethered to in the video clip.

"They were right there." I raise my hands to the window.

Matt tugs on my hand and leads me away. "We need to keep moving."

Around another corner, the hallway changes. Cell doors run the entire length, farther than I can see. No metal bars, but there are thick, solid doors with a small square window and a slot for food trays.

I glance in one. Empty. We dash to the next. A man in an orange jumpsuit with ice-white hair bangs on the far window that overlooks the grassland we crossed.

The next cell reveals another man lying on his bed, ignoring the red lights completely and tossing a ball up and down, but the ball doesn't move like a normal ball.

It stays in the air for a fraction too long before dropping back to his hand. The cell after that shows another man with horns on his shoulders. The tip of each horn tapers to a wicked point and pokes through his prison jumpsuit. He's using them to gouge at the cement in the wall, as if he can dig his way out.

The thud of several heavy boots sounds at our backs.

"Guards!" Matt hisses, flattening against the wall.

I tug him around the next corner, bypassing several cells, and pick the first one that's out of sight. With bulk power, I snap the lock and push us both inside and shut the door behind us. The wailing siren immediately mutes and for the first time since I've been in the prison, I can think straight.

"Matt? Silver? Is that you?"

I swivel toward the familiar voice. The room is another cell, but it's not just any cell; it's strewn with lab equipment and a laptop. My father sits at a small wooden desk in the middle of it all. He wears gray clothes that have been boiled to an inch of their life and a pair of flimsy slippers. Bloody and bruised, a swollen lump straddles his right eyebrow. A long slash splits the back of his shirt, revealing a raised and angry whiplash.

"Dad!" I rush toward him and throw my arms around his gaunt frame. Tears stream down both our cheeks. "Thank God."

Dad wraps his arms around me and relief pours out of me.

"It's good to see you, Dr. Melody," Matt says, shaking his hand.

Dad grins and releases me. "Why is one of your arms a foot longer than the other?"

I draw back and grab his shoulder. "I think you know why." I'm not angry anymore. I know he did it to protect me, and now that I have all these abilities, I can use them for good.

His eyes roam my face, pupils widening as he takes in my appearance. "What do you mean? Did you take something?"

I shake my head and let my arm reduce to its human size. My fingers find his swollen eye and the healing glow spills over his skin into him, easing his pain. I push more of the healing goodness into him, healing him everywhere. His injuries aren't severe, so it only takes a minute.

"You changed my DNA," I say.

Dad gapes. "I did, but it's been so long…"

The red light falls over Dad's face through the square of window. It's hard to tell, but I think I detect the hint of a flush. "I didn't think it had worked."

I pull my hands away and rest them in my lap. "What did you do to me?"

"Chameleon, right?" Matt asks, keeping his eyes on the window.

Dad's hand flies to his chest. "Partly, and cephalopod, the masters of disguise. I gave them to you in vitro."

"But why is it only working now?"

"I'm not entirely sure," Dad says. "There were lots of side-effects we weren't allowed to test."

I perch on the table. "Like some sort of God-factor."

"That's right." Dad knocks the table with his knuckles. "It's what we say when we don't really have an answer."

"Can we talk about this later?" Matt asks. "We need to get you out of here and find Silver's mother."

Dad pushes himself out of his chair. "Margaret isn't here."

The blood drains from my face. "Where is she?"

"I don't know," Dad replies. "Bear decided to separate us as soon as he made that video." He pulls me close once more. "He knew you'd come."

My voice turns to steel. "He knows I have abilities. He saw me."

At that moment, the loudspeaker crackles and a voice booms through the speakers, almost as loud as Joe's.

"What a touching reunion," President Bear says. "I'm so glad you could join us, Silver. I've been waiting for the time to continue our little chat. I would so like to learn how you took on all my abilities. Please come up to my office. There's tea. Third floor. That is, if you don't get interrupted by my little friends first."

The speaker goes quiet.

I glance at Dad's desk, strewn with so much lab equipment. "What has he got you doing?"

"Finding an answer to the aggressiveness problem," Dad says.

"There is no answer," I hiss, shoving paper off his desk. "They're all nuts."

Dad joins Matt at the window in the door. He wraps an arm around my shoulder. "Do you have a plan?"

"Yeah," I say. "Run like hell, and avoid that third floor with the poisoned tea."

Matt checks the hammer of his gun. "Let's go."

Dad shakes his head. "We need to go to that office first. He has something of mine."

I whirl to face him. "What?"

"He's got my flash stick." Dad shoots us an apologetic look.

"The one you took from the lab at home?" I ask. "What is it?"

"During the time I wasn't working on Bear's insidious projects and building more ridiculous nanite pills, I was researching a cure." The last few words are barely above a whisper.

Matt snaps his head up. "It's possible? A way to turn the altereds human again?"

Dad tilts his head. "I think so. I'm still trying to figure it out."

"Can't you do it without the flash stick?" I ask.

"Maybe," Dad says. "But I'd have to start from scratch. It could set me back months, maybe longer."

"Then we're going to Bear's office," Matt says, inching close to the door.

"Yes, we are," I say with renewed determination. "We're starting a coup. And not a peaceful one."

Matt holds his gun in one hand and a grenade in the other. He cracks open the door. We glance up and down the hall and I catch sight of running soldiers.

"What do we do?" Matt asks.

Before the soldiers appear, I charge down the hallway and use my telekinesis to release the locks on all the cell doors. It doesn't take much effort and now the soldiers will have a riot to control. "You. Are. Brilliant!" Matt sticks his thumbs up.

Orange masses appear in the hall between us, and the marching feet of several guards grow louder.

CHAPTER THIRTY

The man with the horns appears and charges down the hall, opening his mouth to release a tremendous war cry. He disappears around the corner and is met with the sound of gun fire. There's a dull thud.

The rest of the prisoners emerge from their cells, opportunity in their eyes mixed with a deadly determination. One man with a gleaming bald head and burn marks scarring his cheeks releases a breath of fire that plumes out a good six feet. Heat rushes by my face and singes the ends of my hair. He's quickly followed by another man with a head of hissing snakes, snapping and biting at the other inmates. A third man with a whip-like tail lashes out and circles the snake-man around the neck, yanking him out of the way. The fire man breathes again and singes the hair off a man half my height who seems to possess a teleporting power. He flashes next to us and Matt's eyebrows catch fire. Matt slaps at his face, putting out the small sparks.

At the other end, the guards stream around the corner. Ten trolls armed with assault rifles.

"I reckon we take our chances with the prisoners," I say.

"Agreed. There's a staircase around that corner." Dad points.

We edge out of the room, ducking the snapping snakes and weaving away from the gusting breaths of fire. Bullets slam into the walls at our backs. Several of the prisoners throw us glances and swivel toward us. One of the snakes snaps out at me.

Dad goes down, shoved by a prisoner with tentacles for arms. I haul him to his feet. The man with fiery breath brushes by, the skin of his forearm connecting with mine. The pain hits immediately. A white-hot fire whips into my lungs and scorches my throat. Matt grabs my hand, pulling me along as I stumble and cough. A small orange flame flicks out of my mouth.

"Holy…!" Matt stares at my lips. The pain in my lungs eases and I pull in a breath. I cough again and another flame forms, but I will it away and it flickers out. We reach the other end of the hall.

Matt unpins a grenade. "Get into that stairwell."

Dad and I push through the door. Matt throws the grenade and ducks into the stairwell with us. We make it to the next floor when the explosion shakes the building.

"Third floor." Dad pushes open the door to a carpeted

hallway. Watercolor prints of landscapes line the walls. Elevator music plays from hidden speakers.

"I think it's safe to say we're out of the prisoner area," Matt says, turning in a slow circle.

A door opens to our left and I raise my knife, but it's just Joe and Sawyer.

"Thank God," Joe says, the relief on his face palpable.

Dad tenses.

"These are our friends," I say to Dad. "Joe saved me after that hellhound attack."

Dad reaches out and shakes Joe's hand. "I'm eternally grateful."

"What are you guys doing here?" Sawyer asks.

"President Bear has something my dad needs."

Sawyer swallows hard.

"This way." Matt gestures down the hall. Two large, glossy photo prints of President Bear frame a thick oak door.

Something shifts in the air around us. The hairs on my arms stand on end. Before we can take another step, a growl winds down the hall.

"What the hell was that?" Sawyer asks, sidestepping to the wall.

We all glance the length of the hall. It's completely empty, but that growl sounded so close.

Joe takes a couple steps down the hallway, leaving a deep tread in the thick carpet.

Matt holds a hand up. "Go easy."

The growl turns to a terrifying roar that blows Joe's hair away from his face. Whatever it is, it's close and it's invisible. Paw prints less than a yard away press into the carpet.

Something flashes into existence and I catch sight of robotic red eyes and a shaggy brown mane. It shifts along the wall. Camouflaged. Taking on the background it stands beside. Once I've spotted it, I keep my eyes fixed and can finally make out its shape.

A flash of memory niggles in my brain. A drawing of a horrifying lion that I burned in my father's lab before we fled to the cave. Earl invented hellhounds. His next project must've been invisible hellcats.

For a second, the animal flashes into full visibility. A towering male lion with wide jaws. Half of the hair on its head has been shaved off, and gleaming metal takes the place of its skull. Combined with the red mechanical eyes, this is something beyond mere creature. This is a chimera of beast and machine. Earl hasn't just manipulated DNA; he's thrown in manmade parts too.

"What the hell is that thing?" The crotch of Sawyer's trousers darkens.

Instinctively, Joe and I step closer to protect Dad. I turn full bulk. Joe raises his machete, and I grip my knife. A second roar streams toward us from farther up the hall. A flash of movement, and the second beast launches toward us.

Its reeking breath blows past my cheek as I duck under it. It slams into Sawyer, eliciting an agonized scream. Blood drips from Sawyer's shoulder. I dive toward the massive animal and dig my knife into the back of its neck. I stab and stab, but I can't find any purchase past its metallic parts. Its eyes whir in striations of red. Matt skids toward us and shoots the oversized cat with a handgun. A spark sizzles from one of its red eyes, but no more. It turns on Matt and crunches its massive jaws on his arm.

Matt screams, knees buckling.

"No!" I yell, wrapping my fingers around its jaw, trying to yank it open.

The color leaches from Matt's face. Blood pools on the carpet.

The door at the end of the hall opens. President Bear looms in the threshold and thumbs a remote. The cats instantly quiet and slink off toward the president. When they reach him, they turn and sit at his feet.

"Aren't they lovely?" President Bear asks, stroking one on the head.

I edge to Matt, tear off a corner of my shirt and wrap it around his wound. The healing glow ebbs at my fingertips, but I push it away. I need to stay on the defensive. Matt will have to wait.

President Bear raises a hand toward us. "Won't you come in? I've just made a pot of tea."

Pushing the bulk power away, I march down the hall, rage building in my heart, webbing lacing at my fingers. "Where's my mother?"

"Now, now, Silver. First things first."

I storm past him into the room, the others close on my heels. With everyone inside, I slam the door. I don't want those cats coming back in. President Bear fiddles with their remote control.

"How nice of you to join me." President Bear shoots webbing from his palms in quick succession. Sawyer is pinned beneath a mound of white, which turns red with his blood. The venom will be seeping into his body. Matt is tied to a chair in the corner and gagged with the silk. Joe gets trapped against the door. Sawyer and Joe start yelling but stop when I remind them of the venom.

"Sit, Dr. Melody," Bear says, gesturing to the chair near the desk.

My father hesitates, then obeys. His hands get tied to the chair's legs. I'm the only one untethered.

"Won't you sit down?" President Bear points to a second chair in front of his gargantuan desk. He pours tea from a china pot decorated, incongruously, with tiny pink flowers. The rich odor of an assortment of dark chocolates fills the space between us. I don't sit. This isn't the time to play to his ego or ask him questions about his terrifying chimeras.

It's time for him to die.

Edging closer to the desk, I shoot out twin webbings from my palms that wrap around Bear's wrists. The teapot falls from his grip and smashes on the desk just as I leap forward with my knife aimed at his throat.

I'm met with only resistance and a smile. He has bulk skin, and I've missed the weak spot, if he even has one.

He tuts and frowns at me, turning his tied palm toward me. Before he can shoot webbing, I wrap his hands in my own silken thread.

"Clever girl." But he smiles a knowing smile, and my venomous ties dissolve from his hands.

"How did you—?"

President Bear stands. I'm tempted to call the bulk back, but I need to be careful; I've used over twenty minutes of abilities and have taken on a new one. I'll need every shred of energy I have left.

He presses his fingers to the desk. "I would really like to know, before I dispose of you and your friends, how you took on my abilities."

The abilities cycle through me, my body looking for a way to deal with my rage, but I push them back down. I need to conserve my energy. "I'll never tell."

"Well, it seems we're at something of an impasse. If we possess the same abilities, we are equally matched."

Tea drips from the table in a slowing stream. The shattered china remains on the desk.

"I have more than you," I snarl.

Bear's red eyes glare at me, but I think I detect a hint of fear. "A pair of blue wings can't hurt me."

I twirl the knife in my hand. "Maybe we should find out."

"Leave her alone," Dad snaps. "It's me you need."

The blade lifts from my fingers and flies to the ceiling. It sticks there. Bear must have telekinesis too. No amount of my telekinetic probing makes it budge, and that's when Bear makes his move.

With my eyes still searching for a way to release my knife, he sweeps out my legs and ties them with his webbing. Claus would be very disappointed in me. *Never lose your focus.*

Searching for the power inside that can dissolve my bonds, I leap to my feet as the webbing loosens around my ankles. I come up firing, my own silken thread shooting at President Bear. But as quickly as strands wrap around his neck or head or wrist, they dissolve. I need a different approach.

Behind me, a slight movement draws my eye. Sawyer. Using his power to wiggle out of his binds. A force slams me against the ceiling. I stretch for my knife, but it's still out of reach.

President Bear stands beneath me. His eyes lock on

371

mine. Something dark flashes across his red pupils. Some power I haven't realized is about to erupt from those murderous eyes. Before he can gain an advantage, I open my mouth and release a jet of fiery breath. Bear's hair catches fire. The stench of burnt hair fills my nostrils.

I stretch again for my knife. A quick glance at Sawyer and I note he's managed to get a hand free of the webbing. The others follow the battle, tied and unable to help. Joe strains against his bonds, but the others won't risk the venom.

My knife skitters across the ceiling to my fingers. Sawyer. The pressure on my limbs releases. Just as my fingers grasp the hilt, I drop to the ground and launch myself at Bear, my foot colliding with his jaw.

He stumbles back, smashes into the window and teeters on the edge. I dash closer, exhaling more fire. Before he can grip the ledge and pull himself back into the room, I leap for his throat. The movement is just enough to send us tumbling out the window.

"Silver!" Dad calls as my hair whips away and the stormy air rushes to meet me.

We fall, but I know Bear, with his bulk skin, won't die from the impact. I flap my wings, following him to the ground. He lands on the broken glass from the window. Rain soaks us both.

Rolling to his side, Bear tries to get up, but I drive the

blade into the back of his knee, praying he has the same weak spots Joe does. I'm rewarded with the give of flesh and an arterial spurt of blood.

Bear gasps, his hand going to his knee, webbing trying to fill the wound. He must be immune to his own poison.

"You'll never find your mother," he says, defiance glinting in his cold pupils, rain splashing on his hairy cheeks. In his hand, he holds the remote for the hellcats. He presses a button.

"No!" I yank the remote out of his hand only to find it has a biometric identification screen. I jab at it, but it's as useless as a muzzle on a hellhound.

Above, screams barrel out of the window. Matt hunches in the empty frame. A shaggy mane fills the space behind him.

"No!" I pump my arms and half run, half fly.

The hellcat's massive paw swipes at Matt's head. He falls out the window, somersaulting in midair. With my wings beating frantically, I direct more speed into my feet and push the teleporting power through my limbs. I'm not fast enough and I still have Bear to deal with, but I can't let Matt die from a fall like that. Bringing out my telekinesis, I break his fall. He lands hard and I reach him just as he thuds on the ground. Blood trickles from the corner of his mouth.

"No!" I slide to his side.

He raises one finger. "Silver." His eyes shift to something behind me.

I swivel around. Bear hobbles in my direction, closing the gap, splashing through the wet grass. He raises his hand. Anger floods my veins and charges my limbs. He stole my mother. He tortured my father. Now he's hurt my best friend.

Fire escapes my throat and curls out of my mouth. Steam clouds between us as I heat the rain. My wings beat a powerful rhythm. Webbing forms on my palms, but I push it away. I need something else, something stronger.

Bear aims his venomous threads at me. I raise my hand, black smoke puffing from my fingertips. All the emotions I've felt during the two years since my mother was taken consume me. The anger at the injustice, the desperation over losing her and wanting her back, the anxiety of never knowing if she was alive, the frustration of being able to do absolutely nothing, the rage, the pure hot rage at the one person who twisted my life into a painful blur.

I march toward him. My heart beats a steady rhythm, powered by the need to see him dead. The black smoke plays over my fingers until it becomes something else entirely. In my mind, I picture President Bear's tyrannical heart, beating without a shred of humanity. With my telekinesis, I squeeze it. Harder and harder, until his face turns as red as his eyes. All except the jagged white scar, which brightens on his cheek. He gasps and drops to his knees. The streams of webbing taper off into thin white threads.

I squeeze his heart tighter. A streak of blackness erupts from my palms toward Bear, tunneling into his chest. This power is new and unexpected, and I have no idea where I acquired it. Gritting my teeth and fighting the fatigue flooding my limbs, I pull at his heart with the black tendrils. They're more smoke than cord and move faster than the eye can see, but they don't dissipate in the air.

Bear's eyes widen. His mouth drops open. He reaches for the black tendrils but can't find purchase. Clawing at his chest, he tries to stop the attack, but I yank the heart from Bear's chest and pull it into my hand.

President Bear falls forward. Dead.

The black, smoking tendrils surround the heart. It shudders out its last sign of life and turns black. Crumbling to ash in my hand, the wind picks up the flakes and disperses them in the air.

My body trembles as I try to rein it all back in. The black smoke puffs out of existence and my knees threaten to buckle. But I have to get to Matt. *Matt.* Who lies unconscious under the window, drowning in a puddle.

CHAPTER THIRTY-ONE

Blinking the rain out of my eyes, I skid to Matt's side and place my hands on his chest. Weak breaths stutter in his lungs. The warm healing glow flickers over my fingers, taking the last of my strength as it ebbs into Matt. I don't think it's enough, but then he blinks and turns his head. I collapse against him.

An earth-shuddering roar snaps me back to reality, filling my ears to almost bursting. My friends surround Matt and me. All of them. Joe and Hal reload their guns, Erica nocks an arrow, one of her wings shredded to nonexistence. Paige supports Sawyer, now unconscious from Bear's venom. He won't have long left. My father hunches next to Kyle.

Gray clouds twist and thunder shakes the ground. The red laser beams sweep the sky, sizzling the rain into steaming, scalding drops. A hellcat stalks us. It opens its jaws and roars. Erica releases an arrow, which finds a purchase in the cat's chest. Blood pours, but it doesn't fall.

"We need to go," Matt says, leaning heavily against me. My wings shrink into my back, and my bulk frame deserts me. My abilities are spent, but I can still run. I hope. I pull the last two regeneration pills out of my pocket and hand them to Sawyer and Erica. It takes a moment while Hal keeps his weapon trained on the hellcat, but eventually Erica's wing re-knits and Sawyer's lips and eyes flutter open.

"Did you get the flash stick?" I ask Dad.

He nods and pats his pocket. "And these." He pulls out a crumbled mess of pills. "Invisibility. Remember, it only lasts half an hour."

The hellcat roars again, and this time it's met with a series of responding roars. There are more out there. We need to get out of the prison. The hellcat before us stands there, dazed, its breath misting red in the rain. Handing Matt to Hal, I step over the hulk of President Bear's corpse. So much smaller in death. Threat extinguished, it's hard to believe he ever held the strings to my life.

"You can never force anyone again to pay for what they don't want," I say to his lifeless body. "I destroyed you. Take that, you son of a bitch."

Rain saturates the cat's shaggy coat and runs in small rivers from its flanks and shoulders. The hellcat shudders, then collapses, giving us a brief reprieve. But I know the others will come.

"This way." Joe waves us forward. We reach the electric fence only to find the whole thing shorted out. We all tumble through, parting the wires without hesitation. At the tall brick wall, instead of climbing over it, Joe and Hal run at it together, leaving bulk-sized shapes in the crumbling brick. We pile through in a haphazard mess that Claus would stroke his mustache at and clump together on the other side.

Several cat-shaped shadows with blinking red robotic eyes fill the recently vacated hole.

"We need to run," Matt says, shoving the useless remote in his pocket. He takes a couple of steps, then falls.

I didn't have the energy to heal him completely, and I pray I've cured the worst of it. Hal returns and picks him up.

We charge across the grass, hellcats thundering behind us. They jump and snatch with their jaws and swipe with their claws. My abilities have deserted me. I can only run at a normal human speed. Hal with Matt, Sawyer and I form the back line, my dad just ahead. Sawyer glances over his shoulder and pushes at them with his mind, making the hellcats stumble.

I go down in a slick of mud, spinning like a top over the drenched grass. A hellcat leaps at me, its jaws wide. I swivel on my butt and kick out a foot, connecting with its teeth. It howls and spins away, giving me just enough time to jump to my feet.

Ahead, the river looms, white and frothy, angry in the storm.

"Into the river!" Dad calls over the shuddering thunder. "The cats won't follow us there."

We run faster, straight for the twisting current. Sawyer tumbles into Hal, and all three slide across the ground, straight into the river's waiting jaws. A hellcat chases me. I leap away from its gnashing teeth and smack straight into a boulder in the middle of the river. I'm the last one into the water.

My breath bursts out of my lungs and I cling to the rock as the current tugs at my heels. The hellcats skid to a halt on the muddy bank. They raise their heads to the bickering sky and roar.

I heave a small sigh of relief. At least Earl hasn't taken their fear of water out of their DNA.

Sawyer screams, swirling downstream. Joe splashes toward him and grabs his arm. Matt and my dad swim through the water with Hal's help. Erica half-flies with her saturated wings, half-leaps from rock to rock, and Paige doesn't fare much better. Kyle blitzes across and waits on the other side.

Dragging myself around the edge of the boulder, I reach for Matt's outstretched hand and he hauls me out of the water. I fall onto him.

Rain streams down my cheeks, and maybe a few tears. I wrap my arms around him. "I love you."

Matt kisses my cheek. "We can't stop now."

"We need to keep moving!" Hal calls. The others are already fifty yards closer to the woods.

We run as a group, with Hal helping Matt and Joe throwing me over his shoulder when I stumble for a third time. It's three miles to the cover of the forest. We charge forward, not pausing until we reach a tall oak tree, under which we huddle away from the rain. Floodlights light the prison in the distance. The hellcats remain on the riverbank, stalking up and down, looking for a way across. I catch a few glints of bright orange jumpsuits.

"Where's Mom?" I ask.

Dad hugs me. "We'll find her. We will."

I crawl over to Matt. "Are you OK?"

Matt nods. "I think you healed the worst of it. When we get back to the cave, I'll rest."

We walk a couple more miles into the forest and finally the rain abates. The sun appears from behind the dissipating clouds and warms the back of my neck. Water drips from the leaves above our heads, and my teeth chatter from my drenched clothing.

We stop to take stock. Matt lights a fire, which we all gather around, warming our frozen hands.

The reality of what we've done finally dawns on each of us. Smiles begin to spread from face to face like a contagious yawn. Murmurings of "*Did you see that?*" and "*I can't believe...*" as we relate the part that scared

380

each of us the most. Mutterings of congratulations, hugs and handshakes. Joe picks me up and throws me in the air. Hal scrunches Kyle on the top of his head. Sawyer blushes so hard under all the praise for freeing everyone in Bear's office that his cheeks turn a lava red.

Around the fire, I have a little time to think. I killed President Bear. But how? Was there some ability I picked up along the way? Bear didn't seem to have it, as surely he would have used it on me. I can't sense it anymore, like it's crawled into a dark depth within me. Maybe I created my own power. I've been filled with so much hatred that something else erupted out of me. Dad said there are a lot of unexplainables when it comes to the nanites. Is it possible for powers to evolve?

Whatever it is, it's gone now. I'm OK. I won't ever need something so dark again.

When we get going, Erica flutters nearby. "What are you going to do?" When I snap my head up, her eyes are on Matt. "You love him?"

Despite my weariness my heart fills with yearning. "Yes."

She steps down to the ground and walks beside me. Unexpectedly, she touches my hand. "You need to tell Joe."

I nod. "I will, then maybe you and he…"

"Let me stop you right there. He doesn't feel that way about me." Her violet eyes brighten. Pain or fatigue? Then she flies away.

Matt limps up to join me. "What was that about?"

I keep my eyes on my feet. "Just Erica being Erica."

"Are you OK?" Matt places a hand briefly on my waist. There's hope in his eyes. Did he even hear what I said?

"Yeah. Just about. You?"

"Just about." He smiles, but it's too brief.

My hand goes to my neck and toys with the pendant.

We walk through the morning. Paige joins us. "Do you think we need to worry about what's waiting for us at the cave?"

"Because of Addison?" I ask.

Paige nods.

"We don't know how far her betrayal reaches. We need to be careful," Matt says.

"I knew you would say that. I was hoping you wouldn't, but I knew it." Her lip quivers. She must be thinking about Jacob. Did he return to safety, or something else?

"Poor Addison," Erica says. Her shoulders are hunched and her arms circle her waist.

"She betrayed us," Kyle snaps, his eyes glinting harder than I've seen before.

"It wasn't her fault," Erica mutters.

Kyle snorts. "She could have killed us all."

Erica looks away. Her wings flutter a deep ocean blue. "I'm sorry."

"What for?" Joe asks.

She refastens her damp hair and smooths her hands down her trousers. "Addison. We were friends. I should have known."

"It's not your fault, Erica," I say. "She played us all."

Erica folds her wings away.

"Leave it," Matt says. "We can't change what happened. We're OK. Her actions didn't change anything."

Kyle kicks at the ground in a blur of speed. "We were almost killed. If it wasn't for Silver…"

"Kyle," Matt says. "If I've learned anything during the past few months, it's that we can't dwell on what might have been. You're good, and now you have a good story to tell the girls." He winks.

Kyle blushes. "Yeah, well…"

Joe claps Kyle on the shoulder. "Let's go. We need to get back to the cave so you can score some action with your new story." The group erupts in laughter. Kyle blushes harder.

Dad chuckles. "I really hope this cave isn't running awry with teenage hormones."

Everyone laughs, and Joe respectfully tells him about Claus and Francesca and the other grown-ups.

"But how did you take out President Bear?" Kyle asks when the laughter dies down.

Everyone's eyes swivel to me.

"Yeah," Sawyer says. "You held his heart in your hand. And then it just… poof… disappeared."

"Dude, that's pretty hardcore," Kyle says, his feet still for once.

"I don't know." I look at the awe on my friends' faces. "I don't know how I did it. I was just so angry."

"I've never seen it before," Dad says.

A thread of fear shivers through me. "What does that mean?"

"It means your abilities might be unquantifiable." Dad's eyes hold an ocean of sympathy and regret. "But we'll figure it out. I promise."

Matt nudges my arm. "He's dead. That's the important thing."

We walk for a couple of hours, gritting teeth against exhaustion and aching muscles, ignoring the blisters on our feet. But the farther we walk, the lighter I feel. There's no sign of anyone chasing us.

When dusk descends, we reach the edge of the valley. We're still a day's hike from the cave, but we can walk through the forest along the ridge line to get there. How much longer will the cave be home?

We stop to watch the sun set over the horizon. Majestic hues bleach the land of color, turning the grass into golden thread, transporting the valley into the rich pastures of a promised land, pregnant with hope. Then the last of the light disappears.

I decide it's time to talk to Joe. I pull him aside as the others take the lead. Erica flutters nearby.

"We need to talk," I say.

Joe focuses his gaze on me. "I'd like that."

I grab his massive thumb, clasping it in my hand, toying with it, suddenly nervous. Then I realize that might send the wrong message and shove my hands in my pockets. A couple of acorns are in there and I finger their reassuring solidity.

"I don't want to put any pressure on you." Joe's arm brushes against mine as we walk.

"I know. You're not. It's time," I say, noticing Erica has fluttered away. "I need to tell you something."

Joe clears his throat and we continue walking together. In the comfortable silence, I try to gather my thoughts. I enjoy just being with him, his booming voice that makes it impossible for him to be quiet, his affable nature, how quick he is to laugh. I don't want to sour any of it with the words I know need to be said.

Yes, I was attracted to him. Yes, I thought perhaps I could love him. But I know now: the corner of my heart that beats so achingly is reserved for someone else.

"It's Matt, isn't it?" He keeps his eyes straight ahead.

I look at the ground. I try to be brave and switch my gaze to his face. "Yes. I'm sorry, Joe. I'm sorry for everything."

"I can't say I'm not disappointed." There's real hurt in his eyes, but he smiles at me. He blows out a loud sigh. "Maybe in another life, heh?"

I resist the urge to hold his hand. "Maybe."

"Matt's a good guy. I think I knew it deep down." Joe's pace slows and we fall back from the group. "I think that's why I tried that second kiss on you. I was trying to leave you with an impression..."

"You certainly did that." I smile at him when he faces me. We stop walking and just stare at each other. I'm almost tempted to kiss him again. A goodbye kiss.

His hand floats between us, but he doesn't touch me. "I was just hoping… well, anyway…" He kisses my cheek.

The sound of a twig snapping breaks my thoughts. No one's walking behind Joe and me. We're the last ones in the group.

I cock my head and listen. Another twig snaps. Something is following us. I look at Joe and unsheathe my knife. He holds his machete ready. Together we turn as a third twig snaps.

A menacing growl fills the air.

CHAPTER THIRTY-TWO

Hellhounds. They're known for their speed. That's why they kill so effectively.

Three pairs of eyes stare at us from the undergrowth. Fangs drip with foaming saliva. Hungry tongues lick trembling jowls. As they lunge, Joe leaps before me and I'm pushed to the ground. I fall backwards and knock my head on a tree root. Dazed, I see double. My head is cocked toward the action, my body unable to move. The three hellhounds jump him simultaneously. Jaws snap at him. Joe slices one way, then the other. The hellhounds maneuver out of the way each time.

They're so fast, faster than the one I killed in the woods. I can barely keep track of them. My mind goes blank. I try to transition to bulk, but I have nothing left. Joe slashes a hound across the paw. It yelps and jumps back, but the wound doesn't stop it for long and it prepares to launch again.

"Help!" I scream, rolling onto my stomach. On my

knees, my vision wavers and I slam back to the ground. I hope the rest of the group returns and equally fear they will.

Joe goes for the gun at his belt. It's a mistake. The two unharmed hounds leap at his throat. Joe's eyes bulge as he tries to fight them off with his hands. Blood trickles down his chest.

One of the hounds finds the weak spot. It digs its teeth into Joe's neck and doesn't let go. Joe swats another of the hounds away, but the third, the last, hangs onto his throat. The hole in his neck rips open. Blood spills faster. Joe collapses to his knees. He grabs at the hound, but he lacks the strength to wrestle it away. The hound with the injured paw leaps into the fray.

I manage to sit up. The black cloud in my vision abates. Joe lies on the ground, blood pouring from the wounds on his neck. He doesn't struggle. The hellhound gnaws at his flesh.

"No! No!" I scream, rising to my feet, stumbling as my vision swims.

Three arrows simultaneously land in each of the hellhounds; one through an eye, one through the heart, the third through the neck. The hounds die instantly. Erica flutters above me. Silent tears run down her face. Joe makes gurgling sounds and clutches his throat.

"No!" I cry again.

I go to him, crawling through the ferns, healer hands

flickering a weak glow. I reach Joe and slap my hands down on his chest, not wanting to touch his wound, not wanting to cause him any more pain. His hands fall from his throat as his eyes dim.

Erica hovers above me. I'm vaguely aware of others in the group approaching. I squeeze my eyes shut and think of Joe. Big, strong, invincible Joe with his wonky nose and friendly nature. And the kiss, our special kiss in the meadow that I will always hold in my heart. The healing warmth splutters in my hands, not strong enough yet, unable to heal.

"Wake up, Joe! You can't die." I throw my hands at his chest again, willing the clouds in his eyes to evaporate.

He stares unseeingly at the sky, his chest still. As I place my hands on his throat, directly onto his wound, lights flicker in the forest. Voices sound in the forest, coming this way.

"Oh crap!" Erica mutters above me, taking to the sky and flying away.

"The army, they're coming." Is that Hal?

"Silver, we have to go." Matt's voice in my ear.

"Silver? Please." Dad holds my arm.

"I can't leave him." I throw myself over Joe's body, tears flowing freely, refusing to give up.

The flashlights come closer. The odd shout echoes through the trees, and twigs snap as the army advances toward us.

"Take the invisibility pill and run across the valley. There's a hollow about two miles down the other ridge. Wait for us there," Matt says to the others.

Paige kneels by my side. "Silver, he's gone. We have to go now, we have to leave him."

I refuse to look in her eyes. I sob louder.

"Go, Paige, I've got this. Take care of Dr. Melody," Matt whispers. "You've got someone to stay alive for, in the cave. Mine's right here."

The lights begin to blind me. I can hear the ragged breaths of the army as they run through the forest. They must have followed us from the prison. Joe's death is all my fault.

Matt pulls me off Joe, shoves his hand in my pocket and finds my invisibility pill. He forces the pill into my mouth and makes me swallow. He downs his own pill, then vanishes. But I feel his arms around me, his breath on my neck, his hand cupping my mouth, willing me to stay silent.

The army arrive. They shine their flashlights on Joe's lifeless body, illuminating the blood covering his neck and chest. The lights beam up into the trees, around the forest, into bushes, and seem to shine straight through Matt and me. I squeeze my eyes shut then, so they won't catch the light.

Matt pulls me backwards, slowly, edging away from the bulks and ogres who stand before us. There must be at least twenty. Are they looking for the missing scout group? What difference does it make? They've found us, found Joe.

"Shame about the hounds," a bulk mutters as Matt and I edge toward the ridge. The soldier squats over the dead hellhounds. A lead dangles from his hand. "Where'd the arrows come from?" He barks his findings into a walkie-talkie.

We reach the ridge, turn our backs on the army and run down the bank into the valley. Matt tugs me along, probably afraid that if he lets go I'll run back to Joe. A gust of wind tunnels across the valley floor and gives me the slap I need. I suppress the image of Joe's lifeless eyes, his inert body, his mangled throat, and the pools of blood for another time and run with Matt, overtaking him, pulling him along instead. No one follows us across the valley. We make it up the eastern ridge and into the trees once more.

Matt pants. I open my canteen, take a swig and offer it to him, or where I think he's standing. His body reappears before me, shimmering, not quite solid.

"This way." He grabs my hand. We walk deeper into the woods, advancing on the cave, looking for the hidden hollow.

Smudges of dirt streak Matt's face. His watery eyes brighten with exhaustion. His clothes are rumpled and his hair matted. My own appearance isn't much better.

I'm covered in blood, Joe's blood, all over my arms and legs. Leaves stick out of my hair. My eyes sting as though filled with sand.

A couple of minutes later Matt indicates a small hollow. No more than a depression in the forest, beneath the roots of a massive tree. Hal, Kyle, Sawyer, Paige and my father wait there, faces expressionless. Matt and I crouch beside them. Paige reaches for my hand and holds me close to her. Matt rips some of his T-shirt into a strip, dampens it with water from his canteen and dabs off the worst of the gook from my face and arms.

"Where's Erica?" Matt asks.

"We don't know. She didn't come with us," Hal replies.

We sit in silence and wait for the lights to appear crossing the valley. I wonder who else we'll lose before we reach the safety of the cave.

But is the cave safe? The army isn't far away. Has it already been compromised? Just how far has Addison's betrayal reached?

An owl hoots occasionally above our heads. Leaves rustle in the light breeze, and the moon falls behind a cloud. I smell dried blood and dirt and earth and horror. I know nightmares will follow.

My head rests on Matt's shoulder, and I nestle into his body. Thank God I had enough energy to heal him. I take a moment to examine him; face encrusted in grime, hair unruly and matted, clothes ripped and torn and covered in his own blood. He is beautiful. And he is mine. I hope. If he'll have me.

When sunlight filters to the forest floor, I realize we must have slept a few hours. The others stir, stretch their legs and climb out of the hollow. The army didn't find us.

Matt opens his eyes and stretches. "We're about two miles away. We'll stick to this side of the valley, follow the tree line until we come level with the cave."

"Once we're there we'll have to watch the entrance for a while to make sure it's still safe. We'll have to wait until nightfall to make a move, in case the army is still out there." Hal gestures to the woods on the far side of the valley.

We rise and trudge along in single file. I allow myself brief moments to think of Joe, but I don't stay there too long. The wound is too raw, the grief too painful to examine. A strange numbness envelops me, making me impervious to the heat of the day and unaware of the blisters on my feet. I think only of the path I follow and where to plant my next footfall. One foot in front of the other, onward. A bluebird circles above our heads, reminding me of my wings. We were ten, now we are just seven. Eight if Jacob made it back safely.

By mid-afternoon the small copse of trees in the valley that hides the entrance to the cave comes into view. We stand and watch for a while.

"Let's sit and wait." Hal ushers us to the ground.

I sit on the ground, cross-legged, watching the valley. Matt and Paige sit either side of me, equally expectant. While we wait, Dad tells us about his plans, so someone else will know if anything happens to him. He thinks he can harness the DNA of a bacteria to change everyone's foreign DNA markers. The bacteria will recognize the intruding DNA modifications and direct the body to attack them, but he needs to figure out how to expose the adjusteds.

Another hour passes and a familiar, barking blur runs up the ridge. Einstein plows into Matt's arms, and both of us shed a tear.

"I missed you, buddy," Matt says, scrunching Einstein behind his ears. "I think it's safe." He stands.

We rise beside him, take one last look at the valley, and walk out into the night. It doesn't take long to reach the small copse of trees and the entrance to the cave. Matt pulls the branches away, revealing the hidden doorway. Hal throws the door open. The familiar smell of damp limestone rushes out at me, making me eager to go inside. Small noises drift up from the passageway, indistinguishable.

We wait a few moments, each of us building up our nerve. We could be met by the comfort of our home, the people of the cave, happy to see us, or by the army and death.

CHAPTER THIRTY-THREE

Einstein woofs and pads into the passageway. Matt smiles.

Together we make our way into the cave, down the passageway and into the main chamber. I link arms with Dad and tell him all about the cave. The dinner hour has passed and it's the time of the evening when people gather to talk.

"They're back!" someone shouts. The phrase catches, spreading around the chamber.

People assemble, staring at our haunted looks, our dirt-streaked clothes, the blood. But there aren't many of them, maybe fifty from a population of four hundred. Francesca emerges from the group, wearing a beaming smile. She hugs each of us in turn, not caring about the muck.

Jacob runs up to Paige and literally sweeps her off her feet. She throws her head back and laughs. There's only a slight trace of a limp.

"Where is everyone?" I ask.

Francesca's eyes flicker cold. "The army came. Some of us managed to hide. Others were taken to compounds."

I scan the crowd. Matt's family pushes through the wall of people, and Megan wheels over people's feet to get to her brother. Claus stands back a ways and bows. His eyes glisten.

"What about Joan?" I ask.

"Joan didn't…" Francesca shakes her head. "People here need your help."

A lump forms in my throat. "Of course," I say. "I'm not quite at full strength, but I'll do what I can."

"Dr. Melody." Francesca reaches for my father's arm. "We're so glad you're here."

"I'm glad to be with my daughter again." He brings me closer to his side. "Now I just need to find my wife."

"I understand," Francesca says. Then she turns to Matt. "Is this all of you?"

Matt nods. "Erica's alive, but she took off. The rest…"

"I heard about Joe on the radio, and your close encounter with the army." Francesca purses her lips, and a clouded expression passes across her face. "I'm sorry."

Matt's sisters approach, launching themselves at him, causing him to stumble backwards.

"I'm coming next time." Lyla punches his arm.

"There won't be a next time." Matt tousles her blonde

hair. His parents wait their turn. Plates of food arrive, riding toward us on a sea of hands. We accept them greedily: hot stew with a dark, nourishing meat. We eat where we stand, too hungry for niceties.

"Wash up, get some rest. We'll talk tomorrow," Francesca says.

After we eat, Matt, Paige and I go to the underground lake to clean up. Paige finds a cloth and dabs at the dried blood and dirt on my body until there isn't a smear left. We check over Matt's injuries and find the worst is healed, just bumps and bruises remaining. The hole in Paige's wing has already begun to knit together.

The cave feels different somehow, as if aware of all the tragedy that has taken place. Loud echoes bounce against unfamiliar, jutting rocks. The walls are drier and crumble under my touch. I shed a few tears. Joe. Addison. Their loss burns inside me. *Mom.*

Matt leads all the injured residents to me. There's an assortment of knife and bullet wounds. Some of them infected. With my limited power, it'll take a few days to bring everyone back to health.

Matt sits beside me and slings an arm around my shoulder.

I pull away and turn to face his startling blue eyes. "Did you hear me? At the river?"

A fragile smile plays on his lips. "There was thunder, a roaring river, and growling lions. Did you thank me for pulling you across?" He winks, and I know he heard each one of those three important words.

I shake my head. "That's not what I said."

Matt pulls on the end of my hair. "I think you mentioned something about killing the hellcat and roasting its meat. Shouldn't be hard with that new fire-breathing power of yours."

A giggle tickles my throat. "That wasn't it either."

Matt cocks his head and scratches his temple in a parody of trying to remember. "Hmm. I guess you better repeat it then."

I don't hesitate. "I'm in love with you," I say. The last few days proved to me there's no more time to waste.

Matt frowns. "What about Joe?"

I stare at my hands. "I won't deny I had feelings for Joe, but it wasn't love." I meet Matt's blue eyes. "It wasn't what I feel for you. Something always held me back with him. I thought it was because he was an altered, but then I ended up being the alt of all alts. It took me a while, but when he kissed me again in the woods… and you were there, watching, I knew it was you I loved." I like how those words roll off my tongue.

Matt's thumb makes a circle on my palm. "I suppose it goes without saying that I love you too?"

I smile. "I was hoping you hadn't changed your mind."

Matt socks me gently on the shoulder. "Diana?

Seriously? You thought Diana and I were going to get together?"

"Now I feel foolish. I missed all the signs." I lean against him.

He chuckles. "Yup, it took you long enough."

"I know." I lift my head and stare at his blue eyes, losing myself in their depths. "I'm sorry." I hold his hands. "It's just that—"

"Silver?

"I couldn't believe... well, I was afraid..." I mumble.

"Silver!" Matt says a little louder.

"Yeah?"

"Shut up already." He pulls me into his arms.

His lips press against mine, soft and welcoming— it feels like coming home. My lips tingle as the kiss deepens. The tingling spreads, like butterflies fluttering against my skin. With our arms wrapped around each other, we fall back onto his sleeping bag. I pull him closer. My need becomes desperate. He's my best friend. I love him with all my heart, and now I want so much more from him.

Matt pauses and pulls away to look at me. His bright eyes communicate desire.

"Don't stop," I whisper, hands under his shirt, stroking the smoothness of his back, willing him to come closer.

"Not yet." Matt puts a hand to my cheek, caressing

the skin there, and kisses me again, gently, and I know I will have to wait.

———

The next morning, while eating a freshly baked roll with strawberry jam that someone procured in our absence, a shadow emerges from the main passageway, hesitating on the threshold.

"Erica?" I say. "Is that you?"

She comes closer.

"Are you OK?" I ask.

"Getting there." Tears shine in her eyes and her long, lavender hair hangs loose. "But I'm here now. I hear your mother needs to be located and a cure needs to be made."

I smile. "It does."

We stare at each other, and Matt gives her a hug.

"You two look good together," she says after a while.

"Thanks," I reply.

Erica's wings remain a friendly yellow. "I'm glad."

Over the next few days, my father sequesters himself in a distant alcove and begins work on a cure. A party atmosphere sweeps through the cave.

"The government has fallen apart," Matt says as we walk in dappled sunshine. "Unadjusteds have broken out of compounds everywhere. Everyone is running."

"So what happens next?" I ask, rolling acorns in my hands.

"We let the dust settle and we see where things fall. We let your father work and we find your mother." The sunlight plays on Matt's hair, making it lighter. "I think she's with Earl."

I frown. "And where is that?"

"I'm working on it, but I think he fled to California," Matt says. "And I've figured out how to make this work." He taps the hellcat remote against his palm. "When they arrive, we'll have six or seven hellcats at our command."

The next day we hold a memorial. The remaining fifty souls of the cave come to mourn, but our numbers are growing as new unadjusteds arrive at the cave every day.

We come to a weeping willow and bow our heads. Its soft branches cascade to the ground and create a private place around its trunk. Matt moves some branches aside and we walk into the coolness of this space. A small wooden cross marks Joe's grave with the words: "Hero to all." I smile. How appropriate. He would have been embarrassed by the accolade. There are several other markers too, including one for Addison. Neither of their bodies was recovered, but fresh mounds show the extent of the army's massacre in the cave.

Kyle, Hal, Sawyer, Paige, Jacob, Erica, and Matt and I stand together beneath the willow tree. We say goodbye. After, Erica nods at me and begins to sing my song.

Our song for freedom. Her voice carries on the air and weaves around my heart.

> *When you hear the lone wolf howling,*
> *When sky comes crashing through.*
> *With all the hellhounds growling,*
> *If it ends, just me and you…*
> *Just close your eyes and breathe in deep,*
> *Look to the new sun's sky.*
> *Because our voice is freedom,*
> *And they will hear us cry.*

A breeze gusts through the trees and makes me shiver. Matt rubs my back. I hold a bunch of wildflowers, picked from the meadows. Kneeling, I lay them on Joe's grave, thinking of the posy he once gave me.

Later that evening, when we wind our way back to the cave, the population is noisy with my freedom song. Someone presses my guitar into my hands and people sing at full volume, their eyes shining with new possibilities.

Paige's wings flutter in time with the passionate chords. Fire sparks in Erica's pupils. With one arm wrapped around Lyla, Sawyer nods his head, the rhythm pulsing through his curls. Everyone sings. Even Evan and Claus.

After dinner, Matt and I are tasked with cleaning the

dishes. We walk to the lake and find my father kneeling at its surface, still muttering the lyrics, his face glowing in the warm light of the lantern.

He looks up at me and smiles. "I found the answer to getting the bacteria to the adjusteds."

His eyes emanate such a strong message of hope that I know: my world is going to change. And this time, the unadjusteds won't be powerless anymore.

ACKNOWLEDGEMENTS

I'd like to thank the following people:

TWP, my most supportive writing friends—and not just writing friends. We've been through it all together and I couldn't have done it without you: Stuart White, Ellie Lock, Caroline Murphy, Anne Boyere, Anna Orridge, Lydia Massiah, SallyDoherty, Jeanna Skinner, Emma Finlayson-Palmer, Emma Dykes and Lorna Riley.

The people in my Curtis Brown Creative Group, who have been a bottomless well of support, especially Lydia Massiah, Mellissa Welliver, Julie Marney Leigh, Sharon Hopwood, Lindsay Sharman, Tasha Harrison and Ralph Browning, and obviously, tutor Catherine Johnson.

Haley Sulich, my fabulous editor at Write Plan, for believing in me and my book and for helping it fly out into the world, and Stephi Cham, for the line edits.

My agent, Yasmin Kane, for helping my book land on the right desk.

My husband, Neil Blagden, for actually reading this one!

My parents, Larry & Rita Woelk, who read everything I write and have encouraged me every step of the way.

A massive thank you to Hannah Kates for being such a rock star and making the lyrics to the freedom song shine.

All my early supporters and friends who read early drafts and encouraged me along the way: Sasha Newell, Michelle Oliver, Nikki & Adrian Kane, Rhia Mitchell, Sarada McDermott, Renate Vapnar. Kathryn Richards, and Mary Bryant.

Diane Hale, who helped put this book on the path it is now.

My cover artist, Fay Lane, who came up with such an amazing concept. I couldn't be happier!

The amazing writing community on Twitter. There is so much support and help, and I couldn't have done it without your encouragement. Special thanks to: Anna Britton, Lorretta Chefchaouni, Charles Femia, David Neuner, Clare Harlow, Amy Avery, Hannah Kates, Jackie Anders, Tammy Oja, Jake Waller, Debbie Roxburgh, Amanda McLachlan, and Sarah Dresser.

My debut 2019/20 group, you are too numerous to name, but navigating the waters with you has been a fabulous experience.

Everyone at #WritersWise, especially Noelle Kelly, Sharon Writes, Viv Conrad and Liam Farrell.

My brother, Christopher Woelk, for giving me a sanity check on all the hard science bits.

My career coach, Kate Brauning, for so much good advice and for helping me to stay focused.

Sarah Lewis and Jo Gatford at Writers' HQ–without them I would never have learned to plot properly, let alone edit!

My A-level English teacher, Michael Fox, who taught me to first think for myself, then to defend my ideas.

Last but not least, all of my readers. Without you this wouldn't be possible, and I hope you stick around to find out the rest of Silver's journey.

Marisa Noelle writes MG & YA SFF & mental health novels, including *The Shadow Keepers* to be released in July 2019 & *The Unadjusteds* in October 2019. When she's not writing, reading or watching movies, she enjoys swimming. In the pool she likes to imagine she could be a mermaid and enter some of her make-believe worlds. There, she can also ignore the real world and focus on new novel plots and scenes. Marisa lives in Woking, UK with her husband and three children.